"I don't want you to be alone..."

Adrian sighed. "James, I *have* been alone, for a really long time."

"I'm sorry," he said. "Adrian...I am so, so sorry."

When he drew her into his arms, she was helpless to stop him. She felt his lips come to rest on the top of her head. His arms wrapped around her back, closing her in, tightening.

He simply held her, for what seemed like ages.

A small eternity passed in the space of moments. Memories stirred, whispering to life, ghosts of what had been.

When his lips touched hers, it felt so natural. The simple press of his lips brought her back to life. Her heart fluttered, lifting and soaring.

She should have pushed him away. After everything, she should shove him back, make him leave. Instead, she let the moment stretch, deepen until she felt him brush up against the soul she'd buried from everything and everyone...

Dear Reader,

Revisiting my hometown, Fairhope, through the eyes and hearts of my characters is something I look forward to every time I write a book in this series. But there's something about Adrian and James that made me anticipate writing this book more than any other. Penning their story was an emotional experience I won't soon forget. Mostly because I wrote this story within a year of having my first child, a blue-eyed boy much like Adrian's.

Writing love stories that involve single parents can be a delicate process. Being a mother opened my eyes to the special bond between mother and child. Even on days when writing had to be put off until bedtime, I wasn't bothered because I knew that the bond he and I have built was the inspiration I needed to do justice to these characters.

And speaking of inspiration...I have to give props to my beloved husband. Not only is he a tall, bearded man in a tool belt—just like James—but his knowledge of engines, mechanics and BB guns was invaluable while researching this book, particularly for a certain scene involving a squirrel and a trip to the emergency room for my unfortunate hero.

I hope you enjoy Adrian and James's story, readers! You can find more about James, Adrian and other characters from previous books in my Fairhope series at amberleighwilliams.com.

Amber Leigh

AMBER LEIGH
WILLIAMS

His Rebel Heart

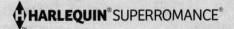
HARLEQUIN® SUPERROMANCE®

Recycling programs
for this product may
not exist in your area.

ISBN-13: 978-0-373-60917-8

His Rebel Heart

Copyright © 2015 by Amber Leigh Williams

Printed in U.S.A.

Amber Leigh Williams lives on the Gulf Coast. A Southern girl at heart, she loves beach days, the smell of real books, relaxing at her family's lakehouse and spending time with her husband and their sweet blue-eyed boy. When she's not running after her young son and three large dogs, she can be found reading a good romance or cooking up a new dish. Readers can find her at amberleighwilliams.com!

Books by Amber Leigh Williams

HARLEQUIN SUPERROMANCE

A Place with Briar
Married One Night

Visit the Author Profile page
at Harlequin.com for more titles.

To my firstborn.... Live always in a world
where dragons fly and fairies dance.
Chase dreams and dragonflies.
Breathe deep and get your hands dirty.
Build wisely and love faithfully.
Listen to stories—and tell a few of your own.

And to Sassy, who we miss....
Dear friend and spirit animal.
Meet you at the Rainbow Bridge.

PROLOGUE

THE NIGHT ADRIAN CARLTON first saw James Bracken naked, he was bloodied and bruised. He'd gone several rounds with a bottle of Wild Turkey 101, then crawled behind the wheel of his father's old Mustang convertible.

The joyride ended abruptly on a backcountry road when the speeding muscle car skated off the pavement, plowed through the entry sign in front of Carlton Nurseries and skinned the side of a giant oak tree before barreling into the glass front of the office building.

From the farmhouse behind the nursery, Adrian had heard the deafening crash and gone running—out the front door and through the rows of her parents' shrubs and saplings, her bare feet sinking into the damp earth. A light drizzle was falling from the leaden night skies and the humidity had swelled at the onset of rain. By the time she reached the nursery's office and saw the cherry-red Shelby that had decimated it, sweat was crawling from her neck to her back.

"Oh, my..." She trailed off as she took in the

scene. Her hands lifted to her mouth as she shook her head. "What in God's name…"

She trailed off at the sound of a grunt and tinkling glass. Her feet unstuck and she took several steps forward. Surely no one had survived this carnage.

The grimacing man unfolding himself from the driver's seat as he struggled to push the car door open suggested otherwise. Swearing under his breath, he grabbed the top of the car for balance. He hissed, lifting his arms away from the glass shards that were littered there, tilting his wrists to the dim light from the street to reveal fresh cuts on the undersides.

"Somabitch," she heard him mutter, the foul words tripping over each other.

Adrian scoffed. The guy was drunk. Her lips peeled back from her teeth in a sneer as she hissed, "You stupid moron! You could have *killed* someone!"

He started at the sound of her voice. His head turned. Through the blood leaking from a large gash close to his dark hairline and the thin cut below his left eye, recognition struck her. Adrian's eyes rounded in surprise. "James?" she said, her voice laden with dread. "James Bracken, is that you?"

He stared at her face for a moment, his eyes moving slowly, sluggishly over her features. Then he staggered forward, his mouth warming into a devilish grin. "Adrian."

As he loped around the trunk of the car, it wasn't just his towering height and lean, muscled form that struck her. Her heart rapped against her chest. He was bloody. He was bruised. He was grinning like a fool. And he was naked as a jay-bird. She took a long step back and swallowed. "James, are you all right?"

He laughed, stumbled a bit. When she dove for him, he pulled himself up to his full height, his blue eyes winking with laughter and not a hint of remorse. She couldn't be altogether sure that he wasn't suffering from a concussion or worse, much less that he was completely aware of his surroundings.

He was six feet five inches tall, easy. Her eyes were level with the wooden cross on his sternum that hung from a leather strap. The religious symbol was so at odds with his devil-may-care persona she frowned, extricating her gaze from his fine, muscled form and, more importantly, his naked hips.

She watched his gaze skim from the top of her head to the tips of her bare toes, and she frowned once more when she felt her red-painted toenails tingle under the smoldering assessment.

"Adrian Carlton," he drawled, swaying a bit. "Damn. Was that an earthquake—or did you just rock my world?"

He was picking her up? Now? For heaven's sake. She pursed her lips, ready to give him the what-for. "Listen, hot rocks, you can't just—"

His eyes rolled into the back of his head and his legs folded beneath him. Cursing, she ducked under his shoulder to catch him but he was too tall. Too damn heavy. She shrieked as they both went crashing to earth. The breath whooshed out of her when his naked form landed on top of her in full supine position. She pushed against his shoulder, couldn't budge him and cursed again.

"Damn you, James Bracken," she murmured, teeth clenched as she yanked his head back with a fistful of his thick, tousled hair. Jaw slack, eyes closed, he greeted her with a gurgling snore. With a sigh, she dropped his head back to her shoulder and groaned. "You're going to be more trouble than you're worth."

CHAPTER ONE

Eight years later

SPRING HAD GONE to the birds, and Adrian didn't mind so much that it had. She encouraged them, setting up bird feeders and birdbaths all around the backyard of her Fairhope cottage. With the weather warming into late March, it allowed for her to open the windows of the house and let the spring breeze waft through the screens. The scents of fresh-cut grass, potting soil and early annuals, as well as the sound of birdsong drifted through the cottage with it.

The squirrels, however, thought the bird food was theirs for the taking.

"I don't think so," Adrian muttered as she watched one such offender—a big vermin with a beer belly—creep down to a bird feeder from one of the overlarge oak trees surrounding the yard. She stood up from the nook table and, using one of the chairs, grabbed her son's BB gun from the top of the cabinets where she'd hidden it.

She crouched next to the half door that led out onto her small patio with the pretty terra-cotta tiles she'd laid herself. Leveling the gun on top of the half door, she closed one eye and sighted it. "I see you," she said, and felt for the trigger.

"Mom!"

Adrian jumped a mile high and shrieked. The sound and movement startled Nutsy the Squirrel and he lit off up the tree, chattering angrily at the spoiled opportunity.

Adrian fought back a curse and stood, raking a hand through her short crop of red hair. "Kyle," she said in as normal a voice as she could manage.

Kyle narrowed his eyes. They were a wild shade of Scandinavian blue. Right now they were scrutinizing her as they scanned the weapon and her long, white nightgown. "Were you shooting squirrels again?"

Adrian cleared her throat. "I was just going to pop one in the butt. Teach him a lesson." When Kyle rolled his eyes, she drew her shoulders back, searching for some dignity. "He was stealing birdseed." Then she waved a dismissive hand. She didn't have to explain herself, no matter how ridiculous she felt in the face of his seven-year-old derision.

"Mom." Kyle sighed. "Please stop doing that. It's embarrassing."

Adrian raised a brow and felt the corners of her mouth twitch. "Oh, is it, huh?"

"Yeah," Kyle said, and scrubbed the backs of his first two fingers over his mouth. It was an endearing habit he'd had since his toddling years. "What's for breakfast?"

"There's some cereal in the pantry," she told him, and waited until he went inside before crawling back up on the chair and replacing the gun on top of the cabinets, out of his reach. Then she got down, carried the chair back to the table and met him at the refrigerator. "Orange juice?" she asked.

"Sure," he said, and took a seat at the table, pouring Cap'n Crunch into a bowl. Adrian topped the cereal with milk, then fixed him a glass of juice.

"Did you know there's a moving van next door?" Kyle asked.

Adrian stopped in the midst of pouring herself a second helping of coffee. "What?"

Kyle craned his neck to look out the bay window over the nook table. "Somebody must be moving in."

The house next door had been for sale for well over six months. The previous owners had left it in a state of complete and utter disarray, so much so that everyone on the street had begun to resent the overgrown property. Adrian leaned over the table, placing a hand on Kyle's dark, tousled head, and peered across her trim, perfectly kept yard into the next.

The grass of the adjacent property had grown as tall as reeds. The mailbox was hanging loose on its stand, the driveway was cracked and mottled and the detached garage was even beginning to fall in. The roof of the house was carpeted in dead leaves and strewn with naked oak branches. The screen door of the front porch had been torn. Adrian was surprised to see the For Sale sign gone and an oversize moving truck parked at the curb, butted up against a sleek, black sportster.

"Somebody finally bought it," Adrian muttered with an unbelieving shake of her head. "I thought they were gonna have to tear it down, the state it's in."

"Maybe they've got kids," Kyle said, eyes widening at the possibility. He watched more closely, nose nearly pressed to the glass now, as the movers milled from truck to house with boxes of varying sizes. "Do you see any toys, Mom?"

Adrian, too, watched for a moment, then frowned, dropping back to her heels and straightening. She wondered how many other neighbors were rubbernecking this morning to get a gander at the street's newest addition. And while, for the most part, rubbernecking was a harmless sport, Adrian knew all too well what it felt like to be the victim of it. "Eat your breakfast," she said with a pat on Kyle's shoulder.

"It'd be really cool if there was a guy my age moving in." Kyle considered as he pushed his cereal around with his spoon, no longer paying Cap'n Crunch much mind. "Then Blaze and I can play two-on-two when Gavin visits in a few weeks."

"What if they have a girl?" Adrian asked coyly, glancing sideways from the counter just in time to see Kyle wrinkle his nose.

The kid positively moped at the idea. "I guess that would be all right, too."

Adrian chuckled. Kyle was firmly entrenched in the cootie phase. "It wouldn't be so bad. You like Harmony, don't you?"

"Harmony's a baby," Kyle told her, referring to their family friends the Savitts' little girl. "Real girls are mean."

Adrian hid a snort in her coffee. "Just concentrate on eating. We've got to get you to school, mister."

"Hey, maybe we could send them something to eat," Kyle suggested, still gazing out at the movers.

"Something to eat?" she asked, brow creased.

"Yeah. Like how we sent the Millers one of Briar's pies when they moved in. Blaze said it was real good. That's how we got to be such good friends."

Adrian smiled as she watched her son's mind work. With a small business to run and being a single parent, her days were so full she had hardly a moment to stop and breathe. But sometimes when she looked at Kyle her heart ached with how much she loved him and at how fast he had grown. "Good idea. I'll talk to Briar this afternoon."

Kyle finally turned his head and grinned at her.

In the light spilling in from the open windows around the room, those wild blue eyes shone like stars and the dark freckles across his nose contrasted with his cheeks. "Thanks, Mom."

She walked to him and touched a kiss to his brow, brushing back the dark hair that was growing over his forehead at a rapid rate. "Take your bowl to the sink. Then get dressed quickly. You don't want to be late."

As Kyle slipped by her, Adrian stole one last glance at the house next door. The movers were hauling in what looked like weights and power tools. She frowned at the license plate of the sportster. Out of state, from the looks of it. Though the tall grass was obscuring her view.

She just hoped whoever was moving in got the old eyesore looking somewhat decent again. How they would manage it all, she had no idea.

Only an idiot would buy a house that run-down. Or somebody with some serious ambition. Hoping for the latter, she turned from the windows and went to help Kyle get ready for the day.

JAMES BRACKEN FROWNED at the cards in his hand. Pocket jacks. He'd always had a knack for knowing what cards were going to show up on the table as well as for reading the people who challenged him to Texas Hold 'Em. Those fine-tuned senses told him that despite the nice, round pile of poker chips between them, his opponent, a scrawny man in a near-to-threadbare work shirt torn at the shoulder, was bluffing.

Scanning the man closely, James wondered when the last time the mover had had a good steak dinner. Not the lean kind of steak. A big, juicy, porterhouse number with fat trimming the edges. He couldn't have been older than thirty but judging by the deep furrows in his brow and his receding hairline, things like luck and plenty had never been on his side.

After leaving home just shy of eighteen, James had found that the former came far more easily to him than most. For eight years, it had brought him a great deal of the latter. Which was why when the dealer, another mover, this one heavy-set around the middle and sweating like a pig in the unaired rooms of James's new house, flicked the river card onto the table, James took pity on his less fortunate opponent.

Ignoring those smiling pocket jacks, he dropped them facedown onto the siding board laid across two sawhorses to make a makeshift poker table and cursed under his breath. "Nothin'," he muttered as hope lit in his opponent's eyes. Reaching for the bottle of water that was sweating as much as their dealer, James lifted a shoulder and leaned back in one of the creaky beach chairs he'd found folded against the wall of the sorry excuse for a two-car garage. "Goddamn, Ripley. The cards love you."

The dealer—Denning was his name, as James had gathered over the course of the busy morning—barked out a knowing laugh. "Bull. Nothing's ever loved Ripley. Least of all Texas Hold 'Em." He reached over to slap Ripley on the shoulder. "Ain't that right, son?"

Ripley was still blinking in disbelief at the poker chips. He'd gone all-in before he realized he was drawing dead. Carefully setting his cards down, he splayed them on the table and looked up at James. "Denning's right. I was bluffing the whole time."

James stared down at the two and the eight. Just as he'd thought. "Hell of a poker face you got there." It was a lie. James had spotted Ripley's tell half an hour ago when the lower lid of his left eye twitched after the man wound up with trip nines. It had been his one well-played hand of the game. Ignoring Denning's answering snort, James pushed the chip pile toward Ripley. "Go on. Count your spoils. I need some air."

Ripley's hand paused before it reached for the pot. "You're gonna finish the game, right?"

James hid a smile by turning to the long line of windows and sliding doors that led out onto the wide deck. This was the reason he'd bought the house. Something about all that glass—smudged and dirty as all get-out at the moment—and that yawning view of the sunbaked deck and the pool and yard beyond it had called to him.

James had always been a sucker for a lost cause. The fact that he'd snatched up this dilapidated house only a short walk from Mobile Bay where he'd grown up was indisputable proof of that. "Sure, I'll finish the game—after we've got all the furniture in." As nice as the companionship he'd found in Ripley, Denning and the other movers was, James was eager to get a move on—to get started making things right here in Fairhope where he'd left his past and all the ghosts that had chased him away.

The past that had haunted him for eight long years. The past that he'd realized he was desperate to finally make right.

A knock on the door echoed from the entryway and James smoothed over the scowl he saw reflected in the dirty window. Turning back to the others, he said, "That'll be the pizza. Let's eat, boys."

THE PIE WAS CHERRY and it was still warm. With Kyle's hope for a new neighborhood friend in mind, Adrian had procured it during that morning's visit to Hanna's Inn where her friend, innkeeper and adept cook and baker, Briar Savitt, lived and worked alongside her husband, Cole. It wasn't out of Adrian's way at all. She owned Flora, the flower shop on the street side of the building next door to Hanna's, a building that also housed their mutual friend Roxie Levy's bridal boutique,

Belle Brides, and Briar's cousin and Adrian's high school friend, Olivia Leighton's bar, Tavern of the Graces, on the bay side.

As luck would have it the midday lull at the flower shop allowed Adrian to slip back to her cottage a few blocks away. Kyle would need his soccer gear for his practice that afternoon anyway, so she'd be saving herself a trip later if she left her assistant, Penny, in charge of the shop and picked up the duffel bag now, in addition to dropping off the pie.

The day was downright gorgeous—it made the gloom of winter feel far away. As Adrian walked from Flora down the sidewalk along the bay toward home, she watched sunlight kiss the water's small crests with golden light. The breeze lifted the bangs off her brow. Over the delicious aroma of cherry pie were strong currents of salt and magnolia leaves. Without sunglasses, she had to squint to see the shadow of silver spires and cranes on the western horizon that marked the opposite shore and the port city of Mobile.

She turned onto the street where she had lived since she left her ex-husband in a hurry years ago while Kyle was still a toddler. The trees on either side of the street grew thickly, merging overhead. Shade gathered around her, sunlight choked out by leaves and heavy waves of Spanish moss. She climbed the hill to the cottage, waving to the few neighbors who were out and about.

She hoped her son didn't have too many memories of those disastrous years she'd spent with Radley Kennard. The man's presence still lurked like a towering wraith at the edge of her consciousness. Run-ins with him had been fewer and farther between as the years passed, mostly thanks to the restraining order she'd filed against him and the fact that her friend Olivia and her husband, Gerald, had given him a non-too-friendly warning the last time Radley had come calling months ago.

Nevertheless, Adrian never forgot he was around. She'd spent many sleepless nights worrying he might show up, drunk and pounding at her door again. Or that he might realize the one thing that would be most devastating to her—losing Kyle.

Adrian shuddered and was thankful when she broke into a patch of warm sunlight again. Dodging around the big moving van and the sportster at the house next door, she slowed. Checking that no one was around, she did a quick perusal of the vehicle. North Carolina plates. As she rounded the car, she caught sight of a Van Halen CD in the passenger seat.

No sign of a car seat, toys, or anything that would denote the presence of children. It looked as if Kyle was going to be disappointed. The sportster was the only vehicle in sight—not exactly a parent-minded mode of transportation. In fact, it was the kind of car she would attribute to a single man. One more than likely going through a midlife crisis.

Add in the Van Halen CD and there wasn't much hope for anything else.

Adrian found herself stopping in front of the run-down house just on the cusp of its overgrown yard, frowning. What kind of a midlife crisis called for a ramshackle house that looked to be far more trouble than the slashed real estate price could possibly have made it worth?

She was about to find out. Straightening her shoulders, Adrian walked into the tall grass. The movers were nowhere to be seen. Beyond the torn screen door with its rusted hinges, the front door was wide-open. As she climbed the sagging porch steps, she heard the hard clash of rock music drifting from within along with clipped male voices and a few choice words.

She took a moment to peer into the house. Through the tattered screen door she saw a wide, empty foyer with scuffed, dark wood floors. The worn hardwood led into a yawning space with windows overlooking a raised, uncovered deck. Though she'd known the previous owners, she had never actually ventured inside the residence. Even from this distance, she saw that the glass was smudged and dirty. Again she wondered who in God's name could have seen the house's potential, as she balanced the pie on one hand and lifted the other to knock on the wood frame of the screen.

Adrian bit her lip. The knock had hardly made a dent in the din of conversation and dueling guitars. She knocked louder and called out, "Hello?"

Something heavy clattered to the floor. She heard more cursing, then the rhythmic clump of footfalls. Adrian watched a long shadow fall across the floor, followed by the solidly built form of a man who, from her faraway estimation, had to stand well over six feet.

Her eyes widened as he neared the door. He was wearing a simple cotton T-shirt and faded jeans that rode his hips well. There were colorful tattoos down the length of one arm and another peeking out of the collar of his shirt, feathering the base of his neck. "Who is it?" he asked in a non-too-gentle voice that had her freezing in place.

She was surprised when her heart picked up the pace, in tune with his approach. Her gaze traveled up over his bearded chin and finally, as he came to the door, to his eyes.

He slowed, reaching for the handle. "Oh," he said, "sorry. I wasn't expecting anyone but the pizza delivery guy. How can I help you, miss…"

Trailing off, he opened the screen and smiled at her in greeting. One of those long, muscled arms held the door open as he stepped down to the sagging porch. The boards groaned beneath him. His eyes were blue. But not just any blue. Maybe it was that his face was so tan or his shaggy head of hair and eyebrows were so dark. But no, those eyes were a fierce, wild, *familiar* shade of blue.

Adrian's lips went numb…as did her legs. The pie tipped over the ends of her fingers and landed facedown on the porch boards with a splat.

That smile was devastating and, again, *familiar*.

It had been years. Back then, his face had been close-shaved, his hair more kempt. Not one tattoo had marked his body, much less the thick cords of his neck. But there was no way she could have forgotten James Bracken's devil-may-care smile.

Adrian watched the smile slowly fade from his features. They didn't stray to the pie on the ground or to her useless fingers, which were spread between them like a supplicating statue. The mirth in those blue eyes faded, too, as they searched hers, pinging from one to the other and back in a quickening assessment. His mouth fumbled and he braced a hand against the yawning screen door. "Adrian?" he asked, finally, the name launching off his tongue.

It made her jump. Suddenly, she could feel everything again. The blood spinning wildly in her head, dizzying her, before it fled all the way down to her toes and left her cold, hollow except for the panicked rap of her heart.

"I'm right, aren't I?" James asked, shifting his stance toward her as hope blinked to life in his eyes—the Scandinavian blues that were a perfect

match for her son's. "Adrian. Adrian Carlton." The
smile started to spread again.

She shoveled out a breath and, on it, one word.
"No."

Puzzlement flashed across his features. "What
do you mean 'no'? I haven't seen you in eight
years, but I haven't forgotten you." He let out
a surprised laugh, reaching up to run a hand
through his thick, dark cap of unruly hair. There
was another tattoo there on the back of his hand.
She only saw a kaleidoscope of color. The shapes
were a blur, as was the new smile that warmed
his face. His eyes cruised over her, fondly, ap-
praising in a familiar sweep that had once made
her libido charge from the gate like a Churchill
Downs Thoroughbred.

"Sweet Christ. Adrian—tell me how you've
been, what you've been up to…everything. I want
to know everything—"

"No," Adrian said when he took a step toward
her. She raised her hands again, this time as a
shield, and continued to back away from him.
"No, no, no…"

"Careful. Don't fall," he said when she tripped
on the first step. She managed to right herself
but not in time to stop him from advancing. He
grabbed her arms to keep her from tipping over
onto the concrete walkway.

She hissed, snatching away from him as if his
touch had burned. And it had. By God, this man

had burned her. Eight summers ago, he had blazed into her life like an impossible sun—bright, beautiful, remote, untouchable. Only she hadn't been able to stop herself from touching. That face. That body. The dark, troubled heart he'd hidden under the surface of it all. The soul she'd thought he had offered up to her on a silver platter.

Then, in a supernova flash, he was gone. He'd left her. Heartbroken. Humiliated. Pregnant. Burned. He'd jetted out of Fairhope so fast that rabid dogs might have been chasing him. Adrian had never heard from him again. Nor had she attempted to find him to tell him about Kyle…

Kyle. Oh, dear God. Adrian glanced at the cottage next door, her hands lifting to her head in horror and disbelief.

James followed her gaze, noted the house, the name painted on the mailbox and turned back to her, jerking his thumb toward it in indication. "Are we neighbors?"

She shook her head, continuing to back away from him. She was knee-deep in grass and weeds, but she needed to retreat. To get the hell away from him as fast as she possibly could lest all those terrible, horrible feelings of abandonment and humiliation she'd tried so hard to forget swamp her once more. "Stay away from me," she told him sternly.

"Adrian," he called, walking toward her to stop her from retreating. "Hey, come back!"

It was the cowardly thing to do, but she turned and bolted. She ran away from him and all the grim implications his reemergence in her life brought.

CHAPTER TWO

ADRIAN'S MAD DASH back to the shop was all a bit hazy. Once there, she immediately sent Penny off to the greenhouse to deal with that morning's delivery, something Adrian usually handled herself. Alone, she turned off the radio, locked the shop's door and paced from one confining wall to the other.

The anxiety attack came crashing down on her like a torrent of icy water, chilling her to the bone and robbing her of breath. After a while, once the attack wore itself and her down, she folded into a chair in the corner and put her head between her knees.

She felt sick and helpless, a grim compilation of feelings she'd fought to escape after the torment of her marriage to Radley. She could have very well shrunk into a ball on the floor and cried, but she straightened, bracing her hands on her knees and breathing deep against the gut-wrenching sobs that were packed tight in her throat. She wasn't going to do this. She'd had enough weakness for one godforsaken lifetime.

When Adrian was sure the sobs had abated, she

made herself stand up. She waited for her legs to steady, cursing when it took longer than she would have liked. Then she propped her hands on her hips and stared through the display window that faced South Mobile Street.

James Bracken. Before that fateful summer, they had been little more than ships passing in the night. Sure, they had gone to the same high school, but that didn't mean they ever spoke to each other.

Though she *had* attended his father's funeral after the beloved town preacher died in a car accident. James had been a passenger. Up until that accident, he'd been known as Fairhope's golden boy, the one who could do no wrong. He'd played football well enough for whispers of scholarship potential. He'd partied, like most other kids who had run in his circles, but not excessively so.

But at his father's funeral, he'd looked anything but the golden boy. Wearing a somber suit of flat gray, sitting next to his sobbing mother, he'd looked helpless against the tide of reality. Adrian hadn't been able to watch Zachariah Bracken's body being lowered into the earth—she hadn't been able to see anything but that lean shell of a boy with the evidence of that horrible crash still scratched and nicked across his face and hands.

After that, James had developed another kind of reputation entirely. He dropped out of sports. He dropped out of life in general. He partied by night, every night, and slept through class by day. The teachers hadn't known what to do with him—neither had his friends. He skirted the ones who reached out and meant well, retreating to the center of a darker, more troublemaking circuit. The drinkers, smokers, joyriders and general hell-raisers.

Which had led him to another car crash, this one at Carlton Nurseries. James was still a couple of months underage at the time of the second accident so he was tried as a minor and sentenced to community service, repairing the damage he'd caused and toiling the summer away under Adrian's parents' watchful eyes.

Adrian remembered the exact moment she first felt the walls of her heart tremble for him. It was an especially hot day and she'd been trying to move heavy bags of fertilizer from the bed of her father's truck to the storeroom. She hadn't heard James come up behind her; he hadn't said a word. All she felt was a hand on her arm, gentle, maneuvering her out of the way. She stepped back, saw it was him and opened her mouth to tell him that she could handle it when, shirtless, without so much as a grunt, he'd hefted a bag over his shoulder.

He'd turned, and his gaze met hers—that wild, blue gaze. There had been beads of sweat on his face, crawling down his chest. He'd looked a shade pale, but there was a determined set to his jaw and, in those eyes, a kind of desperation.

She hadn't known what it meant, but as attraction and answering emotions swam beneath the surface of her skin, she hadn't been able to do anything but step aside, allowing him to pass and do the chore for her.

They worked like that for several days—wordlessly, side by side. Close enough for her to begin to feel the sadness and torment leaking off him in waves. The helpless boy he'd been at his father's funeral was clearly trying to fight past his pretense of badassery and James was wrestling with it, the struggle heightened now without the aid of liquor or drugs.

It wasn't until another moment, when Adrian found James hiding in her parents' barn, that her empathy turned into understanding. James was slouched on the bed of a tractor, flicking a Zippo lighter and watching the flame burn and die, burn and die, over and over again. She remembered how ill he'd looked. His skin had a gray tinge, there was a sheen of sweat cloaking his face and neck and a noticeable tic in his jaw. His foot tapped restlessly against the dusty concrete.

He wasn't coping well with the withdrawals. She knew it as soon as he raised his gaze to hers and again she saw the desperation and more than a touch of helplessness.

Unable to help herself, Adrian had taken him by the hand and led him back to the farmhouse. She fixed him a glass of lemonade, watched him

drink it and talked herself silly. He began to talk
back, haltingly at first. Then their conversation
had flowed easily as they emptied the pitcher of
lemonade. Adrian even managed to work a smile
out of him. He looked loads better, the desperation and helplessness vanquished. The shadows
under his eyes weren't quite so dark as they locked
on hers across the room and snagged her breath.

His effect on her had been disconcerting, but
she'd held that gaze, thrown it right back at him.
Then Adrian's mother came into the kitchen and
eyed James like a hawk. Adrian quickly ushered
him out. As they walked back to the nursery together, James had thanked her.

That was the day they became friends. It was
less than a week later that she drove him home
and he admitted that it was the anniversary of his
father's death. She comforted him. Somehow his
mouth found hers and he kissed her. By God, had
he kissed her. And their relationship, as it was,
had blazed on from there like the doomed supernova it was.

The summer romance ended abruptly when her
father was attacked.

It was after hours at the nursery. James had
crawled up to her second-floor room in the farmhouse and woken her. Sometime in the early hours
of morning, he had snuck out while she slept,
spent from his loving.

The next day brought upheaval.

During the night, her father had been assaulted by an unknown assailant. All Van Carlton had been able to remember as he lay in a hospital bed with his head and arm heavily bandaged was that his attacker had been wearing a letterman jacket.

All signs pointed to James. Her mother had been the first to say so. The police dragged him from his father's moored boat, where he had been sleeping, down to the station to question him. When Adrian found out that James had been arrested, she drove to the police station and, demanding to see the detective on the case, made it known that James had an alibi.

James was released. Her parents were shocked and disappointed by the fact that she and James had been together. It had taken her father months to look Adrian in the eye again. The real perpetrator was never caught.

As the weeks wore on and she neither saw nor heard anything from James, Adrian became deeply disturbed. When she went to his mother's house, Mrs. Bracken informed Adrian that when his community service time was over, James had skipped town.

Adrian waited for word from James, becoming more frantic when she realized she was pregnant. That franticness eventually warped into devastation. From there, her own brand of desperation had taken over. There could have been no other explanation as to why she married a man like

Radley after knowing so little about him. All that had seemed to matter at the time was that he appeared to be a kind man. At her weakest point, she'd latched onto that kindness in the face of her parents' deep disapproval.

It had taken years for Adrian to dig herself out of that hole of bad decisions, to regain the respect of her parents, her peers, to put the abuse she'd suffered at Radley's hands behind her and—hardest of all—to forget how hopeless she had felt when she realized the boy she loved would not be there for her, even after all she had done for him.

Eventually Adrian's heart did harden and turn cold. Thoughts of James Bracken and the hot summer they spent together grew fewer and farther between as she threw herself into making a new life for Kyle and herself.

She never counted on seeing James Bracken again, much less his moving into the house next door.

Growing restless once again, Adrian paced the shop before shouldering out the front door.

Spring air greeted her. Drinking it in, she veered around the silver buckets of blossoms and the chalkboard easel she'd set out announcing today's sale. By the time she reached the worn wooden door of Tavern of the Graces, she was muttering to herself.

The bar was empty. Her footsteps echoed in the absence of boisterous conversation and jukebox rock that usually blasted through the tavern. Knowing where to find her friend Olivia, Adrian made her way behind the counter and past the swinging doors. The first door to the left in the hallway beyond was open, the light streaming out.

Blowing a relieved breath, Adrian entered Olivia's office with its cluttered desk, large wall safe and sagging, green couch. "I have a problem," she announced, then stopped short, feet halting when she saw her friend sitting in the desk chair, hands on her knees, head hanging.

"Liv?" Adrian asked, alarmed when Olivia didn't look up or stir. "Are you okay?"

Olivia lifted a hand. The fingers trembled a bit. "Fine. I just…oh, crap." Her head lowered farther between her knees, her blond curls falling forward as she braced her hands on the arms of the chair. "Hang back… I may hurl on your shoes."

"What's wrong?" Adrian asked, taking a step into the office.

"Oh, just sick as a damned dog."

"The flu's still going around," Adrian warned her. "Maybe you should go home."

"I'm not contagious."

"Are you sure?" Adrian narrowed her eyes.

Olivia waved it off and finally, after some hesitation, sat up, slumping against the back of the chair. She looked pale, tired, but the corners of her lips twitched in something of a smile. "What's up? I need a distraction."

Adrian scanned Olivia closely. Her friend still looked a little green around the edges, but despite her weary movements, her eyes were alert and her eyebrows raised in expectation. Adrian cleared her throat and went ahead. "You won't believe this, but…do you remember what I told you last November? About how Radley isn't really Kyle's dad. It's—"

"—sexy James Bracken." Olivia's expression warmed several degrees. "Oh, yeah. I remember."

Adrian took a deep breath, as if she were about to plunge deep underwater. Then she blurted, "He's here."

Olivia's smile faded after a moment. "Who's here?"

"James!" Adrian exclaimed. "James Bracken. He's back—in Fairhope!"

Olivia's brows drew together and she lifted a hand to rub them, closing her eyes as she did so. "Wait a minute. James is *here*? He's been gone, like, eight years."

"I know that," Adrian pointed out, fighting impatience. "I'm telling you, Liv, that he is, at this very moment, moving into the house next door to mine."

Olivia's jaw dropped. "Holy crap, Batman."

"Yeah," Adrian said with an asserting nod, resisting the urge to pace Olivia's office. "Olivia, *what do I do*?"

Olivia's eyes scanned Adrian's face closely and

she rose carefully from her chair. "Okay, first of all, you need to calm down. Here. Maybe *you* should be sitting."

Adrian shrugged off the offer. "No. I need to *do something* about this. I need to call whoever it is who's in charge of selling that damn house. If they knew who they were selling it to, they'd back out. Escrow might not have closed by now. There's a chance they could—"

"What?" Olivia demanded to know. "The worst thing James Bracken ever did was run his car off the road into your parents' nursery, and he paid that debt. Getting you pregnant and leaving you high and dry was shitty, sure. But, for one, he didn't know about the baby. And two, it's not a criminal offense to sleep with someone and never call them again. If it were, he and I would both be repeat offenders. Plus, for all we know, he's a model citizen now."

Adrian snorted in disbelief. In rare moments through the years, low moments, whenever she had ventured to think about James Bracken, she'd imagined him in some seedy, twenty-first-century equivalent of a brothel. Her bitterness might have also conjured for him a handlebar mustache and a beer belly like Nutsy the Squirrel's.

Thinking back to the man who had come to the door of the house next door, she frowned. The lower half of his face might have been covered in hair, but the full beard hadn't looked cheesy.

It made James look manly—even sexier than the clean-shaven seventeen-year-old she'd fallen in love with. And he'd definitely not been hiding a beer belly under his sweaty T-shirt. There had been more than a faint impression of pectoral and abdominal muscles...

Adrian shook her head, forcing her thoughts back to the dire situation at hand. "So, what do you suggest?"

Olivia braced her hands on her hips. "Talk to him?" When Adrian looked horrified, Olivia shrugged. "Unless you're willing to pick up and move within the next few days, there's nothing you can do about living next door to him. And ask yourself this—would you rather he find out about Kyle from you or on his own?"

"Kyle?" Adrian shook her head. "No, no. He can't find out about Kyle."

Olivia's expression went blank. "Huh?"

"He won't know about Kyle," Adrian repeated, determined. "I'll send Kyle to live with Mom and Dad at The Farm before I let James find out about him."

Olivia's brow creased. "Adrian, think about this. Kyle's his son."

"He left!" Adrian shouted, unable to hold back the dangerous tidal wave of desperation and anger a moment longer. "If James wanted to know about the baby, he would have stuck around. He would have stood by me. He would have done all those things he told me he would."

"Like what?" Olivia asked.

"Like…" Adrian stopped, breathing hard, and brushed the hair out of her eyes. They had been silly, sweet things that James had said, she thought, looking back now with a bit more clarity. There had been few promises for the future, but she'd been certain James wanted to be with her beyond that summer. For a time, she even thought he was as in love with her as she'd been with him.

Olivia seemed to deflate as she read Adrian's helpless face. "Okay, let's try approaching this from another angle. How did you find out it was him moving in? Did you see him, face-to-face?"

Adrian nodded, wordless. She thought of the pie lying facedown, ruined, on James's front porch. *So much for the warm welcome.*

"So he knows it's you, too?"

"Yes," Adrian admitted. *Unfortunately.*

"And?" Olivia asked. When Adrian only looked at her in question, Olivia lifted her shoulders. "How did he look?"

Adrian frowned deeply. "What does that have to do with anything?"

"Just indulge me," Olivia insisted.

Sighing, Adrian gave in and lowered to the arm of the battered couch. "He looked…like a grown-up."

"Meaning?"

"Meaning he was different," Adrian said, rubbing her hands together. They were sore. During her anxiety attack, she had clenched and un-clenched them over and over. "He used to be long and lean and…well, he's still long and he's in good shape, damn it. But he's bigger here." She lifted her hands to either of her shoulders. "His hair's thicker, a bit shaggier. And he's got a beard and tattoos."

Olivia raised an interested brow. "Oh?"

"A whole sleeve of them, from what I could tell," Adrian said. "And one here." She pointed to her neck. "Though I couldn't see what it was exactly." Taking several, calming breaths, she frowned at the floor. "He looked good. The bone-head."

Olivia looked as if she was trying very hard not to smile. "You know…this could very well be a good thing."

Adrian's frown deepened as she saw the gleam in Olivia's eye. "Don't even think about it."

Again, Olivia's shoulders lifted as she feigned innocence. "What am I thinking?"

"That this is Briar and Cole all over again and you're going to fix James and me up and we're going to spend the rest of our lives driving each other crazy." Adrian rose and walked to the door. "It's not gonna happen for me, Liv. Especially not with a deadbeat asshole like James Bracken."

Olivia turned to watch her walk out. "Aren't you just a little bit curious about what he's been up to all this time?"

"No," Adrian replied. "And you know why? Because he left. He had better things to do than stick around and be with me. Why should I care what he's done with his life or made of it?"

"I don't know. For Kyle, maybe?"

Adrian's hackles rose. Then she realized it wasn't so much a low blow on Olivia's part to say so as it was clear-cut sense. Kyle knew that Radley wasn't his real father. Adrian had worked to find the right time and the right words to tell him just that. She'd told him very little about the man who had fathered him. She'd believed there was little chance James and Kyle would ever meet so she had let Kyle's imagination fill in the blanks.

Every so often, Kyle would ask a question about his father...questions Adrian didn't know how to answer. Even though she'd remained ambiguous through the years, she knew that Kyle's curiosity about his paternal heritage was a barely contained bud she didn't have the heart to suppress completely.

Olivia trailed Adrian from the office into the hall as she headed for the back door that led out onto the inn's lawn behind her greenhouse. "What're you going to do?"

"I don't know," Adrian said wearily. Damn it, she had enough to worry about on a day-to-day basis without a dilemma this size obstructing life in general. "I'll...think of something. I have to." She stopped, propping the door open with her shoulder and knee as she glanced back. She noted the way Olivia was leaning against the wall, the bags under her eyes. "Is Gerald home?"

"Yeah, writing. Why?"

"You should go. Have him take care of you. Seriously. You look like shit."

Olivia frowned over the sentiment. "So long as we're being honest...does it strike you as coincidence that James is moving in next door to you?"

"What do you mean?"

Olivia lifted a shoulder. "Maybe he already knows what you don't want him to know. Maybe he's trying to edge his way back into your life— to be a dad, a man. Not the screwup he was eight years ago."

Adrian pressed her lips inward, rubbing them together as she thought back to their abrupt reunion. James had seemed as surprised to see her as she was him. Though, could Olivia be right? Did James know something about Kyle already? The thought made Adrian's heart race like something preyed upon.

There was no way anyone was going to get to Kyle. There was no way anyone was edging their way into her life and taking her son from her.

Adrian raised her chin. "If that is the case, then he can kiss his chances goodbye. It'd take a heck of a lot more than a new house to convince me that James Bracken has become an honest man, much less daddy material."

CHAPTER THREE

ADRIAN CARLTON. *UNBELIEVABLE*.

After the movers left him alone with the boxes and furniture, James went over to the little cottage next door. It was a charming yellow clapboard house with a well-tended yard and picket fence. He knocked on the red-painted door a few times, then returned home, disappointed, when no one answered.

She must have gotten home late that night. He hadn't seen or heard a car pull in. And she must have left early the next morning, too, because after he rose, showered and had what he could find for breakfast in the nearly empty pantry, he'd gone over again to knock. No answer.

Put off by the fact that she had evaded him again, James got in his sportster and drove into town. The garage on Section Street was another work in progress. Still, it was in better shape than the house. It was an old service station in desperate need of a paint job and some TLC. James had wanted it from the moment he heard it was for sale.

He'd already had several of his old cars brought

down from North Carolina, some favorites he had collected over the years of good fortune. He pulled in next to the cherry-red Shelby he had bought to replace the one his father owned—the one James had plowed hood first into the office of Carlton Nurseries. As he got out of the sportster and walked around the Shelby, his hand automatically reached out to graze the restored hood. He veered around the tow truck the previous garage owner had generously left him and, digging the keys from the pocket of his worn jeans, rounded the front of the building.

Bending over, he unlocked the latch at the bottom of the steel door and, grabbing it from the bottom, shoved it up over his head. The door rolled up and bright morning sunlight spilled into the garage, revealing the automotive and mechanic's tools James had already started to arrange around the room. Taking off his sunglasses, he moved past rolling toolboxes, a couple of jacks, the electric car lift he'd recently spent a weekend installing and even a rough-hewn table covered in wrenches, wipe rags and the Corvette engine he had finally finished restoring after starting the project with his father in his early teens.

James had kept the engine around for luck, mostly. Over the years, it had served him well. He would need that luck to get his fledgling small business off the ground. And it also reminded him of why he had bought the run-down garage in the first place. Back in those early, simple days of adolescence when Zachariah Bracken had still been alive, father and son had talked about opening a garage together when James grew up.

His father might have given up alcoholism and tinkering with boats and automobiles to devote his life to God and join the ministry. James, however, had held on to that dream, and it had never really left him. Not even after his father passed away and James buried himself in seedy, reprehensible pursuits to get away from that reality.

His father was long gone. And those shady years after had left their mark. But James still had a love for cars and all things automotive. His passion and knack for mechanics had served him as well as the lucky Corvette engine through the years. He was to the point in his life where he didn't need money or cars anymore—he had plenty of both. What he needed now was closure. Peace. He had a good sense that launching Bracken Mechanics in Fairhope, the place he began, would be a big step in that direction.

As he set the duffel he'd brought from the house on the work counter beside the dusty screen of his service computer, James caught himself scrubbing a hand over his sternum and the wooden cross that hung beneath his black T-shirt. A tinge of regret flared to life in his chest. He'd been meaning to visit his father's grave since his return. He hadn't yet found a moment to do it. Maybe some part of him was avoiding the painful errand. He hadn't even ventured into the cemetery since the funeral—the funeral he hadn't been man enough to sit all the way through…

He *would* do it, he thought, squaring his jaw. He just needed a bit more time.

Ghosts. The memory of Zach Bracken was just one of those lurking around Fairhope. His mother still lived here, though he hadn't summoned the gall to show up at his old childhood home. There were too many hurts to make up for between the two of them, and he needed to mull a little longer on how best to approach that situation. Anyway, James had found yet another ghost staring him in the face yesterday afternoon in the form of Adrian Carlton.

No, he hadn't been able to forget Adrian. The memory of their summer together was burned into his mind, into his skin. She looked a good deal different, undoubtedly a woman now. She'd cropped her hair short. Eight years ago, it had hung down her back. He remembered how he'd wrapped it in his hands, a thick, red silk rope.

The short hair suited her. It left the fascinating angles of her face to answer for themselves. And answer they did. It made her eyes look bigger, deeper—saucers of dark chocolate. That was exactly what he had thought the first time he'd lost himself in them.

As a seventeen-year-old, Adrian had been built

like a waif. Not too thin but with more angles than curves. As James watched her retreat from him yesterday in puzzlement, his eyes had latched onto the line of her hips, more rounded now in womanhood. He'd wanted nothing more than to chase after her, place his hands on either side of her waist and soothe the stark, white panic he'd seen on her face.

Clearly, he hadn't left things well between them, but James had known that before he encountered her on his front porch. The thought of Adrian had troubled him deeply as he skipped town all those years ago. It didn't matter that he'd been doing the right thing at the time. The right thing for her, at least. But he couldn't understand the sheer level of terror that confronting him again had obviously caused her. Anger would have been a great deal more justified and characteristic of the Adrian he'd known. But fear? James couldn't make sense of that.

He needed to make sure she was okay. Hell, he needed to know how life had treated her. When he decided coming back to Fairhope was the right decision, he'd thought of her, of course. Though he'd figured there was little chance she'd still be living here. Fairhope had seemed far too small a town for both of their wild teenage selves. As they grew to know each other over the course of that summer, one of the commonalities that had struck a fast bond between them was the mutual desire to one day put as much distance as possible between their hometown—and the people in it—and themselves.

Thinking about the firebrand version of Adrian he'd known back then, James caught himself smiling. He scraped the back of his middle and index fingers over his mouth to chase it away and turned at the sound of an approaching vehicle.

Sunshine shot off the black hood of the car. James squinted as the light beamed into his eyes, raising a hand to his brow to shield them as he watched the 1969 Camaro Z28 with white racing stripes pull into the parking lot. He let out a low whistle. "Nice car," he called as he walked from the garage to greet the man who unfolded himself from the driver's seat.

"Thanks." The visitor appeared to be in his midthirties with dark hair growing over the collar of his black business suit. As he approached James, he stood tall and straight. "That's a nice Shelby GT350 over there. You wouldn't by any chance mind a stranger taking her off your hands, would you?"

James cracked a smile. He looked over at the Shelby, reaching back to scratch his neck. "Sorry. She's got sentimental value."

"That's a damn shame." The man offered a hand and shook James's in a firm grip. "Byron Strong. I heard someone bought ol' Cy Witmore's place and had to come by to see for myself."

"James Bracken," James greeted him. "I take it you were one of Witmore's customers?"

"Since I moved over from Mobile several years ago." Byron nodded. "Every once in a while, he'd let me help out around the place. Not that I'm a certified mechanic or anything."

"No kidding," James said. "My dad and I used to come up here when I was a kid and hang out with Witmore. But this was back when he kept glass bottles of Coca-Cola to sell to his customers and his old coon dog, Scout, was still loping around after him. You lookin' for a job? I could use a tow truck driver."

Byron lifted a shoulder. "My day job keeps me busy enough. I'm an accountant. The other reason I came by is because my sister, Priscilla Grimsby, is a reporter for the local newspaper. She has a business column. I thought you'd like to get in touch with her, see what kind of publicity the two of you can generate for this place. I'd sure like to see it do well again."

James took the business card with Byron's sister's name and number on it. "I appreciate it." He scanned Byron's face. "You play any poker, Byron?"

A smile wore into the corners of Byron's mouth as he relaxed his stance and crossed his arms over his chest. "When the occasion strikes."

"I just got back into town," James admitted. "When I get settled in, we should get a game together so that I can repay you for this…" he lifted the card, then gestured to the Camaro "…and for letting me take a peek under your hood."

Byron considered for a moment before his smile widened. "Sounds fair."

Byron even went a step further and let James fire the Camaro up. He revved the Z28 and listened to the ponies work, impressed. The two of them drooled over the engine for a while. Byron obviously knew his way around one. It was no wonder ol' Witmore had let him hang around occasionally.

It wasn't until Byron closed the hood and stepped back toward the open driver's door of the Camaro that he said, "There's already some talk about you in town, you know."

"Huh." James could imagine what residents were saying about him. Eventually talk would lead back to those ghosts of his who still lived and thrived. Not just Adrian, but also his mother. His stepfather. James fought off the shadow that thoughts of his relatives brought about. "Word of mouth's as good promotion as any."

"True," Byron acknowledged. "Word is you were the town riot back in the day."

"I'll go out on a limb and say that everything you've heard is true."

Byron leaned against the driver's door and raised a brow. "Even the joyriding?"

"Maybe. Why?"

Byron grinned. "I'm just wondering if I need to be worried about my ride here."

James laughed despite himself. "If I'm gonna take your Camaro, Strong, it'll be in a hand of poker, along with most of your earnings."

Byron chuckled. "For what's it worth, welcome back to town. And call the number on the card. Let Priscilla fix you up." He gazed over the hood of his car at the garage. "This place deserves a second chance."

James stood back as Byron folded himself back into the driver's seat of the Chevy.

"Anything else I can do, you'll let me know," Byron asserted, rolling down the driver's window.

James frowned. "Actually…how long did you say you've been here?"

"In Fairhope?" Byron reached up to scratch his forehead. "Going on three years."

"You wouldn't happen to know the Carltons?" James ventured.

Byron thought for a moment. "You mean Van and Edith?"

James's pulse jerked at the mention of Adrian's parents. "That's them. More to the point, it's their daughter I'm wondering about."

"Adrian," Byron said and nodded. "Yeah. I know her. Pretty well, as a matter of fact."

With a frown, James wondered what the man meant by *pretty well*. He cleared his throat. "I just moved in next door to her. Do you know where she works?"

"Oh, yeah," Byron said. "She owns that little flower shop on the bay, a few blocks from where she lives. Next to Hanna's Inn. You know it?"

Years ago the proprietor of Hanna's Inn, Hanna Browning, had been close friends with James's mother. "I do. So Adrian's a florist now?"

"A good one, too," Byron said. "She does damn good business, anyway. The apple didn't fall too far from the tree as far as business interests go. Though I'd never say so to her face." When James only frowned at him, Byron explained, "I do the books for Carlton Nurseries so I've come to know the Carltons pretty well. Adrian and Edith don't exactly see eye to eye."

"They never did," James muttered.

"She's a prickly one. Edith," Byron added. "I'm assuming you and Adrian went to school together."

James thought about that, brows coming together. "We knew each other," he admitted.

Byron watched James chew over the words for a moment. "Well, give her my regards. It's been a while."

"I'll do that," James agreed. *If she'll let me.* He shut Byron's door for him as he cranked the Camaro and the engine's horses purred to life. Through the open window, James said, "Thanks for stopping by."

Byron slipped his sunglasses into place and gave James a salute. "See you around."

"ADRIAN?"

"Back here," Adrian called from the cooler as she moved several wedding and funeral arrangements around to make room for today's pièce de résistance—a bouquet ordered by one of the local churches for the altar on Easter Sunday.

Penny peered around the jamb of the open steel door. "Hey, you got a minute?"

"Yeah," Adrian said with a grunt as she hefted the large vase onto the second shelf at the back of the cooler. Wiping her hands on the front of her apron, she turned to her shop assistant with raised brows. "What's up?"

Penny pressed her lips inward as if hiding a smile. Her eyes were a tad overbright. She was nineteen and friendly with customers—the attractive men in particular. Adrian knew by the look on Penny's face that she'd recently encountered one such appealing male specimen.

"There's a man here to see you," Penny answered, confirming Adrian's suspicions.

"What kind of man?" Adrian asked. Then she paused, frowning as her heart rapped hard against her ribs. "Wait," she said, holding her hands up before Penny could explain. "Does he have a beard?"

"Mmm-hmm," Penny said. "And tattoos all down his arm. Very James Dean."

Adrian shook her head. "James Dean didn't have tattoos, Penny," she muttered in automatic response. "Or facial hair."

"I meant he has that vibe," Penny said. She opened her mouth, then stopped and stared at Adrian as the latter began to scrub her hands over her face. "What's wrong?" Penny's face fell. "Oh, my God. Is he Radley, your ex? Should I call the police—or Mr. Savitt?"

"No," Adrian said carefully. "He's not Radley. And there's no need for the police or Cole." She took a deep breath, hoping it would calm her—or at least make her legs stop quaking. "I've got this."

"Are you sure?" Penny asked doubtfully.

Adrian rolled her eyes as Penny's voice mirrored all the uncertain voices in her head. She shouldered past the shop assistant into the prep room of Flora. "Tell him to come on back. Then you can go home."

"All right," Penny said hesitantly. "You're sure you don't need me?"

"Just do it, please," Adrian told her. When Penny returned to the front of the shop, Adrian ran her fingers through her hair, feeling frazzled already. She planted her hands on her hips when she heard heavy footsteps coming toward her and turned to face James as he entered.

By God. With his height and massive shoulders, he filled the room. Hell, he filled the air, stealing it from her. Her alarm and resentment for him rose by twin notches. Crossing her arms over her chest in a shielding stance, she jerked her chin high and met his gaze with a cold look. "James."

He stopped just inside the door, not even bothering to glance around. Those blue eyes latched onto her and seized. "Adrian," he said, his tone a great deal softer and gentler than hers.

There was kindness behind those eyes. And longing. Adrian blinked, frowned and forced herself not to look away. Instead, she scanned his features. She'd always thought he had the face of a Roman warrior—manhood had affirmed that. The bones of his face were long and broad. Beneath his beard, his jaw was perfectly etched. Someone could break a knuckle or two against that jawline and probably already had. The rise and hollows of his cheeks were artfully hewn.

There were three buttons at the top of his black T-shirt and, damn it, every single one was open, giving her a better look at the tattoos underneath. The one most visible was a bit faded, but she could still clearly see a black and red nautical star. *Fitting*. He'd spent a great deal of his childhood on the water. His father had been a boat captain at one point before becoming a preacher. James had inherited Zachariah Bracken's recreational daysailer after he passed away.

Just below his collarbone was more ink, Latin letters. She couldn't make out what they said. Neither could she discern what shape the darker ink below took. It was lost under the cotton and what looked to be a thick growth of chest hair.

Adrian took a gulp of air and hated when it trembled out on an exhale. "What are you doing here?"

One of James's dark brows arched, but his eyes lost none of their softness nor, unfortunately, did they stray from hers. "I guess I figured we should talk."

"About?" Adrian prompted, trying not to sound defensive and failing miserably.

"About how we left things yesterday…or how *you* left things yesterday," James told her. "I need to know that you're okay."

"You want to talk about how I left things *yesterday*," Adrian repeated, incredulity honing the words to a fine point. She felt anger brewing and latched onto it like a lifeline. "That's all you came here for?"

"Yeah," James said with a small nod. "And to make sure you're okay."

"Huh," Adrian said, punching the word out as she walked to the other side of her prep counter. With the raised surface between them, she felt better. Half to herself, she muttered, "I haven't seen or heard from the man in eight years and he's as blind and self-centered as ever."

"Excuse me?"

"You, James Bracken," she said, turning to

face him and slowing the explanation to mocking speed, "are a self-centered jackass."

James stared at her for a shocked moment, jaw slackened. Then his features shifted into an unexpected and equally devastating smile. He took a step toward her, then another. "And you, Adrian Carlton, are the same crazy, beautiful firebrand."

When he continued advancing on her, Adrian found herself retreating backward. Damn it, this was *her* turf. "Stop flattering me, for God's sake," she said, flustered. "I'm trying to insult you."

James chuckled. The deep, rich laughter flowed over her like warm waves. Her heart trembled. "Christ, I've missed you."

"No," she said, as she found herself backed into a corner, his big, rangy body closing in on hers. His friendly gaze locked her into place, cutting off all means of escape. Raising her hands, she planted them on his chest and pushed against the hot, strong line of his torso. "Stop, James. You have to stop." Panic closed up her throat and she could breathe no longer. "Please." Damn it, she hadn't meant to beg. But there it was. *Please.* That weak, useless word she'd grown to hate over her years with Radley.

James's body stiffened and his smile dropped away. He frowned, scanning her face. When he spoke, his words were low, surprised. "You're afraid of me."

Adrian swallowed, unable to deny it with her

voice trapped at the back of her throat. Her heart banged away at her ribs like a wild, caged thing. She stared at those Latin letters on his collarbone, very aware of the rise and fall of his chest as the moment between them stretched, the silence deep. *Don't let him see.*

James's hand lifted and she braced not for a blow but a touch she knew would be just as crippling. She drew back against the wall, every muscle in her body tightening. The rough pad of his thumb grazed the knob of her chin just below her lips before his fingers spread and cupped her cheek.

Adrian closed her eyes to keep from looking at his face and all the things she might see there. Possibility. Light.

Nope, she refused to look at him and let her heart leap at him in the reckless, kamikaze way it had all those years ago.

His words were low again but edged in need that made her bite the inside of her lip. "The past eight years have been a crazy blur," he began. "I've had some amazing highs and some pretty terrible lows. There's been triumph and pain, light and shade. But no matter where I was, or what was going on around me, sometimes I would close my eyes and, in my mind, quiet would take over. For a moment, everything around me would be still and I could breathe. I could think. And then you'd be there. I'd see your face in front of me as clear as it was the last time I saw it. And there with you in the calm, I'd feel at peace again."

Adrian opened her eyes as her lips parted. She gaped up at him and the emotions clashing in his eyes. She had expected pretty, empty words of apology from him. But this was a surprise—and the only thing that could have shattered her defenses. Suddenly, they were standing together and he looked as vulnerable as she felt.

She scanned his face, unable to look elsewhere. His expression, his eyes, all the silent words he communicated to her…they were like an eclipse—too dangerous to look at without some sort of shield but too irresistible not to. Adrian firmed her mouth in a tight line before she whispered, "You can't…" Faltering, she reached up, took his hand, dropped it away and tried to form words again. "You can't just come back into my life, say all the right things and expect me to fall at your feet again."

A flicker of mirth crossed James's face. A corner of his mouth twitched. "Well, the last time you didn't exactly fall at my feet. Women like you, Adrian, don't fall." He moved his hands into the pockets of his jeans. "You're much more resourceful and purposeful than that."

She reached up to knead the pulsing vein in her temple. "You don't know me, James. You might have once. But I'm different. I've changed." *You changed everything.*

His eyes scanned her, heating. "I can see that."

Adrian felt the rush of incredulity again and let it lead her out of the numb, defenseless state his words had bound her in. She scoffed, planting her hands on his chest and using them to move him back.

Normally, she knew that even if she had thrown a shoulder into his solid frame, she couldn't have budged him. But he stepped back for her and she shoved by, scrubbing her fingers through her hair again. This time they mussed more than straightened, but she couldn't bring herself to care. "You need to go."

"You haven't told me whether or not you're okay," James pointed out, bracing his hand on the wall, the other still buried in his pocket. It was a wonder someone as big as he was could look so casually graceful.

"Oh, I'm fine," she snapped. "I'm just peachy. Now are you satisfied?"

"Satisfied?" he asked and ran his tongue over his teeth, considering. "I might be. If you hadn't looked so lost yesterday. If you hadn't run from me as though I was the grim reaper."

"You weren't supposed to come back," Adrian told him, wanting to hit him where it would hurt the most. Maybe then he would know what he was doing to her. "You weren't ever supposed to come back."

"Truth be told," James said, pushing off the

wall and straightening to his full height, "when I left, I fully intended it to be for good."

"So, why are you here, James?" she asked, fighting hard to keep desperation from breaking over her voice. It was like walking on eggshells. "Why *did* you come back?"

James moved his shoulders. "I have unfinished business."

"Me?" she demanded. "Is that why you moved in next door? Because you wanted to fix things with me? Or mess them up for me like you did the last time?"

His face went blank. "I would have messed things up more if I had stayed."

Adrian let out a bitter laugh. "You idiot."

"I didn't ask you to vouch for me that night, Adrian," James pointed out. "You shouldn't have vouched for me."

"But *I did*!" she shouted. "I did. And how did you repay me? You up and *left*!"

James started to argue, then stopped himself, grinding his back teeth. For the first time, a dark light blinked to life in his eyes, a warning glimmer. It was a snatched glimpse of the old James, the dark side of the hell-raiser he'd been. His chest moved as he pulled in a slow, deep breath, seeming to gather himself. He lifted his hand from his pocket and scraped two fingers over his mouth— the exact way Kyle did.

Adrian's heart dropped and she almost reached for the chair beside her for balance.

James didn't notice how much the gesture affected her. *Thank God*. Instead, his eyes cooled, the anger effectively vanquished, and he said, "We both know what happened eight years ago. I'm not dragging it out and picking a fight over it. I did what I thought was right."

"And we both had to live with that," she said, then bit her tongue. Damn it, why had she said that?

"What do you mean?" he asked.

She lifted her gaze back to his, challenging. "You don't know?" she asked, again punching the words out. Unable to help herself now that she'd started.

His eyes narrowed. "What are you trying to tell me?"

"Come on, James," she said, exasperated. "You expect me to believe you moved in next door by pure chance? Am I supposed to believe you closed your eyes, drove in circles and wound up at my place of work, too? Or did you throw darts at the map?"

James shrugged. "Adrian, I didn't even know you were still in Fairhope, much less living next door to the house I bought." He advanced again. "And even if I had known, what would it matter? Why are you afraid me?" Before she could reply, he pointed at her, the muscles of his face tight.

"The Adrian I knew wasn't afraid of anything, least of all me. What the hell's happened in eight years to make *that* change?"

Adrian opened her mouth to retort, to deflect, but the sound of the bells jangling over the entry doors of the shop stalled her. *Crap.* She didn't need customers overhearing this. With a sigh, she tempered the heat of argument inside her and lowered her voice. "These are business hours. If you want to continue this, it'll have to be later."

"Sure, later," James said with a rigid nod. "How 'bout your place at six?"

"No!" she shrieked. "You can't come over!"

"Why not?" he asked. Something crossed his face and it wasn't friendly. "You got a territorial, live-in boyfriend or something?"

"No, but—"

"Hey, Mom, guess what!"

Adrian turned, horrified. Her blood turned cold as Kyle sprinted into the room. "H-how…?" She trailed off as Van Carlton stepped into the room next and laid his hands on his grandson's shoulders. "Dad."

"Adrian," her father greeted her. The warm smile on his face faltered when he turned his attention to the other man in the room. "Bracken?" he asked, surprised.

James didn't reply. His eyes were on Kyle, studying his face. He didn't seem to be breathing.

He wasn't the only one. Adrian felt her face heat

and wondered how. She was so cold her bones ached with the chill. She tried to swallow, but her throat was as dry as dust. Instinct broke through and she walked to Kyle, putting herself between her child and the man she hadn't ever wanted him to meet. "You need to go, hon."

"But, Mom…"

"Take him home," Adrian said, praying her father wouldn't argue.

Her dad considered her for a moment. He glanced over her shoulder at James, then back at her and gave a short nod. "I'll take care of it."

Adrian watched Kyle and her father leave the shop, watched through the glass display window as her father's truck, marked with the Carlton Nurseries logo, pulled out of the gravel parking lot. Only then did she turn back to face James and the secrets of the last eight years.

CHAPTER FOUR

IF JAMES HADN'T known better, he would have thought he was in a submarine. The walls of the flower shop seemed to be pressing inward, bowing under some enormous pressure. The floor seemed to tilt. To keep his balance, he held his arms out slightly as Adrian turned back to face him in the absence of the man and the boy.

The man had been her father. James had recognized Van Carlton well enough despite the new sunspots and creases in the older man's face. He'd worn the same, worn, black Dale Earnhardt cap years ago. But the boy—

The boy was another story entirely. For a split second, James had thought he was staring at a mirror image of his younger self. The mop of hair might have been a lighter shade of brown, but it was just as thick, just as untidy, and it fell over the boy's brow in just the way James's fell over his and always had. James knew instinctively that it grew at an unmanageable rate and had to be clipped every three weeks to keep it from covering the boy's eyes.

His eyes—dear God. They had been the kicker.

James knew those eyes, not just from his own re-
flection. His father had looked at him with the
same eyes, in the same light. Considering. Ami-
able. Curious.

James's stomach pitched. His throat closed. He
reached up. The rafter above his head was close,
close enough for a man of his height to wrap his
hand around it and brace himself. He was afraid
it was the only thing keeping him upright.

The boy had sported a face full of freckles.
They'd been a curse of James's early adolescence.
He hadn't missed them when they began to fade
with time and maturity. There was still a dark
scatter of them across his shoulders and upper
back.

The boy had been tall for his age, too. *Seven*.
James knew he was seven. Not because he was
around children all that often. He just knew…he
knew, damn it.

His gaze finally found Adrian's. Her hands
were at her sides, her back and shoulders straight,
a posture that might have looked calm, composed
if not for the fact that her fists were opening and
closing into white-knuckled balls.

He had a good sense that her nails were scoring
her palms. She'd done that whenever her mother,
Edith, started in on her. After Edith walked away
at long last, taking her dark, rumbling cloud of
disapproval with her, James remembered taking
Adrian's hands in his, opening them to see the

half-moon marks on her palms. Then he'd rub the pads of his thumbs over them, lifting them to his lips, soothing hurts he knew she felt outside and in.

Disappointed mothers had been one of their commonalities. James had deserved his. The eternally disappointed Edith was another thing, and for some reason, once James's relationship with Adrian had heated and gained some tenderness over the weeks they grew to know each other—bodies, hearts, minds—he had been eager to make up for those undeserved hurts...

Now he couldn't have crossed the room to her if he tried. Now he didn't feel like soothing. He didn't know what it was he felt. He'd suffered concussions. He'd been as drunk as ten sailors on a rainy night in Dublin. Still, he couldn't remember ever feeling so off-kilter. So lost.

A maelstrom built inside him. Something burned the back of his throat. Anger. It was his old fallback, that knee-jerk emotion he'd turned to when Zachariah Bracken died—his chief coping mechanism. The one he'd worked so carefully to learn to curb as an adult.

The anger twisted and burned inside him. It grew and he didn't do much to stop it. The boy's appearance had stripped him, left him naked and raw. Suddenly anger was the only thing he had. The taste of it was bitter, but also familiar. And the familiarity was a comfort he couldn't refuse.

James's lips parted. He finally found his breath and sucked it in raggedly. His voice was rough when he spoke. It sounded dark, deadly even to his own ears. "Explain," he said.

Adrian's expression wavered for a moment—one moment of weakness before composure took over again. Practice. That kind of quick, strong composure only came with practice. When she spoke, her words were calm, too. Steady but low, so low he could barely hear them over the pounding in his ears. "I don't think I have to."

James's brows lifted. "You don't?" he asked, punching the words out. It was his turn to ball his hands into fists. The knuckles cracked from the strain. The maelstrom had turned into a hot, fiery vortex of anger he feared there was no escape from. It scared him just as much as the implications of that face, those eyes that were an exact match for his own.

"No," Adrian answered. "I don't."

"He's mine." James wondered where the words had come from. They didn't seek or question. They were just there.

Something flashed in the dark depths of her eyes. Emotion. He was as relieved to see the small puncture in the wall of her composure, as he was satisfied that he had caused it.

"No, he's mine," she said, not raising her voice. The words shook in ferocity. "You might be his father, but you didn't bring him into this world.

You didn't raise him. So whatever *say* you think you have in any of this you can swallow. And you'll forgive me, hot rocks, for not much caring if you choke on it."

The breath washed out of him and he advanced on her as the fiery storm inside him began spitting hail. "What—"

"No!" she shrieked, her composure finally shattering. She was shaking. He wasn't altogether sure if it was from weakness or fury. She jabbed a finger at him as her eyes fired. "You can threaten me, rail at me, curse me all you want, but when it comes to him, I will not budge!"

"For Christ's sake, *he's my son, Adrian*!" The words cracked, his voice shattered and he struggled to hold back a blistering oath. He said the words again. "He's my son. He's my blood. You just admitted it yourself and you expect me to stand here and not say one damned word about it?"

"No," she said. Her eyes hardened to pebbles. Her arms crossed. "I expect you to walk away."

"Walk away?"

"Yes."

"And why would I do that?" he thundered.

Her gaze cleaved into his, but her words softened. Sure and sad at once. "Because that's what you did. Remember, James? You walked."

He faltered, struggled for argument, words, justification. "I didn't know…"

The sadness spread quickly across her face. She blinked and it vanished, contained once more. "I didn't know, either. Not when you left. It wasn't for three or four weeks after that that I began to…" Her breath hitched, throwing her off. She stopped, swallowed, closed her eyes for a brief moment, then opened them and stared hard at his chest. "…before I began to feel the effects. You were long gone."

When James only shook his head, she loosened a breath slowly. "Look, we both know there isn't much room for you to point fingers. We slept together and you were gone two days later."

No, he couldn't argue with that. The waves of anger that had been pounding at the shore of his control rolled back on themselves until they were a distant rumble. His incredulity splintered and cold seeped into the cracks where fury had been boiling minutes before.

Still, he couldn't get around the fact that eight years had gone by. His child had lived and breathed and thrived here in his hometown and he hadn't known about it. James began to shake his head in denial. "You could've—"

"What?" she demanded when he trailed off. She lifted her hands when his mouth only hung open, wordless. "You were gone. You didn't even tell your mother where you were going. Nothing."

"Wait a second," he said, holding up a hand. "You went to my mom?"

"Well, yes, of course," she said. "I thought she would know where you'd gone."

He reached up to scrub a hand over his temple. "Did she know—about the baby?"

Adrian hesitated for a moment, then she nodded. "Yes. She knew."

"Son of a bitch," he said. He had to resist the urge to sit down. "All this time…" His eyes zeroed in on Adrian's face again. "Who else? Besides your parents and my mom, who else knows?"

"I didn't tell anybody else that you were the father," she told him. "My friends know now, but I told them in confidence. You and I were together for just a handful of weeks and we kept it quiet so my parents wouldn't find out. You were gone before the news that I was pregnant became common knowledge."

Adrian lowered her eyes as she went on. "Your mother pitied me, James. And she wasn't the only one. There were a lot of people who pitied me when I began to show, and that was the worst part. Worse than the disapproval I got from others. Almost as bad as my parents' disappointment. Once it sank in that you were gone and didn't want to be found, I was heartbroken. But worse, I was humiliated."

James looked at her now, the tears shining through the steel of her eyes. He saw the girl she had been. The seventeen-year-old firebrand. And he was ashamed. He cursed. "You stayed here?" he asked. "You could've gone anywhere, started over…"

Adrian's frown deepened. "I thought about it… but then…" She combed her hair back from her brow and shook her head. "Things happened. I stayed. I'm not getting into it now. I landed on my feet eventually and people finally stopped pitying me, even if some of them still whispered behind my back. The most important thing to me, then and now, is that my son is healthy and happy."

"Our son," James corrected. When Adrian only sighed, he raised himself to full height, unable to yield. "You can tell yourself whatever you want, Adrian, but he *is* my son."

She looked at him, expression saddened again. "You don't even know his name."

James's brows drew together. Damn it all to hell, she was right. "Right now all that matters is that I want to know it." When she only looked at him, expression unchanged, he fought another curse. His voice dropped to a whisper. "I want to know, Adrian," he said. "Please…tell me his name."

Adrian combed his features with her eyes. When he didn't so much as blink, she seemed to deflate, the rigid line of her shoulders bowing under the strain he saw in her hands as she scrubbed them over her face. In defeat, she locked her arms over her chest once more and said, "Kyle. His name is Kyle."

"Kyle," James repeated, bringing the boy's freckled cheeks and bright eyes back to mind. As they came into focus, the face did for James what he had admitted to Adrian that her face had done for him through the years. The stillness, the unexpected calm, made breathing a great deal easier. For the first time in what seemed like an eternity, James pulled in a deep, cleansing breath. It cleared his head, stilled those few waves still roiling listlessly somewhere inside him. It brought the first real blink of clarity. "Kyle Carlton."

"Yes," she said. The single word seemed to hang like a challenge in the air. She backed it up by lifting her chin, daring him to contradict it.

James gave a small nod. Despite everything, he was relieved to see the light that challenge brought back to her eyes, easing the strain and fatigue the confrontation and revelations had caused. "That's fair."

She blinked in surprise, thrown off by the easy concession.

James stepped toward her, eager to catch her while her guard was down on one point, at least. "I won't say that leaving you was a mistake. I did it because I thought it was the right thing to do." When she scoffed, he held up a hand. "I won't make excuses, either, because at this point I'm not sure they would mean that much to you, anyway. I doubt, after everything, that you'd be able to take me at my word." When she said nothing to contradict that, James crossed to her. He didn't touch her, but he did lower his head toward hers. "But know this. I will *not* walk away this time."

Adrian's forehead creased. "But—"

"Whatever you want from me, I can't forget," James said evenly. "I never forgot you. I certainly won't forget the child we made together. And however selfish you might think I am for saying and doing so, I'm not slinking away and pretending that this never happened. I'm not staying out of the way. I want to meet him, Adrian." Alarm broke apart in her eyes and he hurried to say more. "I want to talk to him. Know him."

"James, you can't."

"Why not?" he demanded.

"Listen to yourself," she said. "All I hear is *I* want. What about what *he* needs?"

"He needs a father," James stated. When a lightning flash of indignation crossed her face, he lifted his brows. "Are you telling me he's never asked about me? He's never been curious about where he came from? Did you tell him I died—fell off a building, got trampled by bulls…?"

"Of course not. Don't be ridiculous!"

"But he has asked, hasn't he?" James knew he had her there. "He is curious." When she was silent, he swallowed hard because his next thought perturbed him quite a bit. "Is there someone else—another man you've shared him with, trusted him to? Someone he thinks of as a dad?"

Her eyes turned thoughtful and his heart banged away at his chest, knowing the answer.

"Yes."

When he cursed again, a small smile ticked at the corners of her mouth. It was the first waver of mirth he'd seen from her. "Only…he calls him Granddaddy."

Van. She was talking about Van. Inwardly, James breathed a sigh of relief. "That's good," he said after a moment. "I always liked the old man… despite everything. But it's not enough. Tell me it's enough for the kid and I'll walk away right now."

"It *has* to be," Adrian told him. "For his sake, James, *it has to be.*"

"For his sake…or for yours?"

She gaped at him. Then she raised her hands to her head. Her fingertips kneaded at her temples as she huffed in frustration. "I know what's best for him. I'm his mother. You left and—you're right— I couldn't care less what your reasons or excuses for it are. You can't take it back, no matter what you say. There's nothing you can do to fix it."

"That may be true for us—you and me," James acquiesced. And wasn't that a crying shame? "But Kyle is another story, and you know it."

"What I know is that you have to respect my wishes, as his mother."

James blew out a breath, prayed for patience. "Damn it, Adrian. Kyle needs me. Some part of him needs me."

"You don't know him," she said, leveling a finger at him. "So don't for one minute think that you know what's best for him. You broke my heart, James, but I'm a grown woman—I learned to deal with it and move on. He's just a boy, and if you think you're going to get close enough to break his heart, too, you've got another think coming!"

He advanced on her, closing what little space there was between them. "You know what? The same goes for you if you think I'm capable of hurting a kid, particularly one who belongs to me."

"He'll never belong to you," Adrian shot back. "Not if I have anything to do with it."

He smiled because he knew without a doubt that he would prove her wrong. He'd prove his worth, both to her and Kyle. He'd earn his place in their lives, just as he'd earn his place in Fairhope. "We'll see about that." And just because it would catch her off guard, he hooked an arm around her waist. She stumbled into him, navel to navel, and gasped as his lips lowered to her ear. "By the end of this, you'll both know you can count on me. I promise you that."

She balled her hands against his chest and twisted out of his grip. "Let go."

James obeyed. Spurred by the awareness that had flashed briefly across her face, he let his smile soften. "See you around, li'l mama," he said in an undertone as he slipped by her, close enough to get a whiff of her scent. It was the same as it always had been—subtle, sultry with just a touch of sweetness. He trapped it in his lungs on his way out, striding confidently as he faced the blinding streams of sunlight.

"HE'S INSUFFERABLE."

Briar Savitt sipped her tea, not responding to Adrian's heated words. The tea was infused with chamomile. Adrian's friend had taken one look at her when she brought Kyle to Hanna's Inn that evening and ordered her to sit while she put the kettle on the stove.

In her checkered apron and high-necked silk top, Briar looked every bit the calm and collected innkeeper. Which was why Adrian had sought her out instead of Olivia, the matchmaker, or Roxie, the hopeless romantic. She'd needed a place to go that evening to avoid home and, more to the point, her neighbor. The inn offered the warm light of comfort and good food, and Briar was always willing to lend a sensible and sympathetic ear.

As an added bonus, Kyle loved picking her husband's brain. Adrian could hear Cole's deep voice from the next room, followed by Kyle's laugh and the squeal of Cole and Briar's baby girl, Harmony.

The homey noises soothed some of the frazzled edges Adrian had been struggling with for hours. She picked at the corner of the lemon square on the plate in front of her. She didn't know how much she would be able to stomach tonight with her insides twisting and turning. Briar lifted the kettle from the trivet in the center of the round kitchen table to refill Adrian's mug.

"James Bracken might be a lot of things," Briar said thoughtfully, "but I don't think even he'd stoop so low as to drop the paternity bomb on Kyle out of the blue, if that's what you're worried about. Not without your say-so. He'd be a fool to, at any rate. Especially if he's telling the truth about wanting to earn a place in Kyle's life. You don't do that by force."

"I wish I could believe that," Adrian said, drinking the soothing tea. "You don't know him like I do. He used to be rash, impulsive…he certainly didn't listen to authority."

"I remember," Briar said with a nod. Adrian sometimes forgot they had gone to the same high school. Briar and Olivia had graduated a couple of years ahead of her. "My mom and his were both involved in the church. The reverend's death hit us all hard. And I'd hear the gossip about James when I came home from college for summer and holidays." A line appeared between Briar's brows as she studied the place mat in front of her. "Grief isn't an easy thing to bear, especially when it comes suddenly."

Adrian pursed her lips. Briar would know all about grief, as her mother, Hanna, had died of cancer when Briar was fresh out of cooking school. "Be that as it may. It's been eight years since he left. Longer since his father died. He's a grown-ass man and I'd be a moron to buy that as an excuse for his behavior anymore. And besides, he didn't leave me in the lurch because he was grieving."

"I know," Briar acknowledged. "I'm not trying to make excuses for him. And I do agree that caution is your best plan of action as far as he's concerned—particularly for Kyle's sake. However, I have a hard time believing he'd come back to Fairhope unless he really did think he had something to prove, something to fix. It takes a great deal of courage to come back or to redeem yourself. Especially in a place where you experienced or were the cause of as much upheaval as he was eight years ago."

Adrian shook her head. "I don't have it in me to feel sorry for him. I spent two months as his coping mechanism because his arrest cut off his other means of dealing with his problems, those of the substance variety. It took me a long time to accept the fact that that's all I was to him."

Briar frowned, glancing toward the living room where they could both see the baby crawling haltingly across the rug, encouraged by the dark-haired man and the enthusiastic boy. She sighed and lowered her voice. "That's justifiable. But after seeing Cole cut off from his son the way he was for so long, knowing what it did to him… I'm sorry, I have a hard time agreeing that you shouldn't at least let James try to earn a place in Kyle's life, even just a small one."

"This is different," Adrian told her. "Cole didn't deserve to be apart from Gavin the way he was. Nothing in James's past tells me that I should trust him."

Briar took a sip of tea and added, "So what are you going to do? You aren't really going to send Kyle to The Farm to live with your parents, are you?"

"No," Adrian agreed.

"You can't keep them from seeing each other," Briar pointed out.

"I realize that," Adrian said darkly. "And I'll deal with that, too. Even if I have to set up an electric fence on the property line to zap James if he gets within five feet." She felt too tired now to contemplate that particular quandary. "Is Liv still sick?"

"She was here this morning," Briar said. A small smile pulled at her mouth. "Asking about ginger. For nausea."

"So she *is* still sick."

"Yes, but…" Briar let out a laugh as she set down her mug with a clack. "Come on, Adrian. You and I have both been there. The first trimester is hardly a walk in the park."

"First tri…" The words trailed off as Adrian finally put the pieces together. She gasped and sat up straighter. "*No!* Olivia's pregnant? I can't believe this."

"Neither can she, bless her heart," Briar admitted. "But she and Gerald are married. They're happy. They just bought all of her grandmother's land in Silverhill. It's not like they don't have the room, the heart or the capacity for a baby…"

"Sure," Adrian said. "But it's Liv." She shook her head when Briar raised a brow. "I guess I just never thought of her as a mother. Especially not so soon."

Briar tilted her head. "Did you think of yourself as one?"

Adrian blew out a breath. "No. Not until I was." Glancing toward the living room again, she felt the knots in her shoulders loosen. "Not until I felt the first flutters, those first kicks. And then not completely until I held him the first time, until he looked at me…"

Briar smiled warmly. "And look at you now. The best mother any little boy could ask for."

"Thanks for that." She'd needed the vote of confidence, Adrian realized.

"Bring Kyle for breakfast tomorrow," Briar said. "There will be quiche and beignets. Olivia and Gerald will be here, as well. You can avoid

James for a bit longer and we can tell Liv she has another shoulder to lean on."

Adrian nodded. The promise of breakfast at Hanna's surrounded by friends who were as close as family cheered her immensely. "We'll be here."

"Hey, ladies!" Cole called from the living room. "Come see this."

Briar and Adrian walked into the living room in time to see Harmony standing on chubby bowlegs, her tiny hands clasped tightly in Kyle's. The boy's eyes were wide and bright on hers as he called out words of encouragement. Cole, grinning like a fiend, hovered close at Harmony's back. When she took a halting step toward Kyle with little assistance, Briar shrieked and clapped her hands.

Cole looked to her and they exchanged proud, bittersweet smiles before his eyes found Adrian's. "She did it for Kyle."

They made a picture, the two giggling children. Adrian's heart gave a little squeeze.

"She loves him," Briar said when her daughter held her arms up insistently for Kyle and he obliged by picking her up with a "Hoorah!" for her efforts. "Every time she sees Kyle, she lights up. And no wonder. He'll be a bona fide heartbreaker before long."

"I know," Adrian muttered sadly. "What the heck am I going to do?"

"I'm still trying to get over the fact that my

baby's eating solid foods," Briar said woefully. "I can't imagine her growing up, dating, getting married…"

"Liv's right. Denial works wonders sometimes," Adrian told her. "I'll be sticking to it."

Cole walked to her, the proud papa smile not quite worn off. "Everything all right?" he asked, seeming to read past the nostalgic gleam to Adrian's troubles.

Adrian patted him on the arm. He was a damn good man. It hadn't taken long for her to grow to love him, too. "Nothing a trip to Olivia's tavern won't cure."

His expression sobered as he narrowed his eyes on her face, a glimmer of doubt flickering in his dark eyes. "What do you say we all meet there tomorrow night? Liv mentioned it's Monica's night off, so Briar's helping out behind the bar and her dad's coming by to spend a few hours with Harmony." He wrapped an arm around his wife's shoulders, bringing her in close to his side. "I know *we* could both use a night out."

Adrian could, too. "I'll talk to my parents, see if one or both of them can watch Kyle for a few hours. Anyway, it's getting late. I know you've got to put Harmony down for the night and bedtime is fast approaching for her knight in shining armor, too."

"I'll walk you out," Cole offered. He followed

them to the door of the inn. When Kyle bounded ahead down the front steps of the porch, Cole grabbed Adrian's arm. "You sure you're okay?"

She hitched the strap of her purse higher on her shoulder, avoiding his gaze. The man could spot turmoil from a mile away. Probably because he'd been through the worst of it. Adrian had a fair sense that if she told him not just what was bothering her but *who*, he'd go storming off to take care of her business for her. "I'm fine, Cole. I promise."

Unconvinced, he searched her face. "You know if you need anything…"

"I know," she said with a small smile and patted his hand. "Good night."

CHAPTER FIVE

CONCENTRATING ON ANYTHING but his son proved to be problematic for James, even with the grand opening of Bracken Mechanics right around the corner. The morning following the bombshell at Flora, James met Priscilla Grimsby at the offices of the local newspaper to talk about Fairhope's newest business venture.

Fortunately, the reporter skimmed the more sordid details of his past, even after she learned that he had been born and raised there. Though she did seem interested in the fact that his father had once been the town preacher.

James frowned as he drove back to the garage, wondering just how many of those gritty details about his past would end up in Priscilla's business column. Like her brother, Byron, she'd seemed quite interested in generating as much positive press as possible for Bracken Mechanics. He hoped for the best and put it out of his mind.

The latter part proved easier than the first with Adrian and the blue-eyed child they had made together lurking at the forefront. He hadn't the first clue how to prove to Adrian that he could be a good father, much less that he deserved her respect and trust.

Regret was a barb he'd come to know all too well—regret over his father's death, over how badly he had let things get between him and his father before the accident, over how far James had gone to avoid the resulting grief and loss...

However, none of it compared to the regret he felt now knowing that Adrian had had to raise their son alone while also dealing with the heart-break and humiliation she'd spoken of the day before. She'd faced it all on her own. Suddenly, his leaving looked an awful lot less like doing what was right and a lot more like the coward's way out...

Hell, if only he had known. Things could have been different. He would have made things different.

His thoughts circled and spiraled, then circled again until the sun was hanging low in the west and he'd done all he could at the garage for the day. Scowling, he took one last look around. It was coming together, no mistake. Still, there were things that needed to be done, including hiring a couple of guys to help out. A fellow mechanic. A tow truck driver. Maybe somebody to man the phone and handle administrative tasks.

As he locked the doors and pulled the grate over them, a mud-caked Dodge pulled into the parking lot and parked next to the tow truck. James noted the gun rack in the truck bed and the two nuts hanging by a silver chain loop off the back exhaust pipe. He crossed his arms as the driver door opened and a familiar figure jumped to the ground from the raised cab. James scanned the faded jeans, the plaid shirt and the red-bearded face and shook his head. "I'll be damned," he said as a smile stretched across the man's mouth.

Dustin Harbuck took off his sunglasses as he approached James in dirty work boots. "Jim Bracken," he greeted James. Dustin wore a battered camouflage baseball cap with a shiny, silver fishing hook clipped onto the front of the bill. Stretching out a large hand, he pumped James's fist. "Been gone long enough, brother?"

They weren't brothers. In fact, they'd only been friends for a brief stretch of time. All the Harbuck boys were more than a little rough around the edges and daredevils to boot. A few of them had even served time behind bars, but over the months between the fateful wreck that had changed James's life and his departure from Fairhope, James had grown to rely on Dusty and his bad influence to cope with life as it was then. Through their shared antics, they had grown as close as two small-town rebels could.

In fact, it was Dusty James had gone to at the end of that fateful summer. Dusty hadn't hesitated to give James enough money to get him as far away from Fairhope as he could manage on a limited budget. He hadn't asked questions, either.

James looked at Dusty and saw the first friendly face of all those ghosts he had left behind. Without a word, he embraced him hard. "It's good to see you, buddy," he said, and meant it.

Dusty thumped him on the shoulder. He stepped back and surveyed the beard and tattoos that covered James and laughed. "The big, wide world's left its mark on you."

"Seems so," James muttered, turning his tattooed left hand until the art on the underside was revealed. "How's life been treating you?"

"Decent enough," Dusty said with a nod. He glanced over James's shoulder at the locked garage. "Clint told me he'd heard a rumor you were back in town. As shocked as I was to hear that, it wasn't anything compared to how I felt when I heard you're trying to throw together a new business."

James looked at the garage. "I heard Witmore was retiring. I couldn't let the old place go to waste."

Narrowing his eyes, Dusty pushed the bill of his cap up with his knuckles, then used them to scratch the spot where the hat had been rubbing just below his red hairline. "And, just like that, after eight years, you come flying back into town to rescue it?"

James lifted his shoulders. "Why not?"

"I ain't buyin' it," Dusty said, pinning an inquisitive gaze on James's face. "I figure you've either gone nuts or we've got ourselves a new underground gaming establishment here."

James chuckled. "Nah. All my gaming's above ground these days."

Dusty's head tipped back suddenly, as if he'd been hit. A brief wince crossed his face. "So you're telling me not only are you a legitimate business owner now...you're also on the straight and narrow?"

Smiling, James watched his friend's face as the crystal-blue eyes roved his for flaws. "Believe it, Harbuck."

Dusty bolted out a loud laugh. "You *are* nuts."

"Maybe," James acknowledged. He clapped Dusty on the shoulder. "We all gotta grow up at some point."

"Hmm." Looking unconvinced, Dusty jerked his chin at the tow truck. "Heard you were looking for a tow driver."

"Yep," James said as they strode over to Witmore's tow truck. "You interested?"

"Clint's done with the big rigs. Dad gave him the tow I was using around town so I'm in the market. What kind of pay would you be offering on a part-time basis?"

They haggled for a few minutes over commission, hourly rates, benefits and so on. In the end, they shook on an agreement and James handed over the keys.

Watching Dusty flip the key chain from one hand to the other, James leaned back against the tow truck's grille and frowned. "You've been working for your old man since high school?"

"Here and there," Dusty said with a scowl. "He trusts Clint and Hawk more than me, ever since that little incident involving you, me, a bottle of Johnny Walker and his tractor a few months before that fiasco with the Carltons."

The Carltons. James's heart did a little roll and his shoulders straightened. "So you've been around since then?"

"For the most part."

"You ever cross paths with Adrian and her little boy?" James asked.

"Not so much anymore," Dusty considered. "Not since she and Radley ended things."

James's pulse and jaw dropped simultaneously. "Radley Kennard?"

"One and the same." Dusty nodded. "They divorced about six years back. It ruined him. She told everyone who'd listen that he took a swing at her a couple times. He was a cop. Lost his badge and everything. She slapped him with a restraining order. Poor guy hasn't been the same since."

James took a moment to close his mouth, pressing his lips together hard as he digested this new nugget of information. Adrian had been…

married? And how in God's name had she gotten involved with a creep like Radley Kennard? Radley's younger brother, Scotty, had been one of the guys that ran in Dusty's hell-raising crew... though even James had been wary around him and his family. Word then was the brothers had run cock- and dog-fighting rings in the woods—though James had never seen as much for himself. Even in his eagerness to fly headlong into the abyss, he'd known to steer clear of the likes of Radley Kennard.

As to the allegations of abuse...James's blood ran cold at the thought. However life had treated her, she had never been the kind of person to point fingers falsely. She'd worked and fought for what she was and what she wanted. James couldn't dismiss Adrian's claims of abuse as Dusty had. And the thought of anyone hurting her like that made James's fists clench until the knuckles cracked under the strain.

"Why are you interested in Adrian again?" Dusty questioned. "You should know better than that."

James pursed his lips and took in a long breath—long enough to clear away the fog of rage that the thought of a man like Radley Kennard so much as touching Adrian had stirred. Slowly, his fists unclenched and he relaxed the fingers one by one, lifting one hand and using it to massage the knuckles on the other. "Why do you say that?"

Dusty gave him an incredulous look. "You're kidding, right? The Carltons got you arrested twice. They practically ran you out of town. If I were you, the last thing I'd be thinking about is getting involved with Adrian. That can only lead to trouble." He pushed off the tow to walk back to his truck. "Just ask Radley."

It was more complicated than that. Though, since Dusty hadn't mentioned the kid, James doubted he knew that Kyle was his son. "How do you feel about starting the week after next? I told a reporter over at the *Courier* this morning I was planning on opening shop then. She's doing a feature in next week's paper."

"Sounds good to me," Dusty said and smiled, tipping the bill of his hat to James. "And, hey, for the record, welcome back."

"Thanks," James said.

Dusty climbed up into his Dodge. "I'll see you Monday after next."

ADRIAN HAD NO CHOICE. It had to be done. Just after lunch the following afternoon, Adrian reluctantly asked Penny if she could manage the shop for an hour or two while she went home to work in her kitchen.

Her spring line of homemade candles was selling like hotcakes this year. If she didn't find time to work on a new batch, she would sell out by the end of the week.

It was the slowest day of the workweek. Flora had only received a trickle of calls that morning. Penny could easily handle a fruit basket, a couple of baby arrangements and a spring wreath. Adrian figured it was her only chance to get away from the shop before the weekend Easter rush.

As she pulled into her driveway, she chanced a glance over into James's neighboring one. Yep. There was that black sportster sitting on the cracked pavement. She fumbled her keys as she walked briskly to her front door. Even in her hurry, she avoided the grass she tended so carefully, sticking to the footpath that skirted her front beds. There were the annuals and perennials she and Kyle had planted together. The hydrangeas were blooming like crazy and she was pleased to see Kyle's favorites, the citrus trees, coming back from the harsh winter.

If James saw her come home, he didn't hail her in time to stop her from escaping inside the cottage and bolting the three locks she'd installed on the door when she and Kyle had first moved in. She couldn't avoid him forever. She knew that. But she could damn well try...

Breathing a sigh, she walked back to the kitchen and shed the light crocheted sweater she'd left the house in that morning. Opening the window over the sink to let in the scent of Kyle's sweet olives, she took a moment to indulge in the light, cool breeze that blew through the screens and over her bare arms. She opened the half door to the back porch and smiled at the sound of birdsong. Feeling close to relaxed, she covered her shorts and tank top with a red apron and got to work.

Any mother of an seven-year-old boy knew that silence was a rare thing. So she worked without music, unless the birdsong and the jangle and ting of wind chimes counted. Humming to herself, she melted wax and cut wicks. She dyed the wax, except what she set aside to use with one of her best-selling scents, gardenia. She'd discovered over the years that gardenia had its own hue, turning the wax a lovely shade of green.

Carefully, she measured out her various essential oils. Each reacted differently with the wax and some could even eat through plastic or remove paint so here the process became a bit intricate.

Just as she was beginning to measure and stir, a deep, bass note rent the quiet, making her flinch. The scent, wax and dye mixture she was currently working on tipped over and spilled across the hardwood floor of the kitchen. She shrieked in alarm, then again in anger when the clash of drums and guitars of Audioslave followed.

James was, indeed, home. After doing what she could about the mess, Adrian threw the ruined bits into the sink and glared out the window above it, raising herself onto her tiptoes to look over the fence line. But her honeysuckle vines prevented her from seeing anything. The whine of a power saw joined the musical blast. Her teeth ground together as she fought back a growl.

She had half a mind to go pound on his door. She was a few steps from *her* door when she realized what she was doing...

No. No way in hell was she facing the embodiment of her problems. Balling her hands on her hips, she glared again through the window at the fence and the small bit of James's house that was visible through glossy green leaves.

Muttering, she walked back to the sink and salvaged what she could of the wax. One of the other neighbors would surely be as offended as she was. They'd go over, put an end to it...

But it was early afternoon. Most of the neighbors were at the office. The kids were in school.

She was on her own.

Cursing, she went back to making her candles. As the hour stretched into another and the sounds of Led Zeppelin's "When the Levee Breaks" followed closely on the heels of Van Halen's "Eruption," her movements became jerky. She broke two mason jars, spilled more wax on the floor, cursed up a storm...

Adrian figured he was baiting her. She'd avoided coming into contact with him since his visit to Flora days ago—when he'd promised to prove his worth as a man, a father. This had to be his way of getting her over there, face-to-face so they could hash it out again....

"Moron," she muttered, mopping up another mess. If this was his way of showing her he was a changed man, he was failing miserably. Just as her gardenia mixture failed… She thought seriously about murdering him.

Another half hour. Zeppelin was replaced by Sublime, Guns N' Roses and finally Red Hot Chili Peppers. She scowled as she affixed her labels to the fronts of the finished mason jars. Yep. He knew all he had to do was play a little Chili Peppers for her to remember…

It took her back instantly to that night she'd driven him home. Or, rather, when she drove him to the harbor where his father's boat was moored. He'd invited her aboard for a drink. There had been something different about him that night. All that day, in fact. Where friendship had smoothed the rough edges between them with ease, and even jokes and laughter, there had been something amiss that night, a shift back to the haunted shell she'd found in the barn nearly a week before. She hadn't been able to bring herself to just leave him, so she followed him onto the deck of the *Free Bird*, the daysailer that looked as if it had seen better days. There was a tattered pirate flag flying off the stern and more than a little rust to be seen, but all in all, she was a clean boat, one James took pride in. She could see it in the way he ran his hand over the mast and helm.

She'd followed him belowdecks where he admitted to sleeping most nights. He'd told her how he couldn't bring himself to go home—to his mother, his stepfather, the disappointment and feelings of hopelessness they generally cast in his direction. She'd taken his hand because she understood, at least to some degree. It didn't take a genius to see that her mother felt the same way about her—and she told him as much. His hand had squeezed hers a moment or two before he released it and got up to grab them both a beer.

He'd turned on the radio then, a small portable player. They sat on his bunk. About midway through the drinks, he finally admitted what had been troubling him for most of the day. It was the anniversary of the wreck that had claimed Reverend Bracken's life. She hadn't known quite what to say so she'd simply listened as he told her what happened that night—and why Zach Bracken's death haunted him so.

"It was my fault." Although his voice remained detached and he couldn't quite meet her eyes, she saw on his face enough sadness to wrench at her soul. He talked about how his father had picked him up from a party. It was in the early hours of the morning as Zach Bracken drove James home on a backcountry road in the pouring rain and, after some silence between them, began to talk to James about how drinking and partying wasn't the way, about how it nearly ruined Zach's own life before he found sobriety and the solace of God.

James had let the words roll over him and away, only half listening.

Then something had run out into the road—an opossum, a raccoon, a dog...nobody ever knew for sure. Zach swerved. The car flipped into a ditch. James was knocked unconscious. He woke up in the hospital the next day to his mother's grieving face. She'd told him in broken words how his father had asked the paramedics to retrieve him from the vehicle first, although his father had known he himself was bleeding to death.

"He died before they could operate," James told her, in that detached voice that was almost a monotone by that point. "He used to tell me over and over how God saved him, how the ministry saved him...and he died because I was a stupid kid—too much like the man he was before..."

Adrian had watched him break down in gut-wrenching sobs he'd clearly been holding back for far too long. She'd been able to do nothing but hold him through it. He'd grabbed onto her like a lifeline until it was all over, until the back of his shoulders stopped quaking beneath her cheek, until she lifted his face enough to dry it on her sleeve. He'd looked at her then, all the weight of the world in his eyes. A light flashed into them. Longing and hunger broke through behind that light and he kissed her.

Red Hot Chili Peppers had been playing on the radio—"Under the Bridge." After he left Fairhope weeks later, Adrian hadn't been able to listen to that song again without remembering what she'd felt in *Free Bird*'s cabin as he kissed her and she'd fallen head over heels in love with him.

She'd tried so hard to forget, but damn it, she could still remember how his lips had felt on hers, the little licks of fire under her skin as it went from something stolen and hesitant to something deeper, hotter and very much requited. He'd bitten her, just a little, on the lower lip. She'd thought at that moment that she would burst into flames. She remembered even now how she'd desperately hoped he would keep on kissing her if she did burst into flames so that she'd at least die happy.

His hands had moved over her. Down her back, back up into her hair. She'd had a lot of it then. He'd coiled it around his fists until both her tresses and his fingers were balled tight against the back of her head.

She'd wanted him. The days leading up to that night she'd thought seriously about doing something about it. More than anything, she'd wanted to make him forget about being sad, about being haunted and lonely. She'd wanted to give him something else…

Peace.

Adrian blinked. She was standing in the middle of the kitchen. At some point, she'd wrapped her arms around herself at the onslaught of eight-year-old memories. She could feel everything she'd felt then, every tug of his mouth and hands, every burn and brush with temptation and hunger, every little bit of awakening love had brought.

It was enough. She wrested the apron over her head, threw it onto the floor and left the house. Before she knew it, she'd stomped up to his front door.

She didn't bother knocking. Who in God's name would hear her over the noise of "The Righteous and the Wicked"? Tearing her way through the screen door, she had to throw her shoulder against the sticky front door before it gave and she stumbled into James's house.

The great room opened up beyond the entry hall. Wood floors. Lots of glass and sun. The room was untidy, furniture not quite set to square. Boxes everywhere, overflowing. The stereo and speakers were set up on and around the fireplace mantel. In here the music was deafening.

Covering her ears, she caught movement on the other side of all that glass. On the back deck. A tall, broad frame of a man. Muttering amidst the noise, she walked through the open sliding glass door and stalked up to him. "James!" she practically screamed.

The muscles of his shoulders tightened. His head jerked toward her and he spied her through the clear safety glasses he wore. "Adrian," he said with an affable grin as he disengaged the power saw and turned to face her. "Hey! Did you just let yourself—"

"Are you kidding me, with the noise?" she asked before he could finish, throwing her arms out. "Just listen! Who could possibly think with all this racket?"

The grin wavered for a moment. "Oh, you mean the music."

Her jaw dropped before she clenched it and let out a mocking, "Duh!"

He pulled off the safety glasses and studied her as he tugged off the gloves, too. The grin hitched back up a notch as he reached some conclusion. It was then she realized he was sweaty and smelled like lumber. He wore a sleeveless, white work shirt, cargo shorts…and a tool belt.

She fought not to lick her lips as her gaze flipped to his left arm where all the tattoos were. It was the first time she was able to make sense of the colors and shapes. On his thick upper arm was a ship bobbing on stormy seas, being attacked by a giant octopus—a kraken. The tentacles were rending their way through the sails, pulling the old-fashioned man-of-war down into the depths.

Those depths kept going. Sea life dotted his arm as it wrapped around and down to his forearm where coral took over. She caught sight of a black-inked anchor on the inside of his wrist. On the back of his hand was the ocean bottom where the bones of some long-forgotten sea beast rested.

She swallowed. The effect was quite stirring. The artwork was impeccable. She felt that she could almost reach out and touch those cool waters, the bones resting in the deep, the wood of the ship's bow, the rubbery tentacles of the kraken…

Blinking again, she wrenched herself out of the reverie and moved her gaze up…up, up, up to his face. Another distraction in and of itself, sweaty and flecked with sawdust. His hair was mussed, a few dark curls stuck to his forehead.

God, he was massive. As solid as the breakwaters that kept the gulf at bay. She swallowed hard as it struck her again that this was not the boy who had kissed her years ago. That boy had grown into a man and his effect on her was, unbelievably, twice as debilitating. His eyes seemed to drink her in much as hers were drinking him— like a tall glass of water. They turned sly when he realized she was doing just that, and he drawled in a low, rusty voice, "Howdy, neighbor."

She wanted to punch him. For interrupting what was usually a therapeutic candle-making session. For making her come over here to face him. For making her feel this way. For making her remember what had been. And in equal measure, she wanted to kiss him. She wanted to kiss and punch the hell out of him until he felt as drunk and offbalance as she did around him.…

"Hang on, I thought you liked the Chili Peppers," he said, his eyes narrowing on her slightly.

They turned wry and thoughtful. "In fact, I do believe it was 'Under the Bridge' that was playing when we first—"

"Turn the goddamned music down," she warned, advancing on him in jerky strides. She poked a finger into his chest for good measure. "Or I'll make you wish you had!"

He laughed at her, the mirth stretching across the high-arched bones of his face. "God, I love it when you're angry."

She huffed, exasperated, and spun on her heel, rushing for the exit. She needed a cold shower and a stiff drink....

"Wait," he called after her. His hand wrapped around her arm in a gentle hold that still managed to pull her up short. "Let me show you something."

"Oh, heck no," she said, tugging against his grip. He'd said the same thing years ago when she'd let him get behind the wheel of her car. He'd driven to the beach and parked it right on the sand. They'd made out there, too, rolling around in the backseat of her Camry until the gulf tide banked and the windows fogged over.

"Come on," he said with a laugh. "I want to know what you think about the house."

She frowned at their surroundings. Beams crisscrossed overhead. "What are doing out here?" she asked, more in accusation than curiosity.

"Shade," he told her, lifting his palm. "Sun's

damned hot this time of day. Imagine what it'll feel like in the summer. I figured I'd cover the deck and grill down there on the patio by the pool."

Shielding her eyes with a flat hand against her brow, she glanced at the milky green water. "That's not a pool. That's a bacterial cesspit. You're just foolish enough to go swimming in it, too. Mind you don't pick up an infection while you're at it and get gangrene or something similar." She stopped, reconsidered and turned to his smiling face again. "Or do. That way they can tear the place down and I won't have to worry about you anymore."

"You don't mean that, baby," he said, the laughter in his eyes kicking up a notch. "I'm having it drained and retiled. Pretty sure we'll find a dead armadillo at the bottom."

Wrinkling her nose, she shook her head and faced the back of the house once more. "What do you see in this place?"

"I don't know exactly," James said, studying the house. "It's got something to it, though, right?"

"Yeah—water damage and termites."

He chuckled again. "Birds in the attic and chimney, too."

She weighed his good-natured expression. "You're an idiot."

"So you keep saying. I'd wager you'll say so again before this is all over."

"That's what I'm afraid of," she muttered. "I better get back…" She stopped, glancing down at the hand he still had clasped over her elbow. It was his right hand, the one unmarked by tattoos. The skin was rough on the back side, a bit mottled and pink. "What'd you do there?"

He glanced at the hand. The smile faded from his eyes, though he kept it firmly on his lips. Lifting a shoulder, he released her and let the arm hang at his side—but not before she saw that the burn crept all the way up his arm to the elbow. "That old oven in there's a bitch. Serves me right for trying to make pizza from scratch."

The oven hadn't burned him. He was clearly unwillingly to tell her the truth and covering it up with the good-natured ease that teased up memories and feelings her former, younger and far more foolish and uninhibited self had suffered. She let the subject rest. "Will you turn down the music?"

He licked his lips. "Depends. Are you ready to let me see my son again?"

"James, I'm not doing this with you."

He closed the space between them in one measured step. "Adrian," he said, voice lower and expression more sober. "You will let me see him. At some point…you have to let me see him."

She closed her eyes against the desperation she saw in the wild blue of his eyes. "Not now. I can't…not now." And she turned and retreated.

"Eventually," he warned as she made her way toward the exit.

At the front door she turned back. He was leaning through the sliding glass door of the deck, one hand braced on either jamb. She saw the plea hanging there, at odds with the tense lines of his face. She sighed and shook her head. "Not today."

"Come on," he said, straightening. The first waver of impatience crossed his expression. "What's the worst that could happen?"

Her heart rate kicked up a notch. What was the worst thing that could happen? He could ruin her. All over again. But it wasn't just her anymore. He could hurt Kyle while he was at it—whether intentionally or not. And that was unacceptable.

"I can't afford to gamble anymore," she said, knowing the quiet, weary words wouldn't carry over the din of music.

"What?" he called.

She opened the door, took one look at the front yard and yelled back, "I said cut your grass. It's tall enough for Hobbits to hide in." Slamming the door behind her, she left the house and trudged back next door to her solitude.

CHAPTER SIX

EVERY WEEK, ONCE a week, Adrian took Kyle to her parents' farmhouse for dinner. Every other weekend, they spent a Saturday there with Van and Edith so that they could ride horses and Van could teach his grandson a few new guitar chords.

They were due for their weekly visit; however, it just so happened that she had promised Cole and Briar to meet them for drinks that night.

And the timing wasn't coincidental, not on Adrian's part. Van had seen James. He had no doubt told Adrian's mother that her old flame was back. And Adrian knew for a certainty that Edith had been gearing up for a lecture about the trouble James had gotten them all into the last time.

Avoidance wasn't always the answer. But in the case of both her mother and James, Adrian wasn't afraid to exercise it. So it was that she found herself dropping Kyle off at The Farm with only a brief exchange with her father before driving back to the bay.

Taking a night for herself was a luxury she

rarely indulged in. She liked her quiet nights at home with Kyle—it was a ritual she knew never to take for granted. But in light of recent events, Adrian found herself in need of a beer. And since she didn't keep it in the house, there was only one place to go...

By the time she pulled into the parking lot of Tavern of the Graces, it was well past happy hour. Though she'd had her fair share of loud music earlier that day, Adrian eagerly walked toward the sounds of Olivia's jukebox and the chorus of loud voices, drinking in the fresh, tepid scent of the bay.

Inside, the familiar atmosphere of the small-town bar lulled the knots in her shoulders as a measure of her stress fell by the wayside. She raised her hand to one of Olivia's regulars who greeted her by name and walked to the shiny wood counter lined with stools.

Olivia worked the bar, Briar close at her side. Adrian took a seat and lifted her chin, catching Olivia's eye. Her friend finished serving a tall, foaming glass of draft Guinness before veering toward her.

She was still a little frayed around the edges, Adrian saw. At least Olivia looked steadier on her feet—a lucky thing as she was wearing three-inch platforms. "Feeling better?" Adrian asked.

"Peachy keen," Olivia said with a tight, unconvincing grin.

"How're the nerves holding up?" Adrian questioned.

Olivia inhaled sharply through her nose, looking around to make sure Gerald wasn't within earshot. Finding her husband over by the pool tables talking up some customers, Olivia frowned at Adrian. "They've been better, but the bar's open, it's Karaoke and $1.25 Mojitos Night and I haven't got time to think about it."

"Karaoke?" Adrian asked curiously.

"Gerald finally talked me into getting a machine," Olivia said, taking a hurricane glass from Briar and pushing it in front of Adrian. "Mojito?"

Adrian stared at the glass. It wasn't a beer, but it was alcohol. "Why not?"

"Drink up," Olivia demanded. "There's more where that came from."

"Are you trying to liquor me up?" Adrian asked after taking a sip.

"That's my job."

Briar stepped up next to Olivia. "Guess who went to the doctor today," she said, in as much of an undertone as she could manage amidst the din of music and conversation.

"Oh?" Adrian said, looking back to Olivia in question. "So, what's the ruling?"

Olivia dropped her eyes to the bar and looked

helpless for the first time in Adrian's memory. Keeping her voice tuned low, she muttered, "There's a bun, all right."

Briar beamed and patted the slumped line of her cousin's shoulders. "It's wonderful news! Right, Adrian?"

"I think it is," Adrian said in all honesty and smiled when Olivia's empty gaze rose to hers. "Don't you think so, Liv?"

After a moment, Olivia nodded. "I'm getting used to the idea and it's…it's not as scary as I thought. It's just…"

"Unexpected?" Adrian prompted.

"Completely," Olivia agreed. She glanced at Gerald. "Can you both just…keep it on the hush-hush for a bit longer?"

"When are you going to tell him?" Briar asked. "He's got a book tour coming up. You'll tell him before he goes, right?"

"I think so." Olivia gnawed her lower lip. "It's just…I don't know what he'll say or do. We talked about having kids, of course, but always in future tense, down the road. *Way* down the road. We've only been married a few months…"

"He'll be delighted," Briar assured her. "You're going to be wonderful parents."

"I second that," Adrian said.

Olivia gave a small smile. "Thanks." She looked over Adrian's shoulder and her smile widened. "Hey, Rox."

Adrian glanced over just in time to see Roxie Levy snag the stool next to hers. She lifted a finger and they saw the phone at her ear. After a moment's wait, Roxie lowered the phone with a creased brow. "Drat. I can't get ahold of Richard."

"Is everything all right?" Briar asked.

"Fine, I'm sure," Roxie said in regard to her husband of four months. "With his late hours at the university, it's been difficult getting in touch with him lately." She slipped the phone into the side pocket of her Brahmin bag and folded her hands on the counter. "So…Liv…" She grinned her dazzling, cheerful grin and leaned forward. "What's the news?"

Olivia couldn't quite hide a smile now. "Gerald's going to be a daddy."

Roxie shrieked happily and clapped her hands before reaching over the bar to pull Olivia into a spontaneous embrace.

"Shh!" Adrian said with a laugh. "Daddy doesn't know yet."

"Oh, sorry," Roxie said, lowering quickly back to her seat. Her hands still grasped Olivia's. She lowered her voice in a whispered, "I'm so happy for you!" then untangled them.

"Thanks," Olivia replied. She picked up one of the drinks on standby. "Mojito?"

"Absolutely!" Roxie said, taking the drink in both hands.

"To Liv, Gerald and their little munchkin," Adrian said, lifting her own glass.

"Cheers to that." Roxie tipped her mojito with a clink to Adrian's and they both drank deep.

Swallowing, Adrian saw that her glass was empty and pursed her lips. Before she knew it, though, Olivia had set down another mojito full to the brim. "You're welcome," her friend said before busying herself with other orders.

Adrian lifted a shoulder again and drank. After a moment, she looked around and asked Briar, "Where's Cole? This was his idea."

Briar leaned a bit over the bar and said, "Talking with Dad. It sounded tense. Harmony was down for the night so I came right over and left them to it."

Adrian nodded understanding. It was well known that Cole and Briar's father didn't always see eye to eye. Turning to Roxie, she said, "I need to talk to you about that Oak Hollow wedding coming up."

Roxie lifted a finger. "Nope. Not now. We're off duty, remember?"

"Yeah, but the bride has asked for—"

"A bouquet chandelier for the reception," Roxie finished with a sage nod. "I didn't know how to talk her out of it. I'm sorry."

Adrian propped her chin in the flat of her hand. As a wedding planner and a florist, she and Roxie often found themselves collaborating and recommending each other's services to their customers. "It's not the arrangement I'm worried about. More, how in God's name will we hang something with that much weight? Peonies aren't light, especially when they're all clumped together like that. And I'll have to use something sturdier than my usual wire…"

"Holy Mother of God," Olivia murmured from the other side of the bar.

Adrian started at the shell-shocked look on her face. "What's wrong?" she asked, looking around wildly, expecting to see a fire or a murder in progress…

The problem was just over her left shoulder, approaching steadily. James grinned when she spotted him. "Adrian," he greeted her.

"Shit," Adrian said, not bothering to stifle the curse. Turning back to her mojito, she drank deep.

"James Bracken," Olivia said, expression still frozen in shock.

James stared at her for a moment. His eyes widened in recognition. "Olivia?"

"Yes," she said, beaming. "Wow." Her emerald-hued gaze took an admiring dive over his broad torso. "You look…different."

Adrian glared at her friend while Roxie extended a hand to James. "Roxie Honeycutt Levy," she said as he grasped it. "Very nice to meet you, Mr. Bracken."

James chuckled. "The pleasure's all mine, I

assure you, Ms. Levy." When Adrian groaned, he glanced back at her. "Problem?"

"Um, yeah," Adrian muttered, desperately wishing for another full glass. "You."

"James," Briar said as she walked up. "It's been too long."

"Briar," James said, a bittersweet note entering his voice. "Briar Browning."

"Well, Savitt now," she said, lifting the hand adorned with her wedding ring.

"Congratulations," he said with a nod and an answering smile.

"It's good to see you," Briar said sincerely.

"You, too," he replied.

"Can I get you something to drink?" Olivia interjected. "We've got a mojito special."

"I saw the sign," James said with a nod. "But just water for me, thanks."

"You sure?" Olivia asked. "We've got plenty of draft beer to go around. What's your pleasure?"

He raised a hand. "Nah. I've, ah, actually been sober for four years now."

Adrian peered at him as Roxie let out an admiring "Aw, how 'bout that?"

Briar offered her own congratulations. "You never mentioned that," Adrian pointed out when his gaze found hers.

James cleared his throat and crossed his arms. "You never asked. And you always run away before I can get around to mentioning it…"

"Huh." She saw the others looking at her expectantly and frowned. "Well…good for you," she added in a small voice.

"Thanks."

"Glass of water," Olivia offered, setting it in front of him on the bar between Roxie and Adrian. "And another mojito for Adrian."

"No, I don't need—"

"Drink it," Olivia said, lowering her head and eyeing Adrian sternly. She brightened as she looked at James again. "So, James. Tell us what you've been up to."

Adrian had no choice but to sit and drink her mojito, listening to James explain how he'd gone from Fairhope to the mountains, of all places, then to Florida and finally up to the Carolinas where he found work designing engines for stock cars. She was grateful when someone from the other side of the bar recognized him and he was momentarily distracted by a reunion with the Harbuck brothers as well as a few other members of their high school class. After he excused himself from the girls, Adrian dropped her face into her hands.

Olivia was the first to comment. "Oh, my ovaries," she breathed, clasping her hands over her womb.

Adrian scowled. "Your ovaries have been busy enough as it is lately. Give them a rest."

Briar let out a little breath. "He's so *different*."

"It's the shoulders," Olivia explained. "They make a girl wanna curl up there against him and purr."

"Purr?" Adrian asked derisively.

"Yes, he's filled out quite nicely," Briar said in agreement with Olivia.

"Like a single-cab pickup fills into a frickin' Humvee," Olivia said.

"Kyle has his eyes," Roxie added. "And did you see the way he tilted his head at Adrian when he looked at her? That's all Kyle, too. It's adorable."

"Mmm," Olivia hummed with a considering gleam in her eyes. "And I bet he's hung like a—"

"*O*kay!" Adrian interrupted loudly. "I need another mojito."

"I second that," Roxie piped up. "By the way, Liv, where do we sign up for karaoke?"

"Gerald's got the list," Olivia replied as she busied herself making another round. "But don't worry. You're both already on there."

"What?" Adrian asked, gaping in horror.

"That's right, my friend," Olivia said with a grin. "You're singing karaoke tonight."

Suddenly the mojitos began to add up. "Nope," Adrian said. "Nuh-uh. There's no way you're getting me drunk enough to sing."

JAMES REVELED IN making Adrian uncomfortable in front of her friends a little too much. Still, it didn't stop him from enjoying his reintroduction into Fairhope society.

It went over much more smoothly than he'd have wagered. Then again, most of the people he knew in Tavern of the Graces hadn't been the ones he'd maligned back in the day. He was thankful that the Lewis-Leighton family bar wasn't the type of scene he could imagine his mother or stepfather showing up at—or any of their friends, for that matter.

After speaking with the Harbucks for a while, James returned to the bar where Adrian was still hunched over her mojito, barely tolerating the ribbing from her three friends. Olivia slapped him on the back. "How good is your singing?" she wondered out loud.

"Terrible," he admitted.

"Good," Olivia beamed. "You're in the lineup for karaoke."

"Am I?" James looked over at the jukebox where a makeshift stage had been set up. At that moment, an inebriated young man was singing a bad rendition of "Friends in Low Places." James laughed. "All right, then."

"That's the spirit." Olivia leaned over close and added, "Oh, and you'll be doing a duet. With Adrian."

He pursed his lips. "Does she know this?"

"Nope," she said with a Cheshire-cat grin and a wink as she walked off with a serving tray.

He fought a smile as he took a seat on the vacated stool at Adrian's right. She peered at him for a moment as he sipped his water, then shook her head and finally asked, "What are you doing here?"

"Having a drink," he told her, lifting his glass and feigning innocence.

"You just told everyone you've been sober for four years," she reminded him.

He lifted a shoulder. "Maybe I didn't want to miss karaoke night."

Adrian rolled her eyes. "Like hell."

"Did I miss the sign that said this was your turf?" he asked. "I've been pretty good about staying away from the cottage and your flower shop for the last few days. I figure this is neutral ground."

"That won't stop you from trying to get what you want out of me," Adrian said.

He raised an interested brow. "That sounds a little dirty."

"I wasn't—" She stopped when he cracked a smile. "God. If I didn't know better, I'd say you were in league with Liv to get me shit-faced so I'll sing karaoke for her and let you run off with Kyle."

"Is that what you think I want?" he asked. When she lowered her hands to stare at him, expressionless, he frowned and edged toward her. "All right, let's get one thing straight. I don't want to take Kyle away from you. You're an amazing mom."

"How do you know that?" she blurted.

"Let me finish," James intervened. "The boy loves you. How could he not? All I want is to know him—and, maybe one day, for him to know me for what and who I am. His father. Then, if you let me, I'd like to be for him what my dad was for me."

Adrian scanned his face for a long moment. His pulse quickened when he thought that she might be giving his words the consideration he desperately needed. Then she let out a breath and turned away. "No. Not...not yet."

"Because he's not ready or you aren't?"

"I don't know..." She threw her hands up. "Let's just...change the subject. Please."

James opened his mouth to argue, then thought better of it and reached for his water instead. What else did he have to do to convince her to give him a chance? A single chance.

A man appeared on the other side of the bar. Tall, blond, a bit on the reedy side. He smiled easily at Adrian and spoke in an upper-crust British accent. "There you are, Adrian, lass."

For the first time that night, James saw Adrian smile back and mean it. He felt a tug of envy. "Gerald," she said. "You look happy with yourself tonight."

"I am well and truly chuffed," Gerald admitted.

"You have no idea how hard it was to talk Olivia into karaoke night. I think it's a smashing success so far, don't you?"

"If you can get me off the performing list, I'll sing karaoke night's praises for all to hear."

Gerald shrugged. "I've been threatened by a ravishing and dangerous blonde that if I remove your name, I'll be cut off from certain indispensable pleasures."

Adrian sighed. "Well, it was worth a shot, I guess," she muttered.

"Who's your friend?" Gerald asked, indicating James.

Before Adrian could deny any friendship with him, James extended a hand. "James Bracken."

"Gerald Leighton," the man returned. "You must be the old flame."

As Adrian frowned at both of them, James cracked a smile. "That's me."

Before Gerald could explain himself, Olivia strode up, planted her hands in the back pockets of Gerald's jeans and hissed, "Don't let Adrian talk you into taking her off the list."

"What do you take me for?" Gerald asked, bending down to her level so his lips hovered above hers. "How are you feeling?"

Olivia gave a small pout. "I keep thinking about how long you'll be away once you leave in two weeks. Why do you have to be gone for two whole months? It seems like a long time for a book tour."

"Will you miss me, love?" he asked.

"Well…" She reached up and wound his tie around her fingers. "It is two months…"

"You will miss me," he said, pleased with his findings. He wrapped an arm around her waist, tugging her against him. "Don't worry, Olivia Rose. I'll be back before you can say Big Easy Sazerac."

Olivia's wide eyes softened. "That is the sexiest thing you've ever said to me."

"Big Easy Sazerac?" he repeated, smiling as he lowered his mouth to hers and she tugged on his collar, bringing him closer.

"Again," she demanded when he came up for air moments later.

Gerald's lips grazed hers, nibbled, smiled. Then nibbled some more…

Adrian was the first to speak up. "Y'all 'bout done?" she ventured. "We could both really use another drink over here."

"Never." Gerald groaned, an ardent bar appearing between his brows as he kissed Olivia again. "I'm never bloody done."

James cleared his throat. "So they're…"

"Married," Adrian said with a nod. "Newlyweds, in case you can't tell."

"Oh, they make that pretty clear for themselves," James noted.

Gerald pulled back finally, grinning widely as Olivia hummed her pleasure. Reluctantly he disentangled himself from his wife and turned to Adrian. "All right, Adrian, darling. Let's get you onstage."

She fought tooth and nail, but moments later James found himself standing on the makeshift platform on the other side of the room facing a crowd of tavern-goers, Adrian standing stiff and unfriendly beside him. Behind the karaoke machine, Olivia whispered something in Gerald's ear. He shook his head and smiled as he chose the song for them.

When the intro to Johnny Cash and June Carter's "Jackson" began to play, the crowd cheered and James turned to see Adrian pale. As the first words appeared on the monitor in front of them, he took pity on her, grabbed the mic and swung an arm around her shoulders for comfort. "It'd be best to just sing and get it over with at this point."

She took up the other mic in silent agreement and grudgingly began to sing the duet with him. It helped that, as the first chorus got under way, the crowd started clapping, egging them on. At one point, Adrian even aimed a smile at him. It accompanied the lyrics "you big-talking man." Nonetheless, it was a smile for him and he latched onto it, twining an arm around her waist. They finished the song and took their bows.

"That was great!" Roxie exclaimed as they made it back to their seats at the bar. "You two looked fantastic up there together."

"You mean we *sounded* fantastic together," Adrian corrected.

Roxie smiled slyly into her mojito and lifted an unassuming shoulder. "Potato, potahto."

"Thanks all the same, Ms. Levy," James said to her.

"Nice song choice," Adrian commented as Olivia came back around the bar.

"I thought you might like it," Olivia said. "It was either that or 'Son of a Preacher Man.'"

James found himself laughing with the others, minus Adrian who replied with, "Why don't you get onstage and sing, Olivia? I'm thinking either 'Sweet Child of Mine' or 'Cat's in the Cradle.'"

Olivia blanched, then glanced around quickly. A glare covered her shock as she turned back to Adrian and stuck out her tongue in retort. Then she gestured to Roxie. "Rox. You're up."

"Oh, boy!" Roxie said, hopping up and clapping her hands in anticipation.

"There's something wrong with her," Adrian decided.

Olivia glanced from James back to Adrian and said, "I'm beginning to think there's something wrong with *you*."

Briar beamed as she walked up, oblivious to the tension between her cousin and Adrian. "Cole's popped by for a spell. He looks like he could use a drink. Will you make him a margarita?"

"If he sings for it," Olivia said stubbornly.

"Margarita first," the man they were supposedly discussing said as he walked up behind Briar, placing his hands on her arms. "Then karaoke."

"Deal," Olivia said and went off to put the blender to use.

"James," Briar said, "I don't think you've met my husband. This is Cole Savitt. Cole, this is an old friend of the family, James Bracken."

Cole's eyes landed on James and stilled. James's smile of greeting froze on his face. The man wasn't familiar. He had dark eyes and darker hair, a fixed jawbone that looked hard as nails and a measuring look that was edged with suspicion and intensity despite the tender hands he'd placed on his wife. He might have been wearing plainclothes, with no badge or weapon in sight, but James had run into enough cops to know one on sight.

Briar spoke up, a bit tentatively as Cole's stare hardened and James grew warier, the muscles on the back of his shoulders tightening. "Is everything all right?"

Cole was the first to recover, smoothing a hand over Briar's wrist as he noted the thread of distress in her voice. "Fine." Dipping his head toward James, he said, "Nice to meet you. Bracken, is it?"

"That's right," James said and returned Cole's polite yet taut smile with one of his own.

"Huh." Cole stared at him with narrowing eyes. "Where'd you say you were from?"

"I didn't," James said, lifting his glass to his lips, eyeing the man over the rim.

Adrian frowned at the two of them. "Okay, what's going on—"

"Margaritas all around," Olivia announced as she descended on them with a full tray. "I'd like to make a toast." After Briar passed out the drinks, Olivia waited for everyone to lift theirs—Adrian took longer than anyone else, and Cole hesitated a moment before lifting his, James noticed. Finally, Olivia said, "To James, I'd like to officially say welcome home. We all wish you the best of luck with your new business."

"Hear, hear," a few of the others chorused. Ignoring Cole's penetrating stare, James glanced at Adrian and saw her set her glass on the bar. "You didn't drink."

"I'm tipsy enough," Adrian said, rising from her stool. "Liv, thanks for the drinks and humiliation."

"Anytime," Olivia returned.

"I'll walk you home," James said, standing.

"No," she refused as she reached into her purse. "I'm not that tipsy. Neither am I that foolish."

He placed a twenty dollar bill on the bar before she could retrieve her money. "Drinks are on me, then." He grinned when she only frowned at him. Reaching up, he brushed at the hair on her brow.

It was enough to make her suck in a breath and dodge the sweep of his fingers. "I don't want to owe you anything."

"You don't," he told her in an undertone, leaning close so the others wouldn't be able to hear over the music. Her eyes yawned like chocolate pools under his and he desperately wanted to dive in. Drown. "You don't owe me a thing. Just… think about what I said before. About Kyle."

She closed her eyes, a crease appearing briefly between them. Then she opened them, fixing her gaze on his T-shirt. "I'm not making any promises."

"But you will—think about it?" he asked.

She nodded. "I guess I'll have to."

He wanted to hug her for admitting as much. When he edged a bit closer, she stepped back, alarm crossing her face—as if she could read his mind. "He'll be home by now. I've got to go." And with that, she walked away from him again.

It stung, but he let her go. Tomorrow, he pledged. Even if she didn't decide anything, he'd likely see her tomorrow. And that was enough. For now.

CHAPTER SEVEN

JAMES THOUGHT IT was about time to mow the yard. Pushing a lawn mower around seemed like a good way to burn through some of his frustration.

Adrian hadn't said a word to him since that night in the tavern several days ago. She'd promised to think about his plea for time with Kyle. Clearly, if she'd done what she promised, her answer wasn't the one he'd hoped for.

It took several laps around the yard to cut down the first layer of overgrown grass and weeds. The mower gurgled and protested under the strain, even dying at one point. James cleaned the grass out from under it and yanked on the pulley until the engine gave way and cranked under his none-too-gentle urging. Already sweating, James shed his work shirt.

The chore was taking longer than he'd expected. He paused to guzzle a chilled bottle of water. Sitting on the front porch, he gauged the freshly tended grass. The house was slowly starting to come together. The afternoon before, after returning from the garage, he'd climbed onto the roof to sweep leaves and branches, and clean out the gutters. The day before that, he'd replaced the front screen door and some of the boards on the front steps. Once he'd repainted the shutters and tended the front garden beds, the house would no longer be the eyesore of the neighborhood.

A football sailed into his line of sight. It spiraled perfectly over the fence between his house and Adrian's cottage and came down with a bounce and a roll on the front walk close to his feet. He glanced from it to the two boys who came into sight—one snaggletoothed and wide-eyed, the other cautious, peering at him from a familiar set of blue eyes as he approached.

"Sorry, mister," Kyle said.

James stood, heart thumping a little harder than he would have anticipated. Here he was. His son. Crouching down, James forced his eyes elsewhere and picked up the football. "Hell of an arm," he said for lack of anything better, then frowned over the oath. He probably shouldn't curse in front of the kid.

Kyle's face lit up. "Thanks! It keeps getting away from me, though."

James glanced down at the football, remembering from long ago the wisdom his father had taught him. Shifting his feet, he cleared his throat. "Well…when you pull it back, be sure to lock eyes with your targeted receiver. It'll help."

The kid smiled at him. "Are you the new neighbor?"

"Yeah," James said and handed him the ball. "James Bracken."

"Kyle," he returned. He jerked his thumb over his shoulder. "I live in the cottage next door. This is Blaze. He lives in the blue house just down the street."

"Blaze," James said, with a dip of his chin to the other boy. He turned to Kyle and smiled. "It's good to meet you both."

Blaze nudged his young friend in the back. "C'mon."

Kyle's smile melted a bit as he backed away. "See you around, Mr. Bracken."

"Yeah, see you." James watched them go and felt what amounted to a dumbbell dragging at his heart. Still, his heart rapped violently against his chest. He swallowed. The wall of his throat felt thick, tight. Gathering a long breath inward, he pushed it out and walked to the garage where he kept his yard equipment.

He kept his eyes out for Kyle and Blaze as the afternoon wore down toward darkness. James knew Adrian would be getting home from the flower shop soon. He did his best to trim the unruly fringes of the yard. He had stopped to replace the trimmer line on the Weed Eater when he heard a large dually clatter to a halt. Looking over his shoulder, he saw the red truck, smelled the choking exhaust fumes as it belched black smoke. But it was the man who rolled down the window and poked his head out at the two boys playing near the street who got James's attention.

Radley Kennard was hardly recognizable. His face was bloated, his cheeks tinged red. Underneath close-shorn hair a well-worn sneer pulled at his mouth. He leered at the boys like an untrained dog. James dropped the trimmer and walked over, eating the ground up in several long strides as he crossed into Adrian's yard.

Putting himself between the boys and the truck, James glared at the man. "Something you need, sir?"

Radley frowned and looked at him from a pair of bloodshot eyes. Drunk or stoned. Either way, the man shouldn't be driving. Moreover, he shouldn't be trying to talk anyone into taking a ride around town with him as he'd been trying to command Kyle to.

"Yeah," he said in a gravelly voice that suggested ill use. "That's my boy there behind you, not that it's any of your business, and he's comin' with me."

"You're not my dad!" Kyle shouted from behind James. James had to lock an arm over the boy's shoulder to keep him from advancing. "You're a miserable excuse for a man and a drunken pisspot!"

James's pride began to swell. Then Radley's face darkened and he leaned even further out of his truck. "Don't you talk to me like that, you little shit!"

"Hey!" James shouted, pushing Kyle behind him once more as Radley's fist reached out to cuff the boy.

"If my mom were here, she'd call the cops on you!" Kyle retorted.

"Your mom ain't here, boy, or I'd've knocked her silly," Radley stated, eyes lighting with violence.

James grabbed the man's fist and twisted the thumb around. Radley gave a startled holler, then howled in pain as his face flushed twice over and his head rocked back against the driver's seat. He let out a stream of curses. James leaned in, lowering his voice to a dangerous level. "You feel that, moron? That right there isn't a fraction of what you'll feel if I catch your sorry ass anywhere near the kid or his mother again. Understand?"

Radley hissed in a breath. When he blew it out, James got a strong waft of something sickly sweet. James gave the arm another twist for good measure and growled, "Now get the hell outta here."

As soon as James released his arm, Radley whimpered. He retracted the arm into the cab and used the other to shift gears. James stepped back with the boys as the dually took off with a roar. He watched it blow through a stop sign and turn out of sight. It wasn't until the noise of the truck had faded that he turned to the boys and met Kyle's eyes. The boy's chin was high and his eyes fierce, but there was a quaver in his lips. James's stomach tightened. "He's gone now," James told him.

"I know," the boy replied with a nod. "But I'd better call my mom."

James nodded in return. "Would you mind if I went with you?" No way he was letting Kyle out of his sight now.

Relief spilled across his son's face. "I think she'd want that, Mr. Bracken," Kyle said.

"All right," James said. As Kyle turned and led the way, and Blaze took off for his own home, James lowered his voice and said, "By the way...I think it's best if you call me James."

"YOU HAVE TO contact the police," Olivia insisted in a low voice. "Tell them that Radley violated the restraining order."

"I know. I..." Adrian trailed off, glancing back toward the half-open door to the cottage. Kyle was on the other side somewhere, eating the takeout Olivia had been kind enough to bring over. She kept her voice low, too. "Don't think I won't. Radley's never targeted Kyle like this before. It's always been me..."

Olivia must have seen the blood rushing from Adrian face. She patted her on the arm. "From the sounds of things, he won't be coming back too soon."

"That's what we said the last time," Adrian said.

"And the time before that. But this keeps happening, Liv. And now he's coming after Kyle. I don't know what I would've done if…"

…*if James hadn't been there.*

She couldn't bring herself to say the words. Gathering herself, she said, "I need to get Kyle through the night. Then I'll report it in the morning with a clear mind."

"Do that," Olivia said firmly. "And try and get some sleep."

Adrian doubted very much that would happen. Silently she waited until Olivia had driven off. She took a moment to peer up and down the street. Seeing no sign of a red truck or anything out of the ordinary, she went back into the cottage and shut the door. Taking a deep breath, she turned to go into the kitchen and stopped short, the breath washing out of her suddenly when she found the man standing in her way. "James," she said, her heart pounding.

Adrian had found it difficult to look him in the eye since her return home. Straightening up to her full height—which was ridiculous confronted with his six-foot-five-inch frame—she said, "You can go now, James. Really. We'll be fine."

He shook his head, eyes flat and cool. "Olivia's not staying," he commented.

Adrian frowned. He'd heard every word of the conversation outside, hadn't he? Fighting the urge to massage her temples, Adrian said, "She knows we're fine for the night."

"I'll stay," James told her, then raised a hand when she opened her mouth to protest. "Just until you lock up."

She saw his gaze veer to the three dead bolts on the door behind her. Looking away, she walked around him into the kitchen where Kyle sat at the table. She didn't have the will to argue. Truth be told, everything she had was tied up in knots inside her and she couldn't let either of them see it.

The sooner Kyle was finished with dinner, the sooner she could put him to bed. Then she'd see James out, dead bolt the door, curl up on the couch, watch the windows warily for headlights and succumb to the nerves and panic she felt crawling further and further into the fragments of her mind.

Adrian didn't count on James and Kyle getting into a discussion at the table about school…and then homework. She'd forgotten about the homework, damn it. James, who seemed to have an aptitude for science where neither Adrian nor Kyle did, offered to help. Kyle leaped on the offer before Adrian could refuse for both of them.

So it was that Kyle stayed up past his bedtime. Adrian sorted laundry and had gone through two loads of washing and drying before Kyle started to yawn.

"Maybe you should get to bed, squirt," she heard James say.

"Probably," Kyle said as Adrian hovered by the kitchen door, just out of sight. "It's hard…going to sleep after *he* shows up."

"Hey, listen. He's not coming back. If it makes you feel any better, I'll stay up next door and keep a lookout."

A smile shone through Kyle's voice. "He wouldn't come near you. You scared the piss out of him." Adrian heard his chair scrape back against the floor. "You can stay here, on the couch, if you want."

Adrian chose that moment to enter the room. "Kyle…you should get ready for bed."

They looked at her with matching sets of eyes. Her heart could hardly take it. Kyle's brightened as he asked, "Can Mr. Bracken…uh, I mean, James—can he stay the night?"

Adrian glanced from him to James, frowning.

James rose and clapped a hand on Kyle's shoulder. "I think it'd be best if I went home. Your mom can call if she needs anything."

They both knew the odds of that happening were slim to none. "I laid your pajamas on your bed," she told Kyle as he rose from the table. Indulging, she wrapped her arms around him, holding him against her. Kyle buried his face in her shoulder. They stood that way for a while, leaning one into the other, before he finally moved toward the door, throwing a "Good night, James," over his shoulder.

"'Night, kid."

"Brush your teeth," Adrian called. "I'll check on you in a moment." When no reply came, she hesitated to face James again. If only he'd go. Just go. Moving around him to the table, she picked up the discarded take-out containers. "There's no need to stay any longer. I'll go to bed as soon as he's settled…"

His hands moved over her shoulders. She stiffened. He hadn't broached the subject of Radley since she returned home that evening. She was grateful for it.

Since she came home, he'd been nothing more than a steady presence. She shouldn't resent him. He'd chased Radley off, prevented him from getting to Kyle or hurting him, and he'd stayed. Whether it was for Kyle or her—or both—she wasn't sure. She was too tired to comb his behavior for an ulterior motive. Especially when his thumbs kneaded the place just there at the base of her neck…

Adrian caught herself leaning back into his hands and ducked under his arm. She discarded the boxes and took the plates and cups to the sink, feeling his eyes watching.

Yes, James needed to go. Before she broke down, crossed the room to him and pressed her face into his chest—just as Olivia had said any woman would want to. Adrian, it seemed, was no exception.

In the silence, she watched him go to the window, peer through the blinds. She measured the strong line of his jaw. His shoulders squared. Where once the same hard profile on another man might have made her cringe, she felt not a flicker of fear with him. She knew the difference between the menace Radley had shown her throughout their marriage and the vigilance, the ready urge to protect, that James exemplified. Somewhere deep down, some small, sick part of her was happy for it—happy for him here, crowding her space, her head...

Turning away from him, she went to Kyle's room. She was relieved to see him, covers tucked under his arms and comic book in his hands. His eyes were already heavy with sleep. She bent down, silently pressing her lips to his brow as she swept his hair back. Lingering, she breathed him in, then lifted her head and said, "Don't stay up too long."

He grinned at her as she picked his clothes up from the floor. "I like James."

She snapped the pants he'd been wearing so the legs fell right side out. "You do?"

"Yeah. How do you know each other?"

Adrian frowned over the question. "We were... friends. A long time ago."

"You mean, like in school?"

Adrian nodded. "Kind of. Why?"

"Nothing," Kyle said with a lift of his shoulder. He looked a bit sheepish for asking, but a light sparked in his eyes.

Adrian straightened, folding the pants over her arm. "Ten minutes, lights out. Okay?"

"Okay," Kyle said, turning his attention back to his comic book. "I love you, Mom," he added when she'd reached the door.

She turned back, smiled at the sight of him amidst his Avengers bedsheets. *My God.* What would she have done if Radley had snatched him off the street?

Her breath hitched. "I love you, too, baby," she replied as she stepped back into the hall. Pressing her back against the wall opposite his bedroom door, she took a minute for herself, clutching the clothes he had worn that afternoon. She touched the tip of her nose to his shirt, smelled the little boy who played hard and owned her heart.

That heart gave a swift yank. She reached up to swipe a tear from her cheek.

He was hers, just as she was wholly his. If anything happened to him, there'd be nothing left of her.

Unable to face James just yet, Adrian veered into the laundry room to throw the last load of washing into the dryer. Stalling, she folded what was clean in the basket. Lost in the task, her mind wandered back to the years she'd lived at Radley's mercy.

The pregnancy had passed without incident. It was in the postnatal months that his true nature began to awaken. And with her hormones and postnatal depression raging, she couldn't fight it. She'd sunk deep, deep down into the toxic rut that was their relationship, giving up any sense of self-worth in the process.

It had taken a year of counseling for her to understand what had caused her to live at his mercy, to be abused and to make excuses for Radley's behavior. It had taken longer for her to rebuild any true sense of self.

As she folded the fitted sheet in her hands, she heard a shuffle behind her. She gasped, half turning as she shielded her face with the linens. For a split second, she was back in Radley's double-wide trailer with the stench of booze and the sickly tang of fear coating the inside of her mouth…

When the backhand she'd anticipated never came, she opened her eyes to find James looking down at her, his face as stricken as hers.

Adrian released the breath trapped in her lungs. It sounded like a sob and she cursed, dropping the sheet back into the basket and hanging her head when she saw understanding dawn on his face.

"Sorry," he said in a small voice. "I was just coming to check on you."

She shook her head. Words remained trapped

at the back of her throat so she ducked around him once more, silently tromping down the hall into the kitchen.

He stopped her there, his hand on her arm. "Adrian…I need to know something."

She swallowed hard, still avoiding his gaze. "Yes, okay? He hurt me." She heard his sharp intake of breath. Lifting her chin, she met his eyes. "The last thing I need is your pity. Do you know how long I've been dealing with pity, James? I'm sick of it."

James searched her face, then jerked a nod, his Adam's apple bobbing. "All right," he whispered.

She closed her eyes on a flash of relief. "Now…I need you to go."

"I can't—"

"We'll be fine," she told him firmly. "I just need some peace and quiet so I can—"

"I can't leave you alone," he told her. "Either of you. Not now that I know what you've been through."

"We'll be fine," she said again. "I'll keep Kyle's BB gun close." She paused, wrestling over the next words. "And…and you can come by tomorrow morning. For breakfast, if you want."

James looked at her, his eyes skimming between hers, then over her cheeks, the line of her jaw. "I don't want you to be alone," he murmured.

She sighed. "James, I *have* been alone, for a really long time." *You made sure of that,* she added silently. *When you left me.* The resentment and anger that were usually brought to life by the words didn't stir. Tired. God, she was so tired.

"Adrian, I'm so sorry," he said again. When he drew her into his arms, she was helpless to stop him. She had nothing left to fight him with so she closed her eyes as the chest she had fantasized about burrowing herself against moments before rose up to meet her. She felt his lips come to rest on the top of her head. His arms wrapped around her back, closing her in, tightening.

He held her, simply held her, for what seemed like ages. Long enough for the tension to drain from her body. Long enough for her to lean into the hard, strong line of him without scruples, to breathe in the work shirt permeated with the sweet scent of grass and the slight tinge of motor oil. At some point, her arms rose to his waist, folding around to the small of his back to complete the embrace.

A small eternity passed in the space of moments. A hundred unspoken words. Memories stirred, whispering to life, ghosts of what had been.

He moved first, just enough to move one hand up to the nape of her neck. He made a noise in the back of his throat, drawing her attention upward. When his lips touched hers, it felt so natural for her mouth to receive the firm, yielding line of his.

Minutes before, she'd felt drained. Fatigued. The simple press of his lips brought her back to life. Her heart fluttered, lifting and soaring in a way she hadn't felt since…well, since being with James.

She should have pushed him away. After everything, she should shove him back, make him leave. Instead, she let the moment stretch, slide, deepen until she felt him brush up against the soul she'd buried from everything and everyone.

The kiss was soft…so soft.

He lifted his mouth from hers, easing back just slightly so their mouths were no longer meshed but they still shared a breath. He waited until she opened her eyes and her gaze fused to his. Grazing the tip of his thumb over her cheek, he whispered, "I'll be right next door, if you need me. Okay?"

She nodded slowly, unable to summon speech.

He began to step away, then stopped, framing her face in his big, working hands. Eyes closed, brows drawn together, he kissed her temple. His chest moved underneath her hands as he breathed her in. She actually felt him take a little piece of her with him when he finally backed off and left her alone. And that thought was terrifying.

CHAPTER EIGHT

A FEW DAYS LATER, Nutsy the Squirrel was back for more birdseed. Adrian cursed when she saw her bird feeder swinging drunkenly under the animal's weight.

Cole had taken Kyle with him that morning to go pick up his son, Gavin, from the airport. Adrian had thought it best to get Kyle away for the day anyway, just in case Radley came back. And if Radley followed him out of town...well, Cole, the ex-cop, was more than capable of protecting him. Adrian trusted few other men the way she trusted her friend's husband.

And, with Kyle out of the house, Adrian didn't have to worry about guilt as she clambered onto the kitchen counter to remove the BB gun from the top of the cupboard. When the door to the porch smacked shut behind her, Nutsy looked up, startled.

Gritting her teeth, Adrian sighted the BB gun. Nutsy leaped from the top of the feeder to the tree and dashed, chattering noisily, up the trunk, which crossed over into James's yard.

"Uh-uh," she said, climbing up on top of the

garden bench next to the fence amidst a cloud of Shasta daisies. "You're not getting away this time without a lesson from Mr. Winchester..." Using the top of the fence, she crouched behind the gun, placed the crosshairs over the squirrel's retreating rear, felt for the trigger, squeezed—

"Adrian, what're you—"

Startled, she shrieked and jerked. A shot rang out. Something hit the ground in the next yard and it wasn't Nutsy.

"James!" she cried, vaulting over the fence, leaving the Winchester behind as she ran to the man crumpled on his hands and knees in the grass. Rounding the edge of the pool, she hunkered beside him, placing her hand between his shoulder blades as she peered at his face, which was quickly turning an alarming shade of red. "Oh, God! I'm sorry, I'm so sorry! I didn't see you. What in God's name were you doing in that tree?"

His pained eyes squinted at her. "No. No. First, you tell me why in God's name you *shot me* out of that damn tree?"

"Shot you..." She paled when he groaned and lowered his face to the grass. "I...I shot you?"

"Ah, yeah." James groaned. "Son of a bitch..."

Adrian felt faint for a moment, then shook her head. *Don't panic.* As he rolled onto his side in agony, her hands fumbled over his chest. "Tell me where I shot you."

"In the ass!" he nearly shouted, reaching for the back of his left thigh.

Her mouth dropped open briefly as she bent over his hip to inspect the area. "How did I manage that?"

Panting, he leveled her with something that looked like a glare and a grimace all wrapped up in one red-faced, teeth-baring package. "You know, you could have just knifed me in the back. It would have been quicker, less painful."

"I didn't shoot you on purpose!" Adrian informed him none too gently. "The squirrel was stealing from my bird feeders again and I wanted to teach him a lesson, but he crossed over into your yard and I wasn't letting him get away."

"A squirrel?" he asked, eyes peeling wide in disbelief.

"Yes, a big, bastard squirrel who's mission in life is to drive me completely insane!"

James leaned away from her. "Oh, I think you're already there, sweetheart."

"Let me see," she insisted. When he cringed away from her again, she made an exasperated sound and dug her hand into his knee to keep him still. "We need to find out how bad it is."

"I can tell you how bad it is." He groaned again. Sweat beaded on his brow. "What did you shoot me with, anyhow?"

"Kyle's BB gun," she said as she unlatched

his belt buckle and struggled with the button of his jeans.

"Great," James said, lifting a hand in defeat before scrubbing it over his face. "I have metal BBs lodged in my ass."

"Hold still," she said as she tugged down the zipper and carefully peeled the denim from his hips.

"Listen, baby," he said, voice still tight with pain. "There are easier ways to get a man out of his pants. You don't have to snipe them out of trees."

Her hands fumbled. *James. Naked.* She had *not* thought this through. "I—I need to see the wound. You're simply going to have to take them off."

He wheezed a laugh. "Jesus. You're blushing." As she met his eyes, he grinned. For a split second, beyond the beard, the mop of tousled hair and the red face, she saw the seventeen-year-old boy he'd been. "You've seen me naked before, Adrian."

She looked away. "That was years ago."

"You weren't shy about it then. As a matter of fact, you undressed me faster than I ever could've managed myself."

"You're obviously delirious," she said grimly as she lifted his arm over her shoulders. "Come on. Stand up and lean into me."

What mirth there was in his eyes vanished as she helped him into a standing position. Planting his hands on her shoulders, he hissed, squeezing his eyes closed. "Ah, shit," he breathed, lowering his face into her hair.

She stood stock-still as his ragged exhale blew over her tresses, holding onto his hips to keep him steady. "You okay?" she asked quietly.

"Mmph." His low voice grated deep from his chest. "Yeah, I just need a shot of morphine and a bottle of Jack Daniels."

Adrian frowned. "You gave up drinking."

"I know," he growled. "Damn you, woman. I'm gonna have to call my sponsor."

She took a deep breath. "Okay, well. I'm going to get these jeans off you. Just…try to be still. Can you do that?"

"Mmm," was his only reply.

Choking back the small lick of excitement she felt as she tugged his zipper the rest of the way down, she gripped the waistline of his jeans and gently pulled them down over his hips. Underneath, she found black boxer briefs. *Huh. He wore plain boxers back in the day,* she mused. Then she scowled. That was exactly the sort of thought she did not need.

Jesus…he had the thighs of a Viking. Sucking in a quick breath, she refocused on her task and, making sure he was planted solidly on his feet, circled him.

She'd always liked that space there…just above the waistband of his boxers where his back met…

well, a very nice butt. She had to fight not to trace her finger over the line of his spine or the sweet dimples on either side just above the black band of his underwear. Bending over, she found the entry site in his left buttock through the boxer briefs. "Oh," she said, touching it gingerly. "I got you good, didn't I?"

"Maybe some moonshine," he muttered. "Some of ol' Witmore's moonshine would be great right about now..."

Adrian braced herself for her next task. "Just try and stay still, James." She grabbed the waistband of his boxer briefs.

He hissed and pulled away her hands.

"What?" she asked wildly. "What did I do?"

"Nothing," he admitted. "It's...your hands are like ice cubes."

"Oh." Adrian splayed her fingers apart and frowned at them. She didn't know how they could possibly be cold. She felt warm all over. Clearing her throat, she went back to tugging at the waistband. "I'll pull these down only enough to see the wound."

"Yeah," he drawled. "You keep telling yourself that, baby."

Adrian's teeth gnashed as she revealed the round, upper curve of his buttocks. "Call me baby, woman or sweetheart one more time and I'll go back for that Winchester."

James managed a short chuckle. "You're right. I think I like *li'l mama* better."

She made a noise in the back of her throat. Finally, she peeled the boxer briefs back to find the entry wound. "Um…"

"Bad?" he asked.

Without answering, she quickly moved the waistband back up to the small of his back and tugged his jeans up, coming around to his front to button and zip them quickly. "Do you have your wallet on you?"

"Yeah," he said, brow puckered. "Why?"

Adrian licked her lips. "Because I'm taking you to the emergency room."

FIFTEEN MINUTES LATER, James fought the grappling hands of dread as Adrian pulled into the parking lot of Thomas Hospital. "I told you, damn it. I don't need to go to the emergency room."

"And I told you that the pellets are buried too far in your cheek for me to remove." She parked the car and unbuckled her seat belt. "We're here now. You might as well stop whining about it."

As she got out of the car, James eyed the front of the hospital. His heart rate doubled. *No. Not yet. Not this way.* When the passenger door opened, he gripped the bar over his head. "I'm not going in."

"Oh, my God, men are such babies!" Exasperated, she reached in and gripped his arm, making his weight shift from the careful lean he'd been utilizing to keep from applying pressure to the wound.

Pain rocketed through his lower extremities and he cursed a blue streak. "You're a heathen," he growled through his teeth.

"And you're a bonehead," she retorted, pulling again. "Now, unless you plan on sitting on the right side of your ass for the rest of your godforsaken life, get out of the damn car."

He grabbed the open door, ignoring her helping hands. He stood up on the pavement next to her. Swallowing another groan of pain, he closed his eyes, waiting for the sharp nettles to abate. "I hate you."

"You can press charges later," Adrian told him evenly. She closed the car door, locked it and then tucked herself against his left side to take some of his weight. "Slow," she said as they hobbled together to the whishing automatic doors.

Again James had to lean far to the right in the hard chairs of the waiting area. Then he was forced to strip at the waist for the triage nurse who had hands as cold as Adrian's. By the time he was allowed to lie on his stomach on a bed behind a curtain, his mood had descended into even fouler territory, especially when he was forced to refuse pain meds. "Trust me," he told Adrian when she protested the decision. "It's for my own good."

She sighed but said nothing more as they waited

for the doctor. James tried to calm his racing thoughts as taut silence descended upon them.

Maybe it would be somebody else. Who was to say she worked the ER anymore? If he was lucky, she'd retired to a private practice somewhere far, far away…

In this case, luck wasn't with him. When the curtain swept back and the woman in the blue scrubs appeared, James met the cold gray eyes of Dr. Mavis Irvington straight on and watched as her steps toward the bed hitched at the sight of him.

"James," she said in obvious surprise.

He did his best to sit up without grimacing. "Mom."

For a space of several heartbeats, no one moved. Even Adrian had frozen. Then Mavis seemed to recover, lifting her chin as she pulled air in through her sharp blade of a nose. "How are you?" she asked—the question he knew was routine for every patient. He had a feeling the words didn't sound quite so clipped to strangers.

James shrugged. The place between his shoulder blades itched. In fact, suddenly he itched all over. Itched to be anywhere else but under the gray study of those discerning eyes. "All right, I guess."

"Good," she said with a tight nod. She turned to Adrian and her head rocked back slightly in surprise once more. "Adrian."

Adrian's eyes lowered. "Dr. Irvington."

Mavis recovered from her shock relatively quickly and offered something of a smile. "It's good to see you, dear."

Adrian gave a nod. "You, too. How's Dr. Irvington? Er, I mean, the *other* Dr. Irvington."

James winced. *The other Dr. Irvington* was his stepfather. Dr. Stephen Irvington, PhD. The man Mavis had married a mere ten months after Zachariah Bracken died.

"He's doing well," Mavis replied. "Thank you for asking." Approaching the bed, she asked, "Now...why don't you tell me what happened?"

James's gaze lowered to the floor. There was something pressing...no, sitting on his chest. He was having a hard time breathing. Ah, hell. Sitting here on a gurney facing his mother in his boxer briefs was way more painful than a gunshot wound. Why had he allowed Adrian to bring him here?

He listened with only half an ear as she explained haltingly what had transpired. If his mother was amused, he couldn't tell from her responding *hmms*. As she approached the bed, putting on her gloves, she said simply, "Let's see it."

That hurt, too. She'd said the same thing years ago when he came home from bicycle riding with a banged-up knee or when he fell out of another tree in the backyard of his childhood home and broke his wrist. She'd said it often, in fact, as his daredevil streak led to hundreds of cuts and scrapes and, on more than one occasion, worse things. Only there had been kindness in her eyes then, and no lines in her face.

She looked as ashen as he felt. And those weren't wrinkles in her forehead. Her brow was pulled tight, like his. As if she were in pain.

Yep. This reunion was shaping up to be just as painful as he'd imagined it to be.

As James stood to remove his underwear, Adrian cleared her throat from behind him. "Um, I'll just wait out here." She quickly retreated to the other side of the privacy screen.

As soon as it swept back into place, Mavis asked, "What do you think you're doing, James?"

Placing his elbows on the raised bed, he lowered his face into his hands. "It's not what you think."

Mavis hissed indignantly as she swabbed the entry wound with antiseptic. "You're not home five minutes and you go straight back to where you were before. Harassing Adrian Carlton."

"We live next door to each other," James explained, fighting for patience. "And I'm the one who's been shot. She's unharmed, as you can plainly see."

"Unharmed." Mavis sniffed. James jerked under her ministrations. He tried to tell himself she wasn't purposely hurting him. "She's been anything but unharmed by your interference. Why do you think I hired a private detective to find you?"

"You what?" James asked, straightening. The forceps dug in and he crumbled back to the bed. "You hired a PI?"

"Yes, right after you left," she admitted. "You know, Adrian wound up in the ER with dehydration? Turned out, it was *hyperemesis gravidarum*."

"What the—ah!" The question melted quickly into a cry of pain. Something metal clanged onto the tray beside the bed.

"Severe morning sickness," Mavis said, matter-of-factly, except for the edge trimming the words. "A certain number of women, not too many, are more negatively affected by pregnancy hormones than others. Adrian is one of them. It didn't take a genius to figure out who'd gotten her into such a state."

"So you hired someone to drag me back?"

"Yes," she said. She was swabbing him again. He tried not to think about blood. "I was determined to make you return and, for once, face up to your responsibilities."

"Why didn't you?" James asked curiously, turning his head.

She didn't meet his gaze as she bandaged him. "It took some time, but he found you. Stealing cars and helping smuggle them out of state. I knew you had a misguided streak. But, after everything, I still never thought you would have turned to a life of out-and-out crime."

"I didn't see much choice," he said, "then, at least." He sighed. "You still...you should've found a way to tell me."

"So you could ruin the boy's life, too?" she asked. "I don't think so." Stepping back, she snapped off a glove. "Keep your weight off the wound for two days. Use over-the-counter pain medication to treat the discomfort. It will be tender for a week, maybe more."

James straightened, pulled up his pants and watched her dispose of the pellets. "Mom?" When she finally gazed back to him, he frowned. God, she looked tired. His heart gave a none-too-gentle squeeze. "I would've come back. I would've done them right. Both of them."

Mavis weighed him. "What's sad, James, is that some part of me wishes I could believe it."

"I'm sorry."

"For what, exactly?"

"A lot," he replied. "I'm sorry for leaving. I'm sorry you had to know what kind of life I fell into. But I got out of it." He hesitated, then pushed the words out. "I stopped drinking."

She blinked. Her eyes lowered to his chest. "Well, that's something." He raised a brow as her eyes latched onto his again. "How long?"

"Four years, three months. Give or take a few days. I joined AA. Just like Dad."

She nodded. Her throat moved on a swallow. "I'm glad. He worried you would fall into the same pattern he did. He worried so much for your future, James."

"I know," he said, and his voice sounded choked. "He was right to."

"You're so much like him," she said in something close to a whisper as her eyes raced over him.

He saw the wet sheen in her eyes and began to cross to her. "Mom—"

Mavis stepped back, bringing him up short. She pinned him with a sharp look. "I can't, not yet."

James would have gladly taken another bullet over her reaction, given the choice. It took him a moment to speak again evenly. "I'm opening a garage in town." He rubbed his neck, blew out a breath. "I know you were never really into the things Dad and I did with cars, but he used to talk about opening up a place like this. You should come by and see it. If you want."

Mavis lifted a noncommittal shoulder. "We'll see."

Knowing that was the only promise she could give him, James jerked a nod and veered toward the privacy screen. "Say hi to Stephen for me?"

Behind him, Mavis gave a short, sour laugh. "You don't mean that."

He peered at her over his shoulder, memorizing her face. As if he needed to. "Maybe I do. Maybe I've changed." He hesitated, weighing what he wanted to say next against what they would both be comfortable with. *I love you.* He settled for, "Thanks for the patch-up," instead.

"James."

"Yeah?"

Her face was a mask of warning now. "Don't do anything stupid. That boy's been through enough, and Adrian's been to hell and back herself. The only thing you have any right to give either of them is peace."

James felt the bite of the words, down to the quick. Without a goodbye, he passed through the curtain and escaped.

"ARE YOU OKAY?"

Adrian looked over when a minute passed and James said nothing in return. He was leaning against the car door, the muscles of his face taut and his eyes drilling into the window, not seeming to see much as they passed through the streets of downtown Fairhope.

She licked her lips and faced the windshield again, stopping at an intersection. "Serves you right, you know." When he turned his head to her, she raised her brows. "For not telling your own mother you were back in town."

"Yeah, I'm a real asshole."

The defeated words made her eye him in concern as he turned back to the window. "Well. Why didn't you?"

"Because I haven't spoken to her in eight years, Adrian," he said in a flat voice.

Eight years. The thought of not speaking to Kyle for half that long twisted Adrian up inside. "Why not?"

"Because I thought the whole lot of you were better off without me."

"You were a fool."

"Maybe," he said after some hesitation.

"You were," she told him. She paused over her next question, then decided to go for it. "Are you still upset about Dr. Irvington? The other Dr. Irvington."

"I forgave her for marrying Stephen a long time ago, even the fact that she chose to do it as soon as she did," James told her. "I forgave them both right around the time I stopped downing Jack Daniels and Wild Turkey like water and started looking at myself good and long in the mirror again."

She frowned over that because she'd once had to do the same thing—analyze herself, her life, take stock, rebuild. "Did you think you wouldn't run into them? It's a small town."

"I want to fix things. I just haven't been able to figure out *how*. There's so much there, so much bitterness and regret and mistakes to make up for. Just like with you. It's hard to know where to start."

Adrian swallowed as she turned into their neighborhood. "At least you're willing to give it a shot."

"She told me to leave you alone."

Adrian found a small smile crawling across her lips. "I knew I always liked your mother." He said nothing as they pulled into her driveway. "Come on, let's get you inside."

"No."

"No? You're just going to sit here sulking?"

James sent her a baleful look as he unbuckled his seat belt and reached for the handle of the passenger door. "Today's already been eventful enough as it is, for the both of us. And I'm still man enough to walk myself home, thanks."

She breathed carefully as he struggled to stand. She rounded the hood of the car to grab his arm. "I'm the one who got you into this mess. The least I can do is walk you twenty feet to your door."

When his head lifted and he looked at her, she froze. The anguish on his face was palpable. "You were sick."

Her mouth opened, closed. "I was?"

"The pregnancy," he said. "It made you sick. Really sick."

Adrian blinked. *Oh, crap.* What else had his

mother told him? "A lot of women get sick when they're pregnant, James."

"Not enough to wind up dehydrated in the hospital."

Reading the defeat in his eyes, she closed hers briefly, then straightened her shoulders. She made herself put her hand on his and look at him directly as she said, "There are a lot of things that I regret or wish I'd done differently. But through it all, the one constant has been my little boy. There's no regret there. Kyle might come from you and whatever it was we did or didn't have back in the day. But not one moment of his entire life have I ever regretted. And neither should you."

"Adrian…" He lowered his head until his forehead nearly rested against hers. His eyes were still pained, but they were fierce. "I've never regretted you. Ever. I just regret how I handled things."

"It's done," she told him. Hadn't she woken up telling herself the same thing for years? "Move on."

He searched her gaze. "I tried, when I left before. It didn't work out too well for me."

"Maybe you did it the wrong way."

"Why do you think I'm back? Why do you think I'm standing here in front you?"

"If you've got problems, James, I'm not the answer," she said.

A light entered his eyes, an old flicker of humor. He tucked his hands into his pockets as he straightened. "Over the years, I've had a good many problems. For instance, not being able to close my eyes without seeing your face."

"Stop it," she said in warning.

"*You* were never a problem," he told her. "And it's taken me eight years to understand that maybe you've always been the answer. I just chose not to see before. But I'm seeing now. Despite everything that's going on, you can be damn sure I'm seeing and I'll figure it out."

As he turned and hobbled off toward his house, she crossed her arms over her chest. "James," she called. When he didn't stop, she huffed in indignation.

She didn't want to be his answer. Because if he did come to the conclusion that she was what he needed in life, that meant he wasn't done. She feared he never would be. Not with her.

CHAPTER NINE

JAMES OPENED THE DOOR and pursed his lips when he found the woman on his doorstep. "Briar," he said, opening the screen to let her into the house. "What are you doing here?"

"I brought pie," Briar said, lifting the round, covered platter in her hands as she crossed the threshold under his urging. "I heard about your little accident and…well, I figured you could use something to brighten your day."

James found himself smiling as she handed over the warm foil-wrapped dessert. "That's very kind of you." He glanced around the living room, which was still in a state of chaos with moving boxes and their contents spread over the furniture and floor. "Sorry for the mess."

Briar waved a hand, though her honey-brown eyes did comb the room. "Moving's a never-ending ordeal. Why don't I take that?" Grabbing the pie, she began peeling off the foil. "Would you like a slice? It's cherry, one of my best."

James had heard rumors about Briar's cooking and baking. In fact, he had eaten many of her

mother's pies at church functions when his father
joined the ministry and his mother became ac-
tively involved in Sunday afternoon picnics for the
congregation. The banquet table was a great place
to hang out when trying to avoid conversing with
church folk. "I can't say no to that," James said,
as the scent of the cherry pie washed over him.

Briar bustled around his kitchen as James
settled into one of the dining room chairs. She
brought him a plate with a napkin and fork as
well as a glass of iced tea. "Would you mind me
asking you something?"

"You brought me pie, Briar," James pointed out.
He took another bite and stopped to say, "Mmm,
that's good." He cleared his throat when a small
smile played at her lips. "You can ask me whatever you want."

"Okay, good," she said. "Why did you come
back, exactly?"

James stopped, mouth full. She was staring at
him owlishly and he saw a flicker of speculation
in her eyes amidst the kindness. Swallowing, he
cleared his throat and wiped his mouth. "So that's
what this is about."

Briar shrugged. "What kind of friend would
I be if it wasn't?" Her expression cleared. "I've
always liked you, James. Our families go back a
ways. That means something to me."

He nodded. "Me, too, and I'm sorry about your

mom. She was always nice to me. She was there for my mom, too, in the way I probably should've been."

"Thank you," she said, then her mouth tipped into a frown. "But despite the history between our two families, you've been gone a long time. Now Adrian's practically a sister to me. Kyle's dear to all of us, too. I'd be doing them an injustice if I didn't grill you a little. Especially since she's done the same for me in the past."

James cleared his throat. "Understood." Pushing his plate away, he put down the fork and wiped his hands on the napkin. "I'll be honest. I didn't come back for her. Not initially."

She studied him a moment, then nodded. "I believe you."

Her ready trust in him was a bit off-putting. He couldn't remember the last time someone had placed their trust in him so quickly. It made him look at Briar in an even more affectionate light. "I came back to Fairhope," he said carefully, "because I'm sick of running away from my problems. I'm tired of being haunted by what I left behind. I'm trying to make amends for what happened in the past and with the people I hurt."

"And when you've done that…" Briar lifted a questioning shoulder. "When you feel like you've achieved these goals, will you pick up and leave again?"

"No," James said, determined as he picked up

his tea glass. "I want everyone I left behind to know that I'm here for them—that they can depend on me, always."

"Do you love her?" Briar grinned when he took a sip of the tea and nearly choked at the question. Trying to muffle a laugh behind her hand, she used the other to clap him on the back as he coughed. "I'm sorry. So sorry, but I couldn't resist."

He made a hoarse noise in the back of his throat and took another swallow. "Hazed by interrogation. Nicely done."

Briar rubbed his shoulder before picking up his dish and taking it back into the kitchen. "If it makes you feel any better, you passed the test."

James looked at her hopefully. "Oh, yeah?"

Briar nodded as she covered the pie in foil again. "You have my permission to bug Adrian. Not that you needed it. Just…be careful. There's so much there—so much pain and grief. She's been through a great deal."

Licking his lips, James rose and limped to the counter to lean on it as Briar began rinsing the dishes, right at home. "Briar…" When her eyes rose to his, he asked quietly, "Did Kennard ever hurt Kyle, too?"

The warning light of alarm entered her eyes before she dropped them to the sink. "Why do you think she finally found the strength to leave him?" she asked, lowering her voice so that over the rush of water it was nearly inaudible. "He hurt Kyle and she got the both of them as far away from him as she could. Before that, it had only been her. But, from what I understand, one night I guess he got too drunk or too buzzed off whatever he was into at the time and he pushed Kyle down the stairs."

James's hands hardened in their grip on the counter. "Why did she marry him?"

"Because she was scared," Briar said as she shut off the water and dried the glass with a tattered washcloth. "Because she wanted to get away from her parents. Edith's bitterness. Van's disappointment. Radley was a kind bystander and Adrian latched onto that because, at the time, it seemed like the only positive course in her life. You can't blame her for that. We've all done stupid things because anger or fear got the better of us."

"I don't blame her," James explained. "And you do know that you're preaching to the choir over here?"

She lifted a shoulder as if to say "I know." Then she looked around the kitchen. "Are you sure you don't want me to help you unpack anything?"

James grinned. "If I keep you around much longer, your husband's gonna come looking for vengeance. He didn't seem too keen on me the other night."

Briar waved a hand and smiled. "Cole's harmless. He's overprotective when it comes to me, Harmony or any of the girls. Adrian in particular."

"Does this overprotectiveness have anything to do with the fact that he's a cop?"

"He *was* a cop," she corrected. "A narcotics detective. How'd you know?"

James pursed his lips before sliding his hands into his pockets. "I've had my fair share of brushes with the police. I know a cop when I see one."

"And you run as fast as you can in the other direction?" she asked, raising a coy brow.

"Once upon a time," he said with a nod.

"You can keep your running shoes in the closet. My husband is retired. And he's got no reason to come running after you." Turning, she pinned him with a straightforward stare that almost knocked him back a step. "Right?"

He grinned and tipped his head in agreement. "Right."

"Good." She wavered for a moment, then raised herself on her tiptoes and brushed a platonic kiss over his bearded cheek. "It's wonderful to have you back."

His grin turned rueful. "Thank you."

Leaning back, she pointed at him with a stern finger. "Don't do anything stupid or it'll be me coming after you. Not to mention Liv armed with her granddaddy's shotgun."

"Consider me warned," James told her, trailing her to the front door. He had left it open with the screen in place. As they approached, James saw a man climbing the steps to his front porch.

Briar opened the screen, and James's eyes adjusted to the light beaming in from the outdoors, his steps halted as the man's face took shape and Briar called out a cheerful greeting.

"Dr. Irvington!" she said, grasping the hand of James's stepfather. "How are you?"

"I'm doing all right, Briar," Dr. Stephen Irvington replied, a shade of a smile touching the perpetually serious line of his mouth. "How about you?"

"Great." Briar looked around for James's reaction. Seeing the frown on his face, she quickly waved toward the car in the drive. "I was just on my way out. Please tell Mavis I said hello."

"I'll certainly do that," Dr. Irvington said, stepping aside so that she could pass down the steps into the sunshine.

"I hope we see you soon down at the inn, James," Briar called back to him.

James jerked his chin toward her in answer, unable to summon a passing remark. Still, he watched her drive off in the silence that fell quickly between him and Stephen. He'd be lying if he said he didn't wish he were leaving with her.

Ghosts, James reminded himself. *Gotta face those ghosts.* Meeting Stephen's studious gaze, he jerked his head toward the door. "I guess you better come in, too."

"You don't have to invite me in, son," Stephen told him. He was a tall, reedy man with glasses, and he was always dressed to the nines. When

Mavis first started dating him years ago, James had resentfully referred to him as The Suit. Today he wasn't wearing a suit but what passed for casual attire for a man of his stature—a sweater vest over a pressed oxford shirt and khakis. His loafers were shiny, unscuffed, as if they'd never been worn. "We both know me coming in wouldn't make you any more comfortable than you are now."

James fought a scowl. It was automatic and unmerited. Stephen was right and his honesty was for James's benefit, not his own. Having Stephen Irvington inside his house, scanning the interior and the current mess it was in, would make James itch far more than Briar's questions had. Probably because it was in Stephen's nature to analyze human behavior. He was a clinical psychologist—one of the best in his field. Plus, he would no doubt report everything he saw back to James's mother.

James let the screen door close. Leaning against the jamb, he crossed his arms—a gesture Stephen would probably peg as defensive. But some habits were hard to curb. "Did my mom send you?"

"She doesn't know I'm here," Stephen admitted. If he felt any guilt over the admission, it didn't show on his placid exterior. The man had always been calm. James had bitterly resented him for that. No matter what harsh words he'd spewed in Stephen's face or how loud he raised his voice against him, James had never been able to penetrate that calm facade. James had done his best to hurt Stephen and his mother both when he'd found out they would be marrying.

Those harsh words seemed to echo between them now. James rolled his shoulders back, trying to ease the strain. "Won't she be upset?" he asked.

"She will be," Stephen asserted, "particularly when she finds out why I'm here."

"Why are you here?" James asked.

Stephen seemed to weigh his words for a moment, then the steady line of his shoulders fell. For a split second, he seemed to fall in on himself before taking a breath and gathering whatever emotions he felt, looking James in the eye as he said, "Your mother has cancer."

The statement punctured James through the middle like the tip of a broadsword. He stood against the house, grateful to have something to lean on. "What did you say?" he asked.

"Stage four," Stephen said grievously. "She didn't want to tell you at the hospital. In fact, when I spoke to her later that evening, she left me under the impression that she had no intention of telling you at all. But if you're sticking around, and it seems that you are, I figured you should hear it from me, if not her. Finding this sort of thing out through the grapevine is difficult. And…maybe the news will make you rethink things as far as your mother is concerned."

"Like what?" James croaked. His heart was hammering away at his chest like a sledgehammer on an anvil. The pain reverberated through his rib cage.

"She'll be going through aggressive chemo soon," Stephen told him. "She's going to weaken, and as hopeful as we are, there's no guarantee what treatment will do at this stage. If you have no plans of being a part of her life, that's your decision. But if you intend to see or speak to her again, I'll ask you to do so with the utmost respect and gentility. The last thing she needs in her life right now is strife."

James winced. Lifting his hand to his mouth, he rubbed the back of his fingers over his lips. "Ah…" Unable to think of anything to say, he drilled his gaze into the floorboards of the porch.

Stephen hesitated for a moment. Then he exhaled and moved toward James, lifting a hand to his shoulder. When James raised his eyes to his stepfather's face, he saw emotion. But it wasn't the anger or hurt he'd craved to see on the man's face years ago. It was kindness. And sympathy. The hand on his shoulder squeezed. "She may need you, through this. But being there for her…that's something you'll have to decide for yourself."

James swallowed hard, tasting bile and fear. "I'm not sure she'd want me."

Stephen gave him something of a smile. "She might surprise you. She loves you. Despite everything, she loves you, James. Remember that, whatever it is you decide."

James nodded. Stephen gave his shoulder one last pat before backing away. James didn't stop him from going down the steps and walking back to the Mercedes parked on the street. He stood stock-still, feeling the walls of his life shake for the second time since his return to Fairhope.

ADRIAN HAD JUST finished helping an elderly lady load a large wreath into the backseat of her Cadillac and was waving her off from the parking lot at Flora when, from the corner of her eye, she saw someone approaching. Turning her head, she spotted James coming down the sidewalk.

Adrian began to heave an exasperated breath, then stopped, taking in his appearance. He was walking, head down, hands deep in the pockets of his jeans. Though she couldn't make out his expression clearly, she saw that his mouth was drawn into a deep frown. Something about his posture, the slump of his back and shoulders, and his slow, aimless gait made her steps hitch, made her wait for him to get closer and lift his head to see her.

When he did, she sucked in a breath. His eyes were lost even as they found hers, his expression crestfallen. Her hand rose halfway to her mouth before she dropped it and walked the rest of the way to meet him. "Hey," she greeted. "What's wrong?"

He scanned her face with eyes that looked not

just lost but hurt. Her heart rapped because he looked like that boy she'd seen at his father's funeral, fighting against the tide of grief, sinking under the brunt of reality. She watched his Adam's apple bob once before he lowered his eyes to her shoulder and asked in a voice that was unwavering but hoarse, "Did you know that my mom has cancer?"

Adrian's mouth dropped. "Dr. Irvington…has cancer?"

"Yeah," James said after a moment's pause. "Stage four. She has to go through aggressive chemo. My stepdad…Stephen, he doesn't know if it's going to do her any good at this point…"

She said nothing as she watched the muscles of his face twitch and he trained his gaze on the ground.

He licked his lips. His voice lowered a fraction. "I thought she looked thin. She was always thin, but this was sick thin and I should've known. I should've seen it."

Adrian shook her head. "How could you have known, James? You've been—"

"Gone," he said, disgusted. "Yeah."

"Oh, God." Adrian felt the quaking inside her because it was occurring to her that inside the bearded, tattooed man, the boy she'd fallen in love with was still there and he was hurting all over again. Over the years she'd wished him several ills. A pox. Something itchy and incurable. But this…she hadn't wanted this.

The pain fighting for purchase on his face was too much. She stepped to him and wrapped her arms around his neck, using her hands to pull his head down into her shoulder and cradle him there.

Cars whished by on the street. Birds cried overhead. Adrian didn't know how long she held James. It didn't matter. He breathed against her, into her, deeply, evenly. He wasn't breaking down. Still, he didn't straighten, didn't pull away, and she held on as if both their lives depended on it.

She didn't know when she started caressing his neck or combing her fingers through the hair on the back of his head. He smelled like lumber again. She caught herself touching her lips to the place just above the neckline of his T-shirt, the warm skin there that tasted just faintly of salt and sun.

Stiffening, she sucked in a breath and lowered herself from her tiptoes to the heels of her flats. "She's going to be okay," she told him when he finally lifted his head from her shoulder. Keeping his head lowered, he reached up to run the back of his hand under his nose. "She's tough. She'll fight it."

James dragged his gaze back up to hers at long last. "I thought I might get her something. I wasn't sure what, exactly. The first person I thought of was you."

"Of course," Adrian said. Fighting through her own hesitation, she took his hand and led him into her shop.

CHAPTER TEN

THE GARAGE WAS hopping with activity during opening week. Since James had neglected to hire anyone but Dusty before the grand opening of Bracken Mechanics, he hardly had time to sit and breathe, much less think about everything else that was going on in his life.

However, as he stripped engines and patched tires, ordered parts and chatted up customers, his mind was never far away from Adrian, Kyle, or his mother and Stephen.

A great deal of turmoil roiled around on the underside of his skin and threatened to usurp everything else, but James kept his hands busy. He wouldn't let Bracken Mechanics and the dream he had shared with his father slip away. Beyond that, he knew if he was going to convince Adrian that he could be a real father, he'd need a solid and preferably local business to back him up on that point.

As for his mother...whenever James dwelled on his fears on that score, the turmoil began to burn the back of his throat. When he thought of how much time had gone by, how much time had been lost, and what might happen if his mother's chemo didn't work, he felt sick.

Part of the reason he'd put Fairhope in his rear-view mirror when he was seventeen was to get away from the memories and all the unsaid things that had remained after his father's death. Before he knew about the cancer, he might have continued avoiding his mother. But now, if he lost her, too…living in Fairhope knowing he'd thrown away eight years with her might be too much to take.

And he wasn't leaving. He had a business here now. He was a father and he intended to *be* one. And his mother hadn't seen the last of him. Just as he would for Adrian and Kyle, he would find some way to make up for all those misplaced years and hurts.

Around midweek Bracken Mechanics got an unexpected visitor. James was leaning against the wall, phone pressed to his ear while he filled out a towing request. Out of the corner of his eye, he saw someone walk into the garage. Glancing over, he started to lift his chin in greeting, then stopped.

It was the cop. Briar's husband. He glanced around briefly before his dark gaze fell on James. Then he stopped, crossed his arms and braced his feet apart, waiting.

James cleared his throat and turned his attention back to the phone conversation. "Yeah, I'll call Dusty right away to see if he's en route. We'll get you fixed up in no time, Mr. Bremen…No, it's no trouble. That's what we're here for…All right. You're welcome…'Bye."

He hung the phone back on the cradle on the wall, tore the towing sheet off the clipboard and pushed off the wall. He picked up his cell phone and quickly got in touch with Dusty through the truck link. He told him the name and location of Mr. Bremen's pickup truck, then hung up. Only then did he address the other man in the room. "Is there something I can do for you, Mr. Savitt?"

"In a manner of speaking," Cole replied. "You got a minute?"

James lifted a brow as he turned to look tellingly over the line of cars in the garage. "Not really. Could it wait 'til after six."

Cole jerked a thumb toward the sign outside. "That says you close at five."

"Officially," James said. "I've been staying a little later every night to handle the workload."

"This will only take a second," Cole said. He closed some of the distance between himself and James so his voice would carry over the clash of the radio coming from the work area. "Briar told me she visited you the other day."

"She did," James nodded. "Brought me pie. It was nice of her."

"Yes, it was. That's Briar." Cole's head lowered by a fraction but he didn't take his eyes off James.

"She told me that you're aware that I'm a retired law enforcement officer."

"Narcotics detective," James said, trying not to feel ill at ease. The guy rubbed him the wrong way—wary leftovers of his misspent youth. "Real impressive."

"She happen to mention where I spent my years with the police?" Cole asked.

James reached back to scratch his neck and pulled a face. "You know, we really didn't talk about you that much—"

"Huntsville, Alabama," Cole said without further ado.

James's forced, good-natured expression froze. He measured Cole's stare, saw the knowing gleam there. *Ah, shit.* "You don't say," he replied for lack of anything better.

Cole gave him a grim smile. "Quite a coincidence, huh…Ghostrider?"

Ghostrider. Now there was a name James hadn't heard in a long time. "I'm not sure I know what you're talking about."

Cole chuckled darkly. "Yeah. I'll bet." The smile slowly melted away. "I didn't work grand theft auto cases, but I remember the headlines. I remember how many cars disappeared into the mountains. My partner had worked the GTA circuit for a while. We used to talk about it. I called him after we were introduced at Olivia's tavern, wondering where exactly I'd heard the name James Bracken. I never forget a name."

"Good for you," James said.

Ignoring the offhand comment, Cole went on. "You were Ghostrider. My buddies in Huntsville were sure of it. All they needed was the evidence to convict. Then you up and disappeared, too."

Luckily James had gotten out of the GTA game. He'd left his life of crime and the name Ghostrider far behind him—neither were part of his life anymore. So why was Savitt shoving it all back in his face again? "If what you say is true…" James lifted his shoulders in an indifferent gesture "…you're retired. What's it to you?"

"Adrian," Cole said.

The name all but snapped James's head back. "What about her?"

"You're trying to force your way back into her life," Cole surmised. "And from what I've gathered, she doesn't have a clue what kind of trouble you got yourself into when you left Fairhope. Not really."

James sucked in a long breath. "I take it you're not going to let that slide."

"She's important," Cole told him. "Adrian and Kyle—they're family to Briar and me."

"You have no idea how important Adrian and Kyle are to me," James retorted.

"Then you know what I think, Ghostrider?" Cole asked, once more tossing the moniker in

James's face. "I think you've got some explaining to do to her about the more illicit details of your past." He jerked a thumb toward his own chest. "Or I'll do it for you."

James ground his back teeth. "You stay out of this, Captain Rogers. I'll handle it."

"For their sake, I hope you do, sooner than later," Cole told him. "I'd hate for her to find out who you really are from, say, Briar or Olivia before things get any more serious between the two of you. If you really know Adrian so well, you'll know she values integrity above all else. If you hurt her or Kyle, I won't be able to stand on the sidelines and let you walk away unscathed again."

James threw Cole's menacing stare right back at him, measuring one eye and then the other. "Consider me warned," he said, fighting back every urge he had to throw the guy out of his garage. "Now, if you'll excuse me, I have to get back to work."

"You do that," Cole said, backing up. Before he turned and walked out, he added, "And have a nice day."

James scowled as he watched Cole exit. He reached over and switched off the radio that was still pounding classic rock music through the garage speakers.

He didn't like the guy. But Cole was right. James had to come clean with Adrian. He had to tell her about Ghostrider…and everything else.

"You've got to be kidding me," Adrian said over the phone the following weekend. "Mom, please tell me you're kidding."

"Why in God's name would I joke about this?" Edith Carlton demanded.

No, Adrian thought, closing her eyes as she touched her brow to the cool wall. Joking would require humor, a quality Edith sorely lacked. Breathing deeply for calm, Adrian said, "Every other Saturday Kyle and I come to The Farm. Dad told me two days ago that he was looking forward to it."

"Your father is losing his mind," Edith said dismissively. "We've been scheduled for the festival in Foley for weeks. You should have confirmed with me, not him. But you've been avoiding me."

"No, Mom," Adrian lied smoothly, glancing at the breakfast table where Kyle was downing his morning bowl of Cap'n Crunch and pretending not to listen. "I haven't been avoiding you."

"Ever since that James Bracken got back into town, you have," Edith pointed out.

Adrian spoke up quickly. "So you're telling me there's no way you can watch Kyle today while I deliver flowers to the wedding at Oak Hollow?"

"Isn't that what I just said?"

Adrian sighed, running a hand back through her short cap of hair. A headache was rapidly brewing underneath its roots. "Thanks a lot." She hung up before her mother could say anything else. Rubbing fingertips over her temples, Adrian walked to the table and sat down next to Kyle.

He waited until she reached for the cereal box before asking, "Do I have to go with you to the wedding?"

Adrian looked at him, reaching up automatically to comb his hair when she saw that it was standing straight up in the back. "I'm sorry, baby."

"Ah, Mom," Kyle whined. "Why can't I stay at The Farm? Granddaddy was gonna teach me to ride bareback."

"Evidently, Grandmama and Granddaddy have an exhibition at the festival in Foley this weekend," Adrian explained, topping her cereal with milk and stirring it. "There's nothing I can do about it."

"But I hate weddings."

Adrian smiled at him. Typical boy, she thought. "They have horses at Oak Hollow."

"Not that I can ride," he pointed out. His eyes lit with promise. "Hey, maybe I could stay with James."

Adrian's spoon clattered into her bowl. "What?"

"Our neighbor, James," Kyle prompted. "He's really cool. And he's nice. He could watch me for a few hours."

"It's an all-day event," Adrian told him. "Even if Mr. Bracken knew anything about kids—which I'm fairly certain he doesn't—he's far too busy. His garage just opened."

"I could hang out in town at his garage," Kyle suggested, growing more and more excited by the possibility.

"No," Adrian said and stuffed cereal in her mouth.

"Do you not like James? I thought you two knew each other, back then."

"We did, but that doesn't mean I trust him to watch you for an entire day."

Kyle narrowed his eyes. "But he stood up for me in front of Radley. He could take care of me, Mom. I'm sure he could."

Adrian fought the urge to mash her foot into the floor. "Kyle, my answer is no. Now drop it and finish your breakfast."

FORTY-FIVE MINUTES of bickering later, Adrian pulled her Flora delivery van into the parking lot of Bracken Mechanics.

She'd pulled every last string she'd had to pull before breaking down and coming here. She'd called Olivia and Briar. Both of them had wanted to help but had to work. Cole and Gerald were both tied up, too. Kyle refused to go to Oak Hollow with her. She had one option left.

There were several cars in the parking lot, one attached to a tow truck with the garage logo on the side. She peered into the open building and saw no one.

Kyle piped up from the passenger seat. "Aren't we going in?"

Frowning, Adrian unbuckled her seat belt. "I'm still not sure I like this plan."

"It's perfect," Kyle said. "I can help James out in the garage and you won't have to worry about keeping an eye on me while you work. This way, I'll have more fun, too."

Adrian eyed him doubtfully. "Being a grease monkey is fun?"

"Granddaddy lets me work on the truck and crop duster engines sometimes," Kyle reminded her. "I like it. Everything's got a place and a purpose, as Granddaddy says. Though he's not very good at it. James might be able to teach me a few tricks to help Granddaddy next time we go to The Farm."

"You really wouldn't rather go to Oak Hollow with me?"

"I want to hang out with James," Kyle said with a plaintive pout.

Oh, hell. Not the pout. Adrian looked away and swallowed as her eyes fell on James's black sportster. The man was definitely here. "All right. Just…stay here. There's no guarantee he'll say yes."

"We won't find out until we ask," Kyle pointed out.

She stared at him, then leaned over to kiss him on the cheek. He gagged a little but smiled nonetheless. Opening the door, she planted her feet on the asphalt. "Sit tight," she told him, then closed the door, took a deep breath and approached the garage.

Adrian's nerves heightened with each step. She hadn't seen James in several days, nor heard him doing any work around his house. Word around town was that his business had hit the ground running.

"Can I help you, ma'am?"

Adrian looked around to find a man in a battered trucker hat and coveralls staring at her. She shaded a hand over her eyes. It was a small town. Recognition was nothing rare out and about on a daily basis. But sometimes recognition came with more than a flicker of unease. "Dusty," she greeted him.

Dusty's smile faded. "Adrian Carlton," he said as if it had just struck him who she was. As he skimmed her from head to toe, the palms of her hands began to sweat. "Or do you still go by Kennard?"

Adrian frowned deeply. "It's Carlton."

"Oh, yeah?" Dusty asked, the friendliness dropping from his voice as he scrutinized her.

Adrian jerked a thumb toward the garage, shifting her feet toward the open door. "I was just looking for James. Is he here?"

"He should be inside," Dusty told her. When

she started walking, he called after her, "If I see Radley, I'll be sure to give him your best, huh?"

Ignoring him, Adrian ducked her head and entered the garage. Damn it all to hell. She hated running into any of Radley's old friends, particularly the Harbuck boys.

As her eyes adjusted to the absence of sunlight, Adrian scanned the green pickup truck inside the garage next to a Lexus that had been raised off the ground. Seeing and hearing no one, she cleared her throat and called, "James?"

"Yeah," came a gruff reply. Then, out from under the pickup, a long form rolled into sight. As James emerged, his head lifted from the creeper and he started to sit up. "Adrian."

"Aaaah…" As James straightened, throwing aside the wrench in his hand with a heavy, metallic clank on the concrete floor, Adrian took several steps back, the uneasy exchange with Dusty Harbuck forgotten.

James wasn't wearing a shirt. It was her first gander at his broad chest, the dark hair sprinkled across it, and her first view of all the ink etched into his skin. On an involuntary rush, she breathed in, unable to pry her gaze from the tentacles that wound around the ship and waves on his left arm, fanned up his shoulder and spread onto his left pec. The words on his collarbone were, indeed, Latin.

Off balance, she stared at him in all his male

glory, unable to speak. Where were her words? Where was her brain?

"Er," she said finally. "Never mind. You're busy." With that, she spun around to hoof it out of the garage.

"Wait, wait. Adrian. Hold up."

Turning, she did her best not to stare as he walked to her. "What do you need?" he asked.

She waved a hand. "You're busy…"

"I'm not *that* busy," James admitted, gesturing to the parking lot. "I'm actually not technically open for business today. This first week brought in more customers than anticipated so I thought I'd come in this morning, do some catching up."

"Right," Adrian said. She took another breath. "You're probably going to say no and I completely understand—"

"You look nice," he intervened suddenly.

She stumbled, glancing down at the deep green dress she had picked to wear to the wedding at Oak Hollow Farm. "Ah…thanks." Searching for words again, she added, "It's a long shot, I know, but I have an all-day wedding event I have to get to in, like…" She trailed off, looking down at her watch. "Shit. Less than half an hour, to be on the safe side for preparation. Mom and Dad were going to watch Kyle today, but there was some mix-up…"

She was babbling and he was just watching her with something stirring behind those blue eyes.

Dear God. He needed to stop looking at her like that. And she really didn't need to know what the something was that was stirring there…

"Long story short," she said, holding up her hands to help make sense of the noise inside her head. She would *not* look at those Latin words… or the muscled pecs below them…or, for that matter, the rock-hard six-pack lurking below those—

For Christ's sake, there wasn't one safe place to look, she thought with a flush as her eyes landed on his pelvis and shied away quickly. She thought of the glutes she'd glimpsed the day she shot him.

Closing her eyes, she tried again for words. "I'd take him with me. In fact, that's probably what I'll wind up doing." *Doing. Yes, mmm.* She'd love to be *doing* something else right about now.

Get it together! Adrian cleared her throat and continued. "But Kyle had this crazy idea. I told him you have more important things to do than—"

"I'll do it."

Adrian faltered and her eyes skimmed up to his, shocked. "You…you will?"

"Hell, yeah," James said with a blinding smile. He then checked himself, trying to look serious. "I mean, I could use a hand around the garage. And I'm not so busy that I can't keep an eye on him. That is, if he doesn't mind watching me break down an engine for the better part of the day."

"He does it with Dad all the time," Adrian explained. "They've been trying to get the old crop duster running for weeks now. And before that, it was Dad's old Chevy…" She trailed off with a frown. "Wait. You're not just saying yes to get on my good side, are you?"

"Adrian, he's my son," James pointed out. "I've been meaning to ask you again if I could spend a few hours one-on-one with him. But this…a whole day…this is great."

"He's seven," she reminded him. "Do you know how to entertain a seven-year-old, James?"

"I was seven once." When her face fell, he chuckled. "I think I can manage it."

She was out of excuses. Reaching into her bag, she said, "Here. This is my card. Call the number on the back if you need anything. Questions, emergencies, anything. Don't hesitate. He's allergic to peanut butter and strawberries. Also, I'll probably be back late. He has a key to the house. Take him there when you all are done here. There's some leftovers in the fridge that'll do fine for dinner. Don't let him get into the gummy bears and absolutely no video games until he's spent at least half an hour working on his book report. It's due next Tuesday. You should probably be writing this down."

"I'll remember. Don't worry."

"Right. Oh, and…I know it might not make much sense at this point…but I'd really like him to stay away from Dusty."

"Dusty?" James asked with a frown. "Why?"

"Please, for now can you just go with me on this?"

"All right," James said, a little unsure. "Dusty's done for the day, anyway."

"Okay. Great." Adrian spread her hands, pleading with him now. "Don't make me regret this."

"I've got it," James told her, radiating confidence and barely suppressed joy. She could see the gilded light of it shining, uncontained, under the surface. "Go do what you have to do and don't worry about a thing, okay?"

Adrian lingered, clutching the strap of her purse. "Okay," she agreed, feeling small.

James walked to her. Before she could step back, he planted his hands on her shoulders and rubbed up and down her arms. "Everything's going to be fine," he said. "I promise."

Adrian nodded. Her eyes found the nautical star on his throat. Her lips tingled. They tingled more when her gaze somehow landed on his mouth. She frowned. "I'll just…I'll go get him." And then she did retreat, praying her instincts were right about James and she wasn't making a horrible mistake.

"So after we remove the cylinder heads, what do we do next?" Kyle asked as he leaned over the engine of the green Ford pickup next to James.

James grinned for what had to be the hundredth

time that day. The kid was thirsty for knowledge. And soda. He'd already gnawed through half a pack of Slim Jims, too. And there was the perfect amount of engine grease smeared across his cheek. They'd stood alongside each other like this for over an hour.

The pickup was fixed, running smoothly, but Kyle had had tons of questions about engines and how to rebuild them and James was happy to oblige. So they'd gone over the engine parts one by one, James explaining each of them and how they worked as Kyle drank it all in, never asking a question more than once. "That's when you examine the piston tops and combustion chamber for leaks. Just like with the engine manifold. Remember?"

"Yeah," Kyle said with a quick nod. He peered down into the depths of the engine as James showed him how to check for oil or water leaks as well as melted parts. "They look fine."

"More than fine," James said with a considering nod. "The owner of this truck takes good care of her. Can you tell me what we're gonna do next?"

Kyle pressed his lips inward, contemplating. "Check for cracks in the heads?"

James beamed. "That's right," he said. "While we're at it, we'll check for cracks in the combustion chamber and the engine block, too. Remember, there are some cracks that are invisible to the naked eye. If the engine blew while reheating,

it's a good idea to get the parts magnafluxed."
When Kyle blinked, he said, "When you magna-
flux, you—"

"Is that when you magnetize it and look for pat-
terns in the powder?" Kyle asked.

It was James's turn to blink. For a moment, he
simply looked at the boy. The smattering of freckles across his nose and cheeks. The dark slash of
thick hair on his head that was starting to grow
over the tips of his ears and curl untidily at the
nape of his neck. The wild blue eyes, searching
James's matching set for approval.

James felt his heart stumble over itself. Pride
and a love he hadn't known he was capable of
feeling so soon swelled within him until he felt
the confines of his chest might rupture. He was a
goner. "Yeah, kid," he said finally, a bit choked.
He lowered his head quickly, cleared his throat.
"Ah…will you hand me that socket wrench?"

Kyle reached over to the nearby rolling toolbox
with a young hand, big for his age. A "bear claw,"
as James's father used to call his own. The hand
selected the socket wrench without James having
to differentiate between the others for him. As he
handed it over matter-of-factly, James found himself coughing to clear his throat again. "So you
like engines, huh, kid?" he asked.

"Yeah," Kyle said. "Granddaddy says I've got
the knack. Says I was born for it."

"Huh," James said in reply.

"Can I ask you a question?" Kyle asked.

"Sure, whatever you want."

"Did the tattoos hurt? When you got them, I mean?"

"Some of them," James nodded, rubbing his tatted forearm over his perspiring brow. "It really depends on where you get them."

"Did the big bird on your back hurt?"

"It's a phoenix," James told him, diligently ratcheting something into place. "A firebird."

"Cool," Kyle breathed. "Did that one hurt?"

James thought about the red phoenix spread across his shoulder blades and halfway down his spine. It had been his first tattoo, one he'd gotten mere weeks after leaving Fairhope. He thought about what the phoenix represented. "It hurt like hellfire," he said in a rough voice. "Can you hand me the pliers?"

"Sure." Kyle selected the pliers, handed them over. Wiping the back of his hand over his face, he smudged more engine grease across the side of his nose. Adrian's nose. It was the only thing on his face that screamed *Adrian*. "So…where'd *you* learn about cars and stuff?"

James paused, then realized there was no reason to. "My dad taught me."

"Oh. That's neat."

After several beats of silence, Kyle peered at James. In a quiet and, again, very matter-of-fact voice, he said, "I know you're my dad."

The pliers dropped down into the engine as James's head sailed up, narrowly missing the hood above him. "What?"

Kyle looked sheepish for a split second before he frowned and added, "You are my dad. Aren't you?"

Ah, crap. How did he handle this? Honesty seemed the best course. And not because it was what James wanted. He just couldn't lie to that face. Not if his life depended on it. Praying Adrian would forgive him, he said, "Yeah. Yeah, I am."

"Mom didn't tell me," Kyle explained.

James narrowed his eyes. "Then how did you know?"

"Well, I might have overheard you and Mom talking about it," Kyle admitted a bit sheepishly. "But I could have figured it out for myself. We have the same eyes and the same hair. I don't have any on my face or chest yet, though."

James fought not to let his lips twitch in mirth. "Give it time."

"Griffin Thomas already has a mustache," Kyle pointed out, wide-eyed. "His mom calls them whiskers, but it's a dark line of hair right here on his lip. He's twelve, way older than me, but still… it's weird."

"Don't be too hard on Griffin. You'll be suffering the same before long."

A long pause followed this odd new twist in

the conversation. Then Kyle looked around at the old muscle cars in the parking lot. "Maybe I could drive one of the cars," he suggested, lingering for a moment longingly on the Shelby Mustang. "Would you let me?"

James smirked. "Pretty sure your mother would peel the skin from my body, then slap it on the burner for breakfast." At Kyle's wrinkled nose, James said, "Maybe some other time. With her permission."

"Your dad never let you drive when you were my age? Behind your mom's back?"

James chuckled. "Maybe a little."

"So? Will you let me? Granddaddy's taught me the basics, but he never lets me turn the key."

James considered the face next to his, the smudges on it, the desperate plea in those eyes that blazed trust and sincerity. And he made a decision. "I'll do you one better. You ever fly this crop duster you and your Granddaddy have been tinkering with?"

"It won't even start." Kyle caught on. His face split into a wide grin. "You have a plane, too? A real, working plane?"

James looked around the garage at the work to be done, then stood and shut the hood of the pickup. He threw the cloth hooked through his belt at Kyle. "Wash your face, kid. We're going for a drive."

WHEN ADRIAN RETURNED to the cottage just after dark she was bone tired. The wedding had gone smoothly, but the cleanup with Roxie had been a major undertaking.

Carrying her shoes in along with an armful of peonies, she followed the lights and voices into the living room to find James and Kyle on the couch in front of the television, battling it out via Xbox's LEGO Marvel Super Heroes. For a moment, she simply stood inside the door watching them play and listening to Kyle's victorious shouts as his LEGO Thor pounded on James's LEGO Loki.

Kyle emitted a high-pitched, "Die, Loki, die!" Pitying James's battered Loki, Adrian chose that moment to clear her voice and announce her presence.

Both man and boy startled and looked around. Kyle beamed and leaped up to hug her. "Mom! You're back!"

"I am," she said, eyeing James over Kyle's head as the man stood to face her. "Video games?" she mouthed.

James lifted his shoulders but didn't look remorseful.

Adrian studied Kyle's face as he pulled away. "What's that on your nose?"

"Oh," Kyle said, lifting his fingers to wipe it. "I guess I didn't get all the engine grease off."

"You smell like an airplane hangar," she noted.

James coughed into his hand. "Ah, hey, kid. Why don't you go fix your mother a plate of those leftovers? She looks like she could use it."

"Sure," Kyle piped. He shot into the kitchen with the lightning sounds of Thor behind him. Adrian tossed her shoes on the floor and folded her arms over the peonies. "Please tell me he ate, at least."

"We both did," James asserted with a nod. "And he finished that book report."

Her mouth fell open. "He *finished* it?"

"Yeah. Is that a bad thing?"

"No, it's just…he hates doing book reports."

"It took a bit of coercing," James admitted. "But I bribed him with playing the LEGO video game and he complied."

Adrian watched James lift his shoulders in a modest stance and shook her head. "Well…good. Thank you…for that."

"It's the least I can do." He took the flowers from her arms. "How was the wedding?"

"Long," she said as they walked into the kitchen. "But it was a success. That's all you can ask for." She stopped short when she saw that not only had the table been cleared, they had also done the dishes, and the kitchen looked spotless. "Oh."

"Have a seat," James said, nudging a hand gently against the small of her back. "You want me to put these in water?"

"Just put them in the sink for now," she said. "I'll break them up into arrangements later. Thank you, baby," she said when Kyle set a steaming plate in front of her. She wasn't used to having two men wait on her—it was as disconcerting as it was flattering. "So," she said when Kyle sat down across from her. "What did you do today?"

A ready tumble of excited words spilled forth. Kyle's prediction had turned into fact. He had a blast at the garage. James showed him how to break down a blown engine, giving him tons of tips for Granddaddy. As Adrian ate, she got lost in the lowdown on carburetors and busted radiator caps. After a few minutes of Kyle's wide-eyed explanation, Adrian simply propped her chin in her hand and watched his animated face as he told her more about what he'd learned under James's tutelage. Once, she ventured a glance over his shoulder to find James leaning against the kitchen block, smiling to himself. He met her eyes. She felt the direct gaze like a punch to the gut. Sighing a little, she straightened as Kyle's words finally wound down. "I'm glad you had a good time," she told him.

"We both did," Kyle said, looking back at his new hero. "Didn't we, James?"

"You got that right," James said, beaming at his son.

The ache in Adrian's chest turned sharp. Taking her plate to the sink, she told Kyle, "All right. Bath and then bed."

"Aw, Mom. Can't I stay up and play more LEGO video games with James?"

"It's late enough as it is. Go. Let me know when you're done in the bathroom."

"All right," Kyle said, resigned, as he skulked off.

Before Adrian could do more than reach for the flower stems in the sink, she felt a hand on her arm. James tugged her around and she found herself staring into a second set of enthusiastic blue eyes. She made a noise that was quickly smothered by James's mouth as it descended in a surprise kiss. His hand rose to the nape of her neck as his head tilted over hers and his tongue did a quick, devastating dive into her mouth. Against his, her body quivered like a bow in reaction and she made another noise, this one not the least bit disagreeable.

When he broke away seconds later, she gasped for breath. "Wha... Wha..."

James answered by taking her face in his hands and grinning even more widely. "He's amazing. Our son is amazing."

"Y-yes," she said, gripping his wrists, holding on. This close to him, her equilibrium was off. And she didn't like the way her tummy fluttered warmly when he referred to Kyle as "our son."

"Yes," she said again. "I know that."

"We did that. Together. We made that. I mean, you raised him, of course. You've done all the heavy lifting. And the fact that's he's so amazing is due to you. But did you know that he has a knack for engines? And that he can remember everything? Literally, everything. And…" Here he stopped. He placed his hands on her shoulders and lowered his voice. "Adrian, he figured out that I'm his father."

Adrian's breath left her on a tremulous rush. "Oh…"

"I swear I didn't drop any hints. He just said out of the blue, 'I know you're my dad.' He's smart. Really, really smart and intuitive."

Dear God. *Kyle knew?* How long had that been going on? More, how was she going to handle it?

James went on, undeterred. "And he does this thing with his knuckles, rubbing them over his lips. Has he always done that? Because I've done that since I was a kid—"

"Yes," she said, raising her voice over his. "I know."

He stopped, reading her face closely. His expression fell and his shoulders seemed to deflate. "Right. You've had to live with this, haven't you? You've looked at him every morning over breakfast and seen me."

She didn't confirm it, but she couldn't quite meet his eyes.

At that moment, Kyle's voice came floating in from the other room. "Hey, Mom! I'm done!"

"Be right there," she called back. She forced herself to look at James again. "Tomorrow he's spending the night at the inn with his friend Gavin. We should have dinner, talk things over then."

James lifted his chin in a nod. "All right," he said slowly, noting her dismissal.

"Thank you for everything today," she said. "He had a great day, and it's all because he got to spend it with you. I'll try to find some way to return the favor."

"No favor," he said. "You've done me the favor. Trust me. So, I'll see you tomorrow night. At my place?"

She nodded, nerves stirring in her belly. She thought briefly about meeting somewhere else, somewhere public, but she owed him this. "Sounds fine."

"Good night, Adrian."

She had to stop herself from calling him back, to erase the sullen lines on his face. Tomorrow night, she promised herself. They had things to discuss. Important things. Whether or not she was ready for it, it was time for James Bracken to become somewhat of a fixture in her son's life…and at the same time, hers.

God help her.

CHAPTER ELEVEN

IT WAS JUST DINNER, Adrian assured herself as she mounted the steps to the front door of James's house. Dinner, discussion, done. Then she'd go back home to her empty nest for the night and pour herself a big glass of wine.

Late that afternoon she had dropped Kyle off at the inn so that he and Cole's son, Gavin, could have their prearranged sleepover. She'd sat by the phone for much of the day waiting for either Cole or Briar to call and cancel. Well, hoping they would, anyway. Having Kyle home for the evening would have been a great excuse to cancel dinner next door.

Still, the time came. And Adrian knew she and James needed this time—to talk about Kyle and to set up some ground rules, both for James as a parent and for whatever was happening between him and her.

No reason to be nervous, she told herself as she rang the doorbell. Waiting, she smoothed her hands over the breezy button-up blouse she had chosen to don with jeans and sandals. The outfit said casual. She sincerely hoped it in no way suggested sex or romance—or anything to do with either.

She heard footsteps and straightened, licking her lips when she saw the shadow of him. "There you are," James said as he walked into the entry hall and pushed the screen open. "I was starting to think you were going to stand me up."

Adrian frowned. She couldn't be that predictable. "Sorry," she said absently. He was also wearing jeans, although his were scuffed and faded. The shirt he wore with them was the lightest of blues and short sleeved, leaving the ink on his arm and hand in full view. Her eyes snagged for a moment on the open collar and the tattoos and hair just visible before her gaze fell to his feet.

Flip-flops. Somehow, the sight of the brown leather thongs, his toes and feet bare, made him appear somewhat piratical. Blinking her eyes back into focus, she lifted her hands. "Kyle caught a flounder before I left the inn. I had to take a lot of pictures."

"Flounder," James said, brows raised. "Impressive. He might be eating better than we are tonight."

She glanced over his shoulder into the house. Did it look a bit hazy? "Did you burn something?"

James flashed a grin. "I told you. The oven's a bitch." His grin stretched after a moment's pause drifted between them. Then he said, "Are you going to come in?"

She frowned, glancing down at her feet. Neither one lifted to carry her over the threshold and into his domain.

"Adrian."

Lifting her gaze back to his, she saw understanding there and bit the inside of her lip. "Yes?"

Sincerity blazed from those crazy, beautiful, Scandinavian blues as he said slowly, "I swear if you come into this house, I won't lay a finger on you unless you tell me to."

How had he known she needed that exact reassurance? She searched his expression, admiring the truthfulness behind the words.

James stepped back, edging up against the open wood door behind him. "Now...will you come in? Please?"

Adrian hesitated once more before stepping toward him, bypassing the screen door into the entryway. Her arm brushed his chest and gooseflesh popped up on her skin.

James followed her through the house, taking her purse and setting it on the counter that separated the kitchen from the living room with its high, arched ceiling. For the first time, Adrian noted the exposed rafters and the yawning brick fireplace blackened by time. Although some clutter remained, the boxes had vanished and the furniture was set in place.

"The house looks great," she told him as she walked to the long line of windows. He'd finished the deck. She noticed that the dining room table made of raw wood hadn't been set for dinner. Apparently, he was planning for them to dine outdoors because a new table and chairs had been set up just beyond the windows along with mosquito candles, dishes and flatware. Beyond the deck rail she saw that the yard had been raked and trimmed, the trees bordering the property cut back and the pool had been drained and retiled. The light hum of alternative music was floating from somewhere. She saw the speakers tucked into the recesses of the new deck roof.

She couldn't believe how far he had come in home improvements. She hated to admit it, but under the influence of James's ambition, the house was actually starting to look less like an unmitigated disaster and more like a hidden neighborhood gem.

"You've been busy," she said when she felt him hovering at her elbow. Turning, she accepted a glass he'd filled with iced tea. "Thank you." She took a long sip. "Did you ever find that armadillo at the bottom of the pool?"

James groaned. "Yeah, along with a lot of other things I'd rather not discuss. I'm waiting for the filters to be changed before I fill it up again."

"It'll be nice in the summer," she mused. "The deck, the new pool…you'll have a time keeping Kyle out of the water."

The comment seemed to catch James off guard.

His face turned toward hers. His well-hewn features softened, his eyes going tender, warm. "You think so?"

Adrian nodded. It was her first acquiescence. Thinking about the manila folder she'd brought in her purse, she ducked her head and drank again. She'd spent much of the morning carefully, painstakingly putting together its contents. She didn't know when she was going to give it to him—or if she would be able to hand it over at all. It was a big step. An emotional one. She didn't know if she was ready. Brushing her bangs across her brow, she pivoted toward the kitchen. "Did you burn dinner already?"

"No," James said, looking back at a plate of blackened potatoes. "Well, at least not all of it. The pork chops are still on the grill and I threw some squash on there when it became apparent that we aren't having potatoes."

"Mmm. Do you need some help?"

"Nope," he said, turning to her again. "I want you to relax. It's your night off."

Adrian lifted a shoulder. "I don't mind."

"You're going to let me wait on you," James told her. "I feel like you deserve a good bit of pampering."

Adrian laughed, leaning against the windows. "I don't think I'd know pampering if it hit me in the head, but all right."

James watched her as she sipped her tea. Slowly

the grin on his face melted away. Setting his glass aside, he planted a hand on the sill next to her. "Adrian, while we're waiting for dinner, there's something we do need to talk about."

She pulled in a steadying breath, trying to force down the uneasy feeling the words gave her. Wasn't this what she'd come here for? To discuss things with him and listen to what he had to say. "Okay. Shoot."

"I need to be honest with you," he said, his eyes blazing sincerity and what she feared was need of another kind. Need for her. Whether that need manifested from his desire for her to simply trust him or something deeper and far more costly, she had no idea. "Since I came back home, I've tried to make a clean start. I've wanted a clean living. A clear mind. And since I found you on my doorstep, I've wanted nothing more than to convince you that I've changed and that I'm here for you."

"You mean Kyle," she said quickly, and swallowed when he was silent on that score. "Here for Kyle. Right?"

"For both of you," he said in a deep, quiet tone that reverberated through her. As she glanced out the window, she heard him drag in an inhale. "I haven't lied to you about where I've been these last eight years...but I haven't been completely up front about the darker details of what happened when I initially left town."

Adrian licked her lips. She reached up to scratch the spot between her eyes. "I, uh, think I expected as much." Seeing the slight, crestfallen reaction on his part, she shrugged. "What did *you* expect? Trust isn't exactly my strong suit."

"Not with me," he muttered. He rolled his shoulders back in a restless motion and straightened. "When I left Fairhope, I caught up with some of Dusty Harbuck's cousins in north Alabama. Huntsville."

Her lips parted in surprise. "Huntsville?"

"That's right," he said with a nod. "Your friend the cop's old stomping ground."

"So that's why Cole doesn't like you," she said, measuring him closely now. "You knew each other."

"No," he said. "Not directly. Through his work with the Huntsville Police Department, he knew about some of my activities and recognized my name when we were introduced a couple of weeks ago."

She nodded slowly. "Makes sense." Her arms crossed and she frowned. "You were saying something about the Harbucks?"

"Cousins of theirs," he said again. "I asked them to put some feelers out for me for mechanic work. They came back about a week later saying they might have a job for me. They'd heard from Clint and Dusty that I was a decent driver and that I knew sports cars."

"A decent driver?" she echoed in disbelief. "I'd say my parents' nursery would disagree with you there."

A small smile moved across his face. "I was a decent driver when I wasn't under the influence, I should say. Anyway, they asked me how far under the table I was willing to work. When I told them I'd do anything except deal or traffic drugs, they took me into the mountains. There, in the hills, they had an underground garage where they stored high-end cars."

"Stolen cars," Adrian assumed.

"Yes," James said without hesitation.

Adrian's frown deepened. "Go on."

"There was a path through the mountains, mostly dangerous one-lane tracks that bordered on ravines and cliffs and that went through caves and such. Nothing your average soccer mom could negotiate. So I agreed, for a generous salary, to help drive these cars through the mountains and safely over the state line. There were rules, though."

"As there usually are amongst thieves," she muttered with a roll of her eyes.

"I couldn't under any circumstances get caught," James continued. "I couldn't damage the car in any way. I had to cover up my identity in the event that I was sighted by police or civilians by wearing a mask. If I were ever caught, I had to bail. I also had to wear gloves so that if I did ditch the car, I'd leave no trace of DNA behind. And I had to have a call sign—mine was Ghostrider."

"Original," she drawled.

James pursed his lips. "Kyle isn't the only kid who ever liked comic books."

Adrian tried to digest all the details. "It all sounds very James Bond—that is, if James Bond was a backwoods criminal."

The corner of James's mouth lifted as mirth and mock hurt filled his eyes. "Okay, that stung a little."

"Did you enjoy it, at least?"

"I loved it," he told her. When she lifted a brow, he added, "I promised you the truth. I thought I was lucky to get that kind of work, that kind of money to do something I loved doing—driving the kind of cars I'd only ever seen in magazines and museums. The fact that it was all under the radar and illegal only intensified the excitement."

"So if this was your dream job, why did you get out of it?" she asked. "You did get out of it?"

"Yeah. I got out." His gaze dropped enough for the black curtain of his eyelashes to hide what was behind them. "I worked the same circuit for three years, but things began to escalate. I started to understand exactly who we were delivering cars to. I won't say that I haven't done bad things. I've leaped into shady situations with my eyes wide-open. But these guys…they had the wrong type of vibe, the kind that drips like ice down your spine when you look them in the eye. I didn't want to owe them anything. So I finished my last run and I got out of the life while I could."

Thoughtfully, Adrian lifted her tea to her mouth. "Where'd you go from there?"

"Saint Augustine," he said. "There was a man there who knew who my dad was, who knew his old reputation as a charter fisherman. So he hired me to take tourists into the Atlantic and oversee the fishing."

Adrian glanced over at his arm, the waves, the doomed sea monster and the ocean wildlife circling the soon-to-be wreckage. "That would explain the tattoos."

James lifted a shoulder, smirked. "Well, some of them, at least."

She fought the urge to smile back. "Is that where you cleaned up?"

"The captain saw the signs," James said after a moment's pause, reaching up to rub the skin over the nautical star on his throat. "He knew my dad's alcoholic history, too, and how bad things got for him. He told me he was thinking about buying a second boat and making me captain, but he needed to know that I was on the level. He wanted my guarantee that I would straighten up and quit drinking."

"That's all it took?" she asked. "You didn't hit rock bottom first like everybody else?"

Lowering his eyes again, he said quietly,

"Adrian, my wake-up calls started when I was seventeen. I just spent the next four years ignoring them, one right after the other. Then…I had the wake-up call to end all wake-up calls."

"What happened?"

James rubbed two fingers over his lips to hide a sheepish grin. "Ah…I sank a boat."

She groaned. "Oh, James. Please tell me it was your own boat."

"Not so much," he said with a shake of his head. "I've been lucky more than once. I've survived things that others haven't or likely wouldn't. Yeah, I've been luckier than I deserve. But this was the closest I'd ever come to dying."

"You almost drowned."

"No. There was a fire. That's how she went down."

Adrian found her gaze stilling on the mottled skin of his right arm. It was starting to make sense, as was that doomed ship on his opposing arm. "You *were* lucky," she acknowledged. She sucked in a breath and turned away to roam his living room. She looked around at the furniture. "The house…the garage…the cars…none of them could have come cheap. Did you use the money you got from being Ghostrider to pay for it all?"

"No," James said, his voice flat and dark behind her. "I ran through that cash before I sobered up, which is why I needed the work in Saint Augustine. I bought all this with what I earned designing stock cars and engines for NASCAR."

"How did you go from being a boat captain to working for NASCAR?"

"Luck," he said again with a rueful grin. "There was a well-known stock car designer in my AA group. We got to talking one night. I had some ideas. He liked what I had to say. One thing led to another and before I knew it, I was living in North Carolina and working on the team that designed stock cars for Sprint Cup drivers."

"That is lucky," she said. Almost too lucky. "It paid well, by the looks of it."

"The only thing that mattered to me was that it was honest work," he told her. "It's true you work harder when it's honest, but at the end of the day it felt great. I felt like I was doing some good for once, and eventually that need, that desire to do good, to be good, to show people I had that drive—it all led me back here."

Adrian clutched her tea glass. "Well, I'm happy for you."

His face went blank with surprise. "You are?"

"Of course, I am," she said. Honesty, she reminded herself. It went both ways. "I'm happy for you, not just for leaving the opportunities you had in Huntsville behind and making something honest of yourself. And not just for wanting to do good, which is amazing. I'm proud of you for that, James. But I know what it takes…to rebuild a life.

To hit rock bottom and have to fight and claw your way back to make something of yourself again."

"I know you do," he said, solemn-eyed. He leaned back against the window, tucking his fingers into the front pockets of his jeans. His gaze drank her in slowly and surely. She felt the heat of that look all the way down to her toes.

She swallowed. Her eyes veered over his shoulder. "Um…is your meat burning?"

James's brows shot onto his forehead. "Pardon me?"

Adrian gestured toward the deck outside. "The meat. The pork chops. I think they're burning."

James looked around, saw the black smoke wafting out of the Weber grill. He muttered an oath before shoving the sliding glass door aside and sprinting toward the fire.

"WHAT DOES THE Latin mean?"

James glanced up from his plate. Adrian hadn't spoken much since the revelations about his past. As they sat down to dinner, he'd been able to almost hear the wheels turning inside her head. Her feelings about the more sordid details were a mystery to him. He'd hoped she would say something before the end of the meal. The words she spoke weren't what he was expecting.

He saw her pointing at his collar with her fork. He dropped his head to the front of his shirt and the Latin letters peeking through. *"Non omnis moriar,"* he said after chewing his food and swallowing. He took a sip of water before adding, "It means *not all of me shall die.*"

Her eyes widened for a moment. Then softened. "Oh. So that one's for your—"

"Dad," he nodded and smiled softly.

She continued scanning his collarbone and his throat, a line of puzzlement appearing between her brows after a moment's study. "Is that..." She pointed to her own throat in indication. "The leather string. Is that the same one you wore—before?"

James dropped his fork and reached up to tug the thick brown cord from underneath his collar. The wooden cross on the end of it fell against the front of his shirt, right over his sternum. "I've never not worn it," he told her. "Not since the wreck, anyway."

Adrian took a deep breath. "You used to play with it a lot, tugging and twisting it when..." She cleared her throat, dropping her eyes back to her plate where she picked at her food. "...when the withdrawals would get bad."

James lifted a brow, surprised by her memory. He'd caught himself doing the same when he quit drinking four years ago. When she went back to her studied silence, he all but groaned at the step back. Looking down at the sorry excuse for a meal, he searched for something—anything—to keep that from happening. "Sorry about the pork chops," he said. Adrian had managed to throw together a salad. The squash had had to be thrown out alongside the potatoes. The pork chops had barely been salvageable. "I swear I've cooked before."

"I saw the take-out containers in your trash pail." Adrian eyed him knowingly as she brought a forkful of salad up to her mouth. "It's really not that bad. I like my meat well-done." When he cracked a smile she flushed and pressed a hand over her eyes. "Oh, God."

James drank a bit of water because he'd come very close to swallowing the food wrong and his tongue with it. "I'm the one who took it the wrong way."

"Yeah, well, it didn't take but a moment for me to catch up," she told him. "I guess we're both dirty minded."

James smirked. "Oh, if I remember, you had a very dirty mind and a mouth to match. Remember that time we snuck off to your parents' greenhouse and—"

"Stop right there, James Bracken," she said, holding up both hands.

He laughed again because she was blushing. "Hey, I promised I'd keep my hands off you, not stop myself from thinking about the good ol' days."

"Yeah, well, you don't have to bring them up. Then we both have to *think* about them."

He frowned as she chewed the last tough piece of her pork chop. "You expect me to believe you haven't thought about it?"

"The past is dead," she said.

"What about when I kissed you last night? Was the past dead then, too?"

"James…" She sighed, crossing her arms on the table's edge. "I didn't come over here to talk about the past. And please tell me you didn't delude yourself into thinking this was a date."

He peered over their plates and the candle in the center of the outdoor teak table before letting his gaze climb back up to hers pointedly. The radio was tuned low but he'd made sure to load his Red Hot Chili Peppers playlist before turning it on. It was currently burning through the *Stadium Arcadium* album.

Her frown only grew. "It's not."

"It could be," James suggested.

"It's not," Adrian said again and pushed her plate away.

"All right," he said. Leaning back in his chair, he wiped his mouth with his napkin and asked, "Why did you come over here tonight, Adrian?"

She lifted her water and simply held it as she mirrored his stance, leaning back in her chair. "I guess I came to settle things, in a way. I'm sure you have questions…about Kyle."

"Hundreds," he confirmed. A small grin touched his lips. "Mostly small things. Like what's his favorite board game? What was his first word? And, beyond the physical, is he anything like me?"

Her lips twitched for a moment. Then she replied, "Battleship. Dog. And, yes, minus the delinquent streak, you couldn't be more alike."

He gazed at her, admiring the concession. He could tell it wasn't easy for her to share Kyle. With him, of all people. With anyone. But especially him. "Thank you," he said after a moment. "I have other, more serious questions, too, about him. And about you."

"Such as?"

James paused, thought about it. "Besides the hospital stay in the beginning, was it easy? The pregnancy."

Adrian raked a hand through her hair. In the last light of day, it was the color of a good Bordeaux. "It depends on what you mean by *easy*. He was a healthy baby. He was two weeks late and weighed in at seven pounds, six ounces."

"But was it easy on you?"

She held her water close under her chin and lifted her eyes to his slowly. "Not really, no. I was sick a lot longer than the first trimester. More than I thought any pregnant woman deserved to be. Maybe it was the stress of the whole situation. Maybe it was just the way my body reacted to the pregnancy. I don't know. I didn't put on as much weight as the doctor would have liked. In fact, I don't think anybody could tell I was pregnant until the latter half of the second trimester."

James frowned over his next question, wondering if he had a right to ask. "Did you ever consider…giving him up?"

Something on her face changed. Her eyes turned reflective, seeing beyond him. "Whatever doubt I had about having a child went up in smoke when he was born. Here was this beautiful little boy who deserved all the love and care anyone in the world could give, and I desperately needed to be that person for him—no matter how hard it was going to be." She licked her lips, averted her eyes. "And however much I resented you at the time, he came out of something special. On my end, at least."

His brow furrowed as he steepled his hands under his chin. "Adrian…"

"Don't," she said. "I don't want affirmation of what we had. Whatever it was, it's gone and I can't put myself in that situation again. That's one of the things I wanted to make clear tonight."

"Whether you want to hear it or not, I've wanted to tell you for a while that what we had was extraordinary," he said. And before she could argue, he added quickly, "I want more than anything for you to believe that."

She pinched the skin between her eyes, closed them. "James—"

"Being with you," he went on, "made me the

happiest I ever remember being, and I can't express how much I regret not staying."

"Sure," she said, and swept her hand in a dismissive wave. "If you hadn't come back—if you'd never known—you wouldn't regret leaving. Because what we had might've been extraordinary, but it wasn't enough to make you stick around."

He looked down at his plate. "You know, I've gone a long time convincing myself that I'm content knowing that's what you were led to believe. But I can't do that anymore."

"Maybe it's better that you do," she said and stood, dropping her napkin to the table. "I can't make myself vulnerable to you again. Did you think telling me everything about your time away would make that any easier?"

"No," he said. "I just wanted to put everything on the table. You deserve that."

"It took a lot for you to tell me," she acknowledged, "and it was the right thing to do. But it doesn't change things between us. Twice in my life I've dropped my guard, trusted someone with all that I am. And both times were more devastating than I can say."

She walked toward the sliding door. "Adrian," he called as he pushed his chair back and rose to go after her. "Wait."

"There's nothing left to say," she said, stepping inside.

"The hell there isn't," he replied, following her, reaching for her.

She rounded on him before he could touch her. "I'm willing to let you have time with Kyle. Weekends, holidays. We can work it out. You've cleaned up your life. And Kyle's grown attached."

"I'm not done talking about us," James said.

The sharp words made her scoff and throw both hands up in disbelief. Her voice rose an octave. "Did you honestly believe I'd fall for this again? I'm not as stupid as I used to be!"

"You were never stupid, Adrian," he told her firmly. "And how you managed to lose sight of yourself enough for Kennard to hurt you the way he did is beyond me. The Adrian I knew didn't let anyone push her around or call the shots."

Her jaw dropped, and cold fury etched the lines of her jaw. Her eyes turned to stone. "Let? You think I *let* it happen? You think I just let Radley take swings at me? You think I let him come after my baby?"

"No," he said, trying desperately to gather his emotions. They were jumbling his mind, mixing up his words and meaning. "That's not what I meant."

She planted her hands on her hips. The frigidity on her face was melting away in the face of fresh temper. "Then what exactly are you trying to say to me?"

He took another step toward her, wanting to

touch her. Wanting to make her understand. Wanting her to feel how conflicted he felt whenever he thought of the girl he'd known and what she'd been through. "You had such fire, Adrian. Anybody who looked at you could see it a mile off. Your fire consumed me that summer at The Farm. It stayed with me. I hate that Kennard tried to take it from you, tried to stamp it out and undo everything that made you shine. That fire's still there. I've seen it. He tried to take it from you, but that fire and that woman I fell in love with are still right here in front of me."

Her lips trembled open. "What?"

James stopped. His words echoed between them. He blinked and took a step back.

"What did you just say, James?" she asked, advancing on him.

He backed up until his shoulders found the door. "Uh…" He'd never said the word *love* to anyone. Not to Adrian. Not to anyone. Not since Zachariah Bracken left his life. His lips numbed and his heart pounded at the dawning light of understanding on Adrian's face.

Well, hell. There it was. What he should've stuck around to say to her eight years ago. Only he'd chosen to turn his back on her, instead.

CHAPTER TWELVE

ADRIAN DIDN'T KNOW how long she stood gaping at James as he shifted his feet and tried not to look awkward. But dear God, he'd said it, hadn't he? Along with a lot of other wonderful things. And by the high color in his neck and the sudden awareness in his eyes, she knew he hadn't meant to.

Dear God, he had loved her after all. Her inhale was shaky, as were her hands when she raked them through her hair. "What am I supposed to do with that?" she asked.

"I don't rightly know," he admitted after a moment's thought. "I don't know if I've ever known what to do with it…exactly. But there it is." His eyes were as naked as she'd ever seen them. "I loved you, hard."

It had always been so much easier to believe that she'd loved him more than he had ever loved her, or felt about her, period. It had been so much easier to believe that she had been nothing but a handy coping mechanism. "Why…why did you have to tell me?" she asked finally. "Now we both have to live with it!"

He dug his hands into his pockets. For a moment, he looked lost. "Beats the hell out of me," he murmured.

One look at him and she knew he was as vulnerable as she had been eight years ago. "Damn it, James." She dropped the purse she'd picked up on her way to the exit. "Goddamn it."

He nodded shortly. "That sums it up."

"I shouldn't believe you. After all you've put me through, I should just walk out that door."

He glanced from the exit to the purse she was no longer clutching and back to her, a light entering his eyes. "Then what are you still doing here, Adrian?"

"Complicating things," she said, crossing the room to him. She hesitated briefly before sliding her hands up to his shoulders and lifting on her tiptoes, touching her mouth to his.

The kiss was brushing, tender. He sucked in a long breath. She felt the hands in his pockets twitch. Pulling back, she looked at the bar between his closed eyes, the muscles quaking in his jaw. Smoothing her hand over his cheek, she tipped her mouth up to his again and indulged in another sweet kiss, lingering when he made a noise in his throat.

Cupping his face in her hands, she deepened the kiss, opening her mouth to his for the first time since his return. Yet he did as promised and didn't touch her. He held himself back even as she pulled his tongue into her mouth and suckled. His body hardened under her hands and he hissed. She smiled a bit because she saw that his effort was costing him dearly.

"I think you should touch me now," she told him.

He didn't open his eyes. The muscles in his face were drawn tight under his skin, his voice hoarse. "Once I start, I can't promise I'll be able to stop."

"Just do it," she demanded, "before I start thinking sensibly again."

James's answering kiss was blistering, nearly knocking her off her feet. She wound her arms around his neck as his folded around her waist. They both held on. She tilted her head, letting him delve deeper. He tasted so good. So like James. She wanted to melt into the big, long line of him and disappear into his heat…

Her hands roamed free over his shoulders, arms and back. Lower, under his shirt, her nails dug into the dip of his spine. Hot. His skin was hot to the touch. Her fingertips found the dimples above his beltline. He nibbled at her mouth and she lost all train of thought. It wasn't until he growled in the back of his throat that she realized she'd gone a step further and let her hand wander below his waist to grab a firm hold of his rear.

The laughter trembled out of him. "You're playing with fire, woman."

"Just…shut up and kiss me." She panted and

captured his mouth for herself. He made an agreeing noise and turned her so that his body pressed hers into the glass door. One of his thick, Viking thighs wedged between hers and pushed up against the aching spot between her legs.

Despite the intensity of the kiss and the power vibrating in the muscles beneath her hands, she didn't feel the first lick of fear. Despite the fact that he'd pressed her to the glass as if it was the slide under a microscope, she didn't feel fear—only heat and hunger. God, she was hungry. So hungry she could—

"Ah!" James cried, his head sailing back from hers as he covered the lip she'd sunk her teeth into.

She stuttered in apology. "Oh, God. Are you bleeding?"

James smiled, dabbing his lip with his finger, his wicked blue eyes seeking hers. "You've given me worse."

She let out a tremulous laugh. "I'm sorry. It's… it's been a while. Otherwise, I wouldn't have bitten you."

His eyes went soft again. "Adrian, if you need to take a bite out of anybody, trust me, I'd volunteer."

She couldn't fight another laugh. It washed out of her in a relieved wave.

"BBs, biting…anybody else would move away. Far away."

"I'm not going anywhere," he told her.

She wanted to believe that. Reaching up, she touched the tip of her thumb to the swollen spot on his lip. He touched his hand to the back of hers and held her gaze as he dipped his head and kissed the pad of her thumb. Then, watching her still, he pulled the length of her thumb into his mouth, closed his eyes and gently suckled it.

Lust, bright and burning, lashed at her. She nearly dove at him.

"How long?"

"Hmm?" she asked, lifting a brow absently.

"How long has it been for you?"

She shook her head. "It's not important."

"How long?" he asked again, patient.

She blew out a resigned breath and closed her eyes so she wouldn't have to see his reaction. "Not...not since the divorce."

She opened her eyes and peered at his blank expression. Embarrassment hit her. "And...not very much before it, either."

James's eyes narrowed as sympathy blinked to life there. "Oh, baby..."

She stopped him. "You promised you wouldn't pity me, remember? Don't."

He took a deep breath, then nodded.

"I don't want to talk about the past," she told him. "I don't want to think about the future. I just want you, here and now. I think I've earned that."

"You have," he agreed, touching his brow to hers. "More than you know."

"I'll realize how stupid all this is later," she said as his mouth tilted down toward hers.

"Listen to me, Adrian, and understand this. I will not hurt you."

"I know you won't," she told him, grasping the open collar of his shirt. He could've snapped her in two, as big and brawny as he was. But he wouldn't. Hurting her as Radley had…it wasn't him. She had no trouble distinguishing between the two men. "I know that, James."

"That goes for today, tomorrow and every day after."

"I told you…" She drew his top lip into her mouth. He groaned. "Now. Just give me now."

"Damned if that's enough," he said and returned her kiss before she could argue further. Fusing his mouth to hers, he bent at the waist, hooked an arm under her knees. Using the other to cradle her shoulders, he began to lift.

"No," she said, breaking away from his mouth. "No sweeping."

"Shut up and let me sweep you," he said softly. Swallowing another protest with a kiss, he swept her off her feet. She felt small in his arms, feminine. Almost weightless as he carried her across the den.

The bedroom opened up under an archway. More windows here, she noted, all of them awash with the golden light of the setting sun. The warm glow of it bathed the air until it felt gilded. As he crossed into it, she felt gilded, too. The bed was low to the floor but wide and welcoming, even with the rumpled sheets.

It was a comfort knowing he hadn't expected them to venture this far. When he set her on her feet, she began tugging at the buttons of his shirt.

"Mmm-hmm," he said, grasping her hands in his. "Wait."

"It's almost been a decade and he wants me to wait," she muttered.

He grinned, reaching between them to undo her buttons one by one. His fingers moved slowly down her blouse. Torturously slowly. She opened her mouth to tell him to hurry it along, but then his knuckles skimmed her bare belly. She succumbed and let him slip her blouse over one shoulder, then the other until it billowed to the floor.

She began to reach up for his buttons when he lowered his lips to her exposed shoulder. Surprise and pleasure filtered through her as his mouth grazed the pulse point in her throat, tracing a line to her jaw. Sweeping her hands under the hem of his shirt, she settled for the feel of hot skin under her hands and tilted her head so he could reach the spot behind her ear. The scrape of his beard felt divine. The friction it brought coiled into her core and brought the flame.

So distracted was she by his ministrations, she barely felt the rough pads of his fingers moving around to her back. She did feel her bra loosen, however. He must have felt her stiffen because his hands flattened against her skin, moving up and down in a loving sweep until she relaxed.

James lifted a hand to her chin, lowering until his mouth found hers again. She sank into his kiss, lost herself once more. It felt so natural, the play of teeth and tongue, lips and shared breaths. Her heart gave a tug and she broke away, burying her face in the safe space below his jaw. Giving in, she let him slide the straps of her bra down her arms. It joined her shirt on the floor.

As he nudged her back to look his fill, she fought her self-consciousness. To distract herself she finally tugged successfully at his shirt buttons. One even bounced to the floor. Parting the sides of the shirt, she watched the ink on his chest and arms take shape. The images came to life as she pushed the material from his shoulders. They rolled as he shrugged the shirt free.

Bare but for the jeans snug at their hips, they stood together in the disappearing light. His skilled hands followed the trail of his gaze over her torso. The air between them had gone hot. He took her hand and pulled her with him onto the sheets.

Again, he kissed her as they arched together on the bed. His hand cruised up her thigh to the juncture between her legs and pressed through her jeans to sweeten the ache she felt there. His touch sparked an adrenaline surge that raged through her. Her blood fired, boiled, burned. He must've seen the quick flash of pleasure cross her face because his darkened in answer and his caress hardened just enough to make the ache sail clean into the bone.

It was too much. She was close to peaking and they weren't even naked.

Yes, *naked*. She wanted him naked. She made quick work of the snap of his jeans, leaning over to graze the skin above his beltline with her teeth. His stomach muscles quivered under her lips. She indulged herself by fanning her hands over his abs. As she removed the denim and boxer briefs, the hard rod between his legs drew her attention.

"No," he said, seeing the gleam in her eyes. Before she could reach for the ready shaft, he leaped at her, taking her down to the bed again. There he shucked her out of her jeans, pulling away the undies beneath. Then he covered her body with his again. His sigh washed over her face, flooded with relief and near satisfaction. "I've missed this," he whispered.

I have, too. She closed her mouth tight over the words. The hot ridge of his arousal rubbed against her. Another flash of heat assailed her, forcing her to come up for air. Turning her head away from him, she gasped.

"Easy," he said, touching his lips to the corner of her mouth.

"Sorry," she muttered, shaking her head. She'd

forgotten how overwhelming pleasure could be. How overwhelming James could be while pleasuring her.

"It might kill me, but I can slow it down if you need me to."

Tugging on the leather strand around his neck, she brought his mouth back to hers. "Just kiss me."

He did. Though kissing did nothing to ease or stifle the heat building inside her. It was intensifying, hastening to flash point when his hand crept to the place it had touched before and dabbled. That peak she'd been wary of lunged closer.

Her heart thundered and she begged silently for him to continue. The words wouldn't come to her lips—she'd gone mute. When he bared his teeth and groaned, as if sensing her brush with completion, the fear and wariness broke apart, splintered, and every muscle in her body clenched. She followed his urging into the free fall of oblivion.

Moments passed before she opened her eyes to find him grinning at her. She smiled back. "That was…"

"Wait for it."

Adrian frowned as he clambered off her. "Where do you think you're…" She trailed off when he rolled toward the bedside table. "Oh!"

He glanced over his shoulder, saw her eyeing the tattoo on his back and paused.

Pushing herself up on her elbow, she reached out, wanting to touch the red phoenix fanning its wings across his back. Flames climbed up his spine to wrap close around the bird's shape.

The artwork was…magnificent—the highlight of the canvas he'd made of his body. The phoenix was powerful, dangerous, bold and beautiful. Just like him. But its black eyes looked hooded… jaded. Sad. Drawing her hand to her mouth, she resisted the urge to touch as he leaned over, delving in the drawer of the bedside table.

"What do you think?" he asked quietly.

She heard the drawer slide closed but still he didn't turn. Swallowing hard, she looked into the eyes of that forlorn bird. "It doesn't go with any of the others."

"No," he agreed. He rolled onto the bed next to her, wearing nothing but his tattoos and the condom he'd been busy fixing into place. Turning onto his side to face her, he smoothed his hand over her hip, thumb rubbing a faded stretch mark at the edge of her abdomen. "It's yours."

She lowered her gaze to the Latin on his collarbone and closed her eyes when the letters blurred. "The condom isn't necessary," she said, unable to respond to what he'd said. "I'm on the pill."

"For once, Adrian," he said in a low voice, "let me take care of you."

"I take care of myself," she argued.

"Let me," he said again, dropping his mouth to her collarbone. Lower. She couldn't bite back a ragged exhale. His hand took hers and guided it between his legs. Finding his arousal, she wrapped her hand around him, stroked, squeezed.

His hips jerked, a gruff moan escaping him as his face lowered into her chest. His beard scraped against sensitive skin and she hardened her stroke.

With a noise of growing impatience, he gripped her leg and hooked it over his hip. Rearing up, he held her above him until her legs splayed across his lap. The light was low now, a hushed blue. He pulled her close. Their torsos slid, chafed together. He spread one hand over the back of her head, bringing her mouth down to his. With the other, he cupped her hip and lowered her to meet him.

Together, their breaths quickened as he breached. Her nails dug into his scalp and his arousal slid home inside her. She froze, stretching to accommodate his girth. It was a familiar weight, a familiar push. Still, she hunched forward against him, afraid to move lest she fly apart like shrapnel.

He didn't move. He waited, barely breathing. She took several gulps of air before taking the plunge, moving her lips over his and arching into him. His pant washed over her, ragged, resonant. His arms tightened, guiding her.

So hot, she thought again, as she felt sweat crawl down her back. She saw beads of it on his brow, too, felt the growing perspiration between them. They churned, groaning, gasping, panting until...

"Adrian?"

James's voice penetrated the haze. She turned her mouth to his, hungry, blind. It was wonderful. Too wonderful. "More," she murmured against his lips. "More."

"Sweet Christ." Tucking his face into her shoulder, he drove deep into her again and again. She cried out as she tripped over the edge and fell hard. His head dropped back, exposing the star on his throat as his back arched under her hands, body seizing, then slowly releasing in one, resplendent wave.

They slumped together, limp, exhausted, sated. Finally, he lifted his head from her shoulder. "Almighty." He gasped. "You…nearly killed me." Watching her face, he asked, "Okay?"

She managed something of a nod, studying him. Sweat cloaked his features in a fine sheen. His lips were parted. His eyes smiled, though they looked tired. His heart rapped like a hammer against her breastbone. Hers answered, so insistent she was sure he could hear it.

As his mouth found hers once more for a lazy, languid dip, he made a noise in his throat, this one sweet. It hummed along her frazzled nerves, digging deep into the recesses of her heart. When he shifted, pulling her with him to the sheets again, she wondered vaguely where he found the energy to move at all.

Then his arms wound tight around her and he

rolled to his back, keeping her locked snugly on top of him. Her head found his shoulder, her nose snuggled against the ridge of his jaw. She knew without a word he wouldn't let her go. Not until he fell into the deep cradle of sleep.

Because this was the way he'd held her then, too. This was the way he'd fallen asleep with her the night they made love for the first time.

The night they made Kyle.

Squeezing her eyes shut, she forced back the tears gathering in a storm behind her eyes and did her best to sink into the empty abyss of dreams.

But sleep didn't come for Adrian. It took James into its warm, dark embrace but left her wakeful, restless.

Adrian waited for the sky to dim, for the light to fade completely. She listened for a while to the deep cadence of James's breath. When a tear finally escaped her and dropped to his skin beneath her cheek, she rose, extricating herself from his arms.

She sneaked out of his bed and roamed his room like a thief. She found her clothes and undergarments and tiptoed into the bathroom. Closing the door, she turned on the light. The glass-walled shower snagged her attention. Opening the door, she turned the tap all the way to Hot and waited for it to warm before getting in.

Halfway through the shower, she realized she was crying. Quiet sobs reverberated through her.

Somewhere between the smell of his soap and his shampoo she'd broken down. She'd been trying to wash away the scent of him. But the soap brought him back. Brought it all back.

She lifted her face to the stinging spray. It was the sex, she told herself. It was the vulnerability that came hand in hand with intimacy. Both had hammered at her foundation until it was nothing but stilts on cracked cinderblocks, waiting to crumble.

She did her best to compose herself, to build those walls back and stop thinking about how sweet it had been to lie in his arms with her body still warm and loose. After her shower, she dressed quickly and escaped the bathroom.

In the den she found her purse. Frowning at the manila folder inside it, she was about leave it for him when a sleepy voice behind her said quietly, "Where ya' goin'?"

Adrian jerked around to face him. James was standing in the archway. She shouldered her purse, trying not to let her gaze dance too noticeably over his naked form. There was a tattoo on his hip. A pirate's skull, empty eye sockets and frozen mouth wicked, laughing and silent. It was a wonder she'd missed it while undressing him... "I'm calling it a night," she said, lifting her chin, daring him to challenge her.

"And here I thought we already had," he drawled.

"It's better that I go home."

Any trace of humor fled his face. "No. It's better that you haul your ass in here and dive back into bed with me."

"James—"

"You don't need to be alone in that house with Kennard loose." When she said nothing, he lifted a frustrated hand to the couch. "I'll sleep out here."

"You don't understand anything," she accused. "Nobody calls the shots for me anymore. I'm going home. Right next door with the locks engaged and a loaded BB gun at the ready. That's my decision. There's no use arguing, so…good night."

James scowled when she made a break for the door. "Should I still expect visitation rights to come my way or did you not mean any of that, either?"

Adrian rounded on him. "Did I not make myself clear at dinner? I can't give myself to you completely. It's unfair of you to ask."

"Did I ask?"

"Yes!" she said, and flung an arm toward the bedroom. "In there, when you showed me that stupid phoenix tattoo!"

"What about it?" he asked, raising a brow.

She scrubbed a hand through her hair. "You said it was mine. Like you've been carrying me around with you all this time." Her breath hitched. She didn't stop to gather it, though she felt the onset of sobs again. "I didn't ask you to do that."

"You didn't have to. I carry you with me because that's what I want. No matter what you say or do here tonight, I will always carry you with me, Adrian."

She shook her head, fighting the urge to stamp her foot like a child. "It's not fair."

"To who?" he asked, spreading his arms wide. "I'm the one who has to watch you sneak out of my house."

"Who's to say you won't pick up and leave again tomorrow?" she demanded. "Without so much as a 'See ya, pal! Had fun!' or a high five. Just gone."

Anger forked across his face. James advanced on her in three quick strides. "You want to know why I left the way I did eight years ago? Because I put you in a shitty situation and I thought you were better off without me. If I had stayed and you had stood by me the way I knew you would have, it would've split your family in two. I couldn't do to you and Van and Edith what I'd done to my mom, my stepdad and me. Not after Van forgave me for wrecking his office. Not after what happened between me and you. I put the three of you through enough. The fact that you had me in your room that night hurt your relationship with them and you can't tell me otherwise. I never wanted that."

He stopped for breath. It was like watching a release valve rupture. When he spoke again, the words were strained, resigned. "I took off because I thought it was what was best for your family.

You had so much going for you—college, life...I only would've held you back."

Adrian felt wrecked and bereft all at once. "That wasn't your decision to make."

"I made it regardless," he replied. "You wouldn't have let me go. You would have laughed at me. Thrown something at me. Accused me of being the hero, a caveman, any number of things. Don't think I don't know you. Just as I knew if you asked me to stay, I wouldn't have been able to say no. Because, Jesus, I loved you. I loved you so much."

Adrian raised her hands to her face. Her cheeks were wet. *Damn it.* "Whatever future you thought I had back then, it's not the life I wanted. I didn't want anything but you."

"If I'd known about Kyle," he said slowly, "you wouldn't have been able to get rid of me. If I could go back, you wouldn't have had to go through the pregnancy alone and that dick never would've laid a finger on you. I would have taken care of you. I still want to." James crossed to her then and splayed his fingers over her cheeks as he looked deeply into her eyes. "Adrian, let me take care of you."

She raised her hands to his wrists, unable to say a word. *All this time...*

"Stay with me," he murmured. "Please...stay with me, baby."

She nodded. "Okay." When his eyes widened

in disbelief, she gave in with a tremulous sigh. "I'll stay."

"Thank God." He buried his face in her hair, then rocked her back and forth, slowly but surely, easing her weary soul.

THE NEXT MORNING, Adrian woke to find the hooded eyes of the phoenix staring at her. She jumped a little, surprised, then settled, touching her fingertips to the artwork. It was so alive, so real she half expected the vivid flames to scorch her.

Words he'd spoken the night before came back to her. *You had such fire...That fire consumed me...It stayed with me...*

James's skin tightened under her hands. A second passed, then another, before he rolled onto his back and turned his head to her. His eyes were half lidded, the lines of sleep still etched across his face. His gaze was full of meaning, though, as he rolled closer to her, face-to-face. "Morning," he greeted her.

"Morning." She smiled when the tip of his nose grazed hers just before his mouth came down. There he drank, nibbled. In return, she sipped, combing her nails over his bearded jaw. Drawing back regretfully, she whispered, "I should go."

"But I have bacon."

She smiled wide, feeling the engorged weight of his morning erection pressing against her thigh.

Kissing him again, she lingered, tempting them both. "Kyle's waiting at the inn. I promised to pick him up before ten."

James's eyes sobered. He nodded. "I'd offer to join you, but the detective in residence might shoot me on sight."

She rose, looking for her clothes. They'd gone missing again in the night. She was incapable of sleeping in the same bed as James fully clothed while he...well, wasn't. "I have something for you."

"Bacon?" he asked hopefully.

She shook her head, dressing quickly. "Men and their priorities."

"I have *other* priorities, if you're interested."

Chuckling, she left the room. A moment later, she returned with the manila folder. She stopped for a moment to drink him in.

God, he had to be the sexiest man alive. With his tattooed arm raised above his head and the sheets bunched haphazardly at his waist, he looked like he belonged in some R-rated movie about pirates or gunslingers.

Sitting on the edge of the bed, she waited until he sat up and then passed the folder to him. "It's not breakfast. But it might be better."

He pursed his lips. He undid the clasp and shook out the folder's contents onto the sheets. His hands stilled as Kyle's face stared back at him.

She tucked her hair behind her ear and reached

over to flip some of the photos faceup, doing her best to put them in order. "I thought you might like to see some baby pictures. Well, toddler pictures, too. And some older pictures. Like this one, his first school portrait."

James took the photo and lowered his head to scan it silently.

Adrian took a deep breath and reached for another. "This was when he was about two. Riding his first tricycle. And this one...this was right after his teeth started coming in. He got them a bit late, but they came in perfectly." She watched James lift two fingers and rub the backs of them across his lips. "Ah...this was one of his first photos. He was still in the hospital."

James's shoulders moved on a quiet breath as he lingered over the picture of the newborn. Adrian watched his thumb lift to stroke the baby's cheek and blinked rapidly. Looking down at the pile of photos, she rifled through them. "I labeled most of them, the ones that weren't self-explanatory. Like this one. This was his first ice cream cone. And this was his first horseback ride at The Farm on Stargazer..."

"Adrian," James said in a thick voice. "This is great," he said, finally lifting his face to hers. He grinned wide, his eyes a bit wet around the edges.

A bittersweet feeling passed between them with the collage of their son in front of them. She reached out and took James's hand, squeezing it when he lowered his head again. "What about this one?" he asked, raising it to the light.

And so they went through them all, one by one. There was laughter and a few tears on her part, though she hid them behind her hand, hoping he didn't notice. She watched James turn into a proud papa, not for the first time, as he discovered Kyle as a baby, then a toddler and a young child. A Cub Scout. A soccer player. A junior mathlete.

She shared anecdotes from the childhood James had missed, the notable to the silly. When they ran out of photos, he thanked her. As he began to gather them back into the folder, she stopped him. "No, no. These are yours."

His eyes snagged on hers, round. "Seriously?"

"I have copies of everything," she assured him. "I figured...you know, that you'd want these for your own records."

He kissed her. A quick, hard kiss she felt down to her toes. "You don't know what you're giving me," he told her softly.

"I do, actually," she murmured, nodding. "I never thought I'd share him...especially not with you. But you're his father. He deserves a father, James. A great one. I want him to have that. Just as I want you to have these."

He touched his brow to hers, closed his eyes. "He's incredible. That's all you."

Adrian gave him a small smile. "I'd love to take all credit for him...but I think there's more of you in him than I've admitted to myself until now." She felt emotions biting once more and shifted away from him. "There's, uh…there's just one other thing." Reaching down to the floor into her purse, she pulled out Kyle's birth announcement. "You can have this, too. It's the last one. I mailed all the other copies when he was born."

James's eyes raced over the newborn photos, the printed weight, the height and finally…the name. They stilled. It took him a moment to speak. "His middle name is Zachariah?"

She bit her lip. "Yes. Kyle Zachariah Carlton."

When he remained silent, staring at the birth announcement, she reached for him. "James?"

He blew out a breath. Realizing she'd broken the dam, she put her arms around him and held onto him. His brow lowered to her shoulder and stayed there for some time. Silence and emotions reigned until he inhaled and lifted his head. "You've kept him alive more than any of the rest of us. You know that?"

She managed another smile. "I gave our son his name. We'll see how much of your father lives in him as time goes on."

James beamed. "We?"

She nodded. "Welcome to Daddyhood, hot rocks."

He chuckled, clutching the birth announcement. "Feels good here. Even better than I imagined."

Adrian watched him prop the birth announcement against the lamp on his bedside table so that it was angled toward the bed. The only photo memento in the room. "He'll break your heart a little bit each day," she warned as she stood, slinging her purse over her shoulder.

"I'll walk you home," he told her as he climbed from the bed and grabbed his jeans from the floor.

She insisted that she could manage the walk of shame just fine on her own. Still, minutes later, she found herself hand in hand with him, strolling back to the cottage. "I don't think it's a good idea to tell Kyle about us," she said thoughtfully as they approached her door. "Not yet, anyway."

"Agreed." She glanced at him, surprised, and he shrugged. "He's just getting used to the fact that I'm his dad. It's probably best that we give that time to sink in before telling him anything new."

And, by then, hopefully Adrian would have a better idea of where this thing with James was going. She turned to James on her doorstep. He pulled her in for a kiss, but she pushed back. "James. The neighbors…"

"Screw 'em," he said, then caught her lips and pulled her into him. After a moment's tangle, she realized that her arms had wound their way around his neck and her knee was bent, her foot off the ground. She turned her face away, sighing a little. "Now go away so I can think properly."

He gave her a sexy smile. "Yes, ma'am."

Unlocking the door quickly she opened it and

walked into the house. Shutting the door between them, she locked it, leaned against it and closed her eyes.

Don't hurt us, she thought. *Please, don't hurt us.*

CHAPTER THIRTEEN

MONDAY AFTERNOON, JAMES left the garage at a fairly decent hour considering the steady workload that seemed to be continuing through the second week of business for Bracken Mechanics. As a surprise for Adrian, he went by the local deli to pick up a meal for three. He owed her a decent meal, and he wanted to sit down with her and Kyle for dinner.

It had been a while since he contemplated the meaning of family, what it was like to be a part of that solid unit he'd known in younger years. It had been even longer since he had felt any desire for it.

Suddenly, he craved it—the bond, the unity, the ballast. He knew what it was like to be a family of three. And when he'd had it, he'd taken it for granted. With his lifestyle, he'd never thought he would consider building one for himself. Now he saw that window opening up.

He didn't know how long it would take to form that family. Adrian still shied away from any promises for the future, even after the weekend's intimacy. Her trust was a fragile offering that he was determined to bolster and support until she knew with certainty that she could depend on him in every way. And Kyle knew that he could count on James the way he should've been able to all along.

The pictures of Kyle and the visitation rights were gifts. They were the first step in James's journey to becoming an integral part of both of their lives.

If he'd had any doubt before Sunday night that he was slowly falling in love with Adrian all over again, it had gone up in flames. Great, big balls of flame.

As he pulled into his driveway, James saw a game of baseball in progress on the green lawn of the cottage next door between Kyle, a kid James didn't recognize who wore his hair in a Mohawk…and the cop.

Savitt. James didn't see Adrian's car. She was still at work. Which explained Cole's presence. Glancing at the deli bag in the passenger seat, James frowned.

It'd be best to avoid Briar's husband. But the degrees of separation between the woman James loved and Cole Savitt were limited. James wasn't going to let the fact that he felt cagey around the man get in the way of becoming a part of Adrian's and Kyle's lives.

Grabbing the bag, James got out of the car. Kyle waved and called a time-out and sprinted over. "Hi, James! What's in the bag?"

James held it up for his inspection. "Dinner."

Kyle's face brightened. "You're coming over for dinner?"

Reaching out, James ran a hand over the boy's hair and grinned. "Yeah, I am."

Kyle gave a whoop and a holler before grabbing James's arm and tugging him onto the cottage lawn. "This is my best friend, Gavin," he explained, gesturing to the kid with the Mohawk.

"Nice to meet you, Gavin," James said, nodding at the boy.

Gavin lifted his hand in greeting. He had a striking face, hard-boned and unsmiling. Aside from the eye-catching hazel of the kid's eyes, the resemblance between him and the child was as clear as the resemblance between James and Kyle.

Cole walked over and planted a hand on Gavin's shoulder. "Can we do something for you, Bracken?"

James lifted a brow. "Don't let me interrupt."

"You should join our game!" Kyle said.

James watched Cole's frown deepen. Then Gavin added, "That's a good idea. That way, it'll be two-on-two and Dad won't have to pitch anymore."

"I've got no problem pitching," Cole pointed out.

Seeing Kyle's pleading expression, James shrugged. "Sure. Why not?"

The boys cheered. Cole sneered before Gavin

tugged him back toward the bases. "We can be a team, Dad."

James clapped his hand on Kyle's back, then hugged him around the shoulders as they followed the Savitts to take their places in the outfield. "Come on, kid. Let's win this thing."

"You bet!" Kyle said, picking up his glove and handing James an extra. "Here. This is my lucky one."

James smiled over the battered glove as he turned it in his hands. "Thanks. You wanna pitch?"

"Sure," Kyle decided. "We can take turns."

James hadn't counted on the game being quite so physical. Kyle and Gavin played hard, going so far as to tackle each other to tag one or the other out. And it seemed to be Cole's sole ambition to keep James off the bases. In answer, James swung for the fences and managed several runs and stolen bases.

It wasn't until Adrian's car rolled into the drive that the cop took it a step further. As James attempted to steal third, Cole shouted for the pitcher, Gavin, to throw the ball. He caught it on a flying leap before barreling into James and tackling him to the ground. James tasted grass and dirt. It took a moment for the wind to come back into his lungs. It was then that Cole's elbow dug into his stomach and James wheezed.

A voice in his ear, close and menacing, said

in an undertone, "That's what you get when you play dirty, asshole."

As soon as James regained his breath, he crawled to his hands and knees and glared at his opponent. "It's you who's breaking out the dirty plays, cop."

"Hey!"

Adrian's voice brought both Cole's and James's heads around. "Everything okay over there?" she asked.

"It's fine," Cole told her as James slowly gained his feet. "Just teaching your man here a lesson."

James spun on him. "What the hell's your problem?"

Cole raised a brow. "Oh, I'll tell you what my problem is, Ghostrider. I'm not one to sit back and watch Adrian get herself into a situation she'll regret."

"Who's Ghostrider?" Kyle asked.

James looked over to see that he and Gavin were standing close by, listening intently to the heated exchange.

Adrian walked up behind them. "You boys go on inside and wash up," she told them, eyeing the men grimly as she ushered Kyle and Gavin toward the house. She waited until they were out of earshot before planting her hands on her hips and rounding on the others. "Are you kidding me, behaving this way in front of the kids? Cole, you at least should know better."

James's head kicked back at the insult. "Hey—"

"Sorry I had to bust Bracken's chops in front of the boys," Cole admitted. "But, Adrian, you've got a right to know who this guy really is."

"Yo, Captain Rogers," James interrupted, "sorry to burst your bubble, but the lady's already heard everything from me."

Adrian lifted her shoulders. "Cole, I appreciate your concern. More than you know. But James is right. I know everything about what happened in Huntsville. And you should know that I can take care of myself."

Cole jerked his chin toward her. "Did he tell you about the drugs he was trafficking?"

"You're out of line, Savitt," James said darkly.

"Drugs?" Adrian asked, looking from Cole to James. "You said you didn't have anything to do with drugs."

"I didn't," James told her.

"Oh, yeah?" Cole asked. "Then why, a few months after you got out of the game, did my partner tie the Harbuck cousins and their mountain warehouse to a Columbian drug lord when they found two hundred grams of cocaine in one of their wrecked stolen vehicles?"

James's heart pounded. "I didn't know about the drugs." He looked to Adrian. Her face had fallen and she was staring at him, aghast. "Adrian, I swear. I didn't know anything about the coke until a couple of weeks before I left. That's one of the reasons I left. They'd hidden the cocaine in the cars without telling me. They knew I wouldn't do the job if I found out I was being used to transport the stuff."

She blinked. He saw the trust, that fragile thing she'd placed gingerly in his hands, dim to obscurity as her gaze lowered to the grass between them.

James felt his world tip off axis and took a step toward her. "Adrian, baby—"

Adrian stopped him by backing away, holding her hand up. "Wait. Just wait."

"Guess you should have been a little more truthful, Bracken."

James took a deep breath and expelled it through his nostrils before rounding on Cole again. "You couldn't keep your nose in your own damn business?"

"This *is* my business," Cole asserted. "You're not exactly the kind of guy I'd want hanging around my boy, either."

James jerked his thumb in the direction the boys had gone. "Oh, you mean the kid with the Mohawk?"

When Cole took a threatening step toward James, Adrian thrust herself between them. "That's enough!" she said. When James edged forward, she threw her shoulder into his chest to back him up again. "This is ridiculous. The boys, the neighbors…they're all watching you two act like idiots." Glaring at James, she jerked her finger in his face. "Back off now!"

James sent Cole one last challenging look before backing off a step. The man appeared satisfied until Adrian started in on him. "Go home," she told Cole sternly. "Honestly, what would Briar say if she knew you were picking a fight in front of the kids?"

Cole had the decency to look somewhat chagrined. "I'm sorry," he said again. "I'm just trying to do what's right. For you. For Kyle. I want you both to be okay."

"Thank you," Adrian said in resignation. "But right now I need you to go."

Cole scanned her closely, as if he didn't think she could handle James without him. When she didn't waver, he drew his shoulders back. "I'll get Gavin. Call if you need anything." With that, he shouldered passed James and walked to the cottage.

Adrian stood with her back to James for several, silent seconds. Then she spun on her heel. Without looking at him, she edged around him toward the house.

He reached for her again. "Adrian—"

"I need some time," she said simply, still not meeting his eye.

"You have to believe me," he told her, winding an arm around her waist and turning her to face him. "I didn't know about the drugs."

Adrian closed her eyes and shook her head. Pulling his arm away from her without another word, she walked away.

ADRIAN BIT HER thumbnail as she drove to The Farm on Saturday. She'd made enough excuses. It was time to face the music.

And what better time than now when she and James were at odds and she was cursing herself for putting herself in a vulnerable position with him? What better way to pack on some more self-loathing than to spend the day with her mother?

She didn't know if she believed Cole's allegations that James had known about the drug trafficking. Nonetheless, she hadn't spoken to either of the men since the near-brawl. Cole had tried apologizing to her several times over the last week. She'd done her best to brush him off. James had brought dinner around several times, too, and she'd given him the same treatment.

She didn't know what to do with either of them. Frankly, she didn't want to think about any of it. Either way, she'd gotten herself into this mess— similar to the mess she'd had eight years ago. It was difficult to believe that she shouldn't expect the same results—heartbreak and humiliation.

Kyle bounded ahead of her from the car. Adrian followed him around the farmhouse, eager to avoid her mother as long as possible by steering clear of the indoors. The Carlton family house was a converted barn built from simple clapboard. Set in an old oak grove, it felt tucked away from the world. Sheltered. Almost idyllic. Add in the barn and sprawling horse pasture out back, it looked like something out of a storybook. Van and Edith had lived there all their married lives.

The security and idealism of Adrian's upbringing was something she had taken for granted. Mostly because her rebellious streak had come from her need for independence and a desire to carve her own way in the world.

As Kyle sprinted toward the barn built by Van years ago, where they housed the horses and the crop duster, Adrian stopped for a moment to breathe in the earthy scents of horses and all things green. There were wildflowers and berries growing in the thicket beyond the house and lawn. Birds were nesting in the trees around her. The scents of spring twined thickly in the air. The sun peeking through the trees was warm and a cool breeze kissed her skin.

"It's about time you showed up."

Adrian looked around. So much for a moment's peace. Edith Carlton crossed her arms as she approached Adrian. In her nondescript black sweater, riding boots and jeans, she looked every bit the well-to-do farmer's wife. If not for her cold, shrewd eyes, the lines bracketing her mouth and the disappointed expression—which Adrian believed to be a permanent fixture since the day she was born—Edith might have looked like something out of a catalog.

Adrian took a deep breath. "Mom. How are you?"

"I've been better," Edith said. "Considering how much gossip I've been fielding about you and that James Bracken."

Adrian cleared her throat. "You don't have to worry about James. There's no place for him in my life."

"As if there ever was a place for a man like that in your life," Edith said with a roll of her eyes. "That's the mistake you made before."

"I wouldn't call Kyle a mistake. Would you?"

Edith's eyes flared. "Don't put words in my mouth. These are your peccadillos we're talking about, not mine."

There was that word. *Peccadillos*. The bane of Adrian's existence. "I didn't come here to fight. Where's Dad?"

"In the barn," Edith said. She sniffed in her husband's direction. "Fiddling with that plane again. As if he'll ever get it working. I try to tell him it's useless, but the man never learns."

"I'll go say hi," Adrian said and without any other words, she half sprinted toward the building. Telling herself to brush aside the argument and all the negative feelings and tension that it had brought, Adrian concentrated on Kyle's piping voice and Van's deep, answering chuckle as she got closer to the barn.

Then she heard another laugh, another voice, and stopped cold. After several moments, frowning deeply, she marched through the open archway leading into the stables. She didn't stop to pat the horses as she usually did. Bypassing the stalls and the small tack room, she walked to the back section of the barn that opened into the hayloft. There, just inside the large barn doors, was Van Carlton's pride and joy—the aging, yellow crop duster he'd inherited from his own father. And bent over the engine with him were Kyle, standing on a step stool for a better vantage point… and James. Both men's hands were smeared with engine grease and they looked happy as clams.

"You gotta be kidding me," she groaned.

James's eyes lifted from the engine at exactly that moment, as if he had heard the quiet words. The corner of his mouth lifted in a smile. "Well, if it isn't li'l mama."

Kyle glanced up from the engine, all smiles. "Mom, look! James is here. Isn't that great?"

"Great," she muttered, taking a few steps forward. Van peered at her from beneath the brim of his battered Dale Earnhardt cap. "Dad," she said tightly.

Van lifted a shoulder. "He showed up this morning. Nearly sent your mama into apoplexy. You can't blame me for letting him stay."

Adrian could have admired the sense in that...
if James Bracken hadn't been the tool her father
was using to put a hitch in his wife's step. She met
James's affable stare and threw him all the negative vibes she'd been trying to let go. "Can I see
you for a moment? Outside."

"Sure," James said, innocently enough. "Excuse me, Van."

Van lifted another shoulder to show James his
absence didn't bother him.

Adrian didn't say anything until she and James
were far enough from the barn that neither Kyle
nor Van would overhear. Then she whirled on him.
"Okay, let's skip the part where I ask why you
showed up today of all days. You've got a lot of
nerve coming here to get under my skin."

James reached into his back pocket and pulled
out a white cleaning cloth to wipe his hands. "Kyle
mentioned your father has been trying to get his
plane running. I thought I'd lend the guy a hand."

"You know his opinion means far more to me
than anyone else's," Adrian accused. "So you're
cozying up to him. Admit it."

James considered, then lifted a wry brow.
"Well, I think we all know I don't have a chance
in hell with your mother." When Adrian only
groaned again, he laughed it off. "Look, your old
man called me last week to ask if I could come
by and lend him a hand. He would've come to the
garage, but the plane isn't exactly something he

can tow. I didn't know you'd be here today until I showed up."

When he shrugged, she frowned. "So this has nothing to do with what's between us?"

He smirked. "Well, maybe a little." He chanced a step toward her, lowering his head. "And I like the sound of that."

"What?" she asked.

"What's between us," James repeated. His smile gentled and his eyes sobered. "At least you admit there is something."

"There was," she pointed out. "Before you lied to me."

"I didn't lie."

"You weren't exactly truthful, though, were you?" she asked. "About the drugs."

"Listen—"

"I don't want you to stay for dinner."

He pulled a face. "Sorry. I'm here at your father's invitation. If he wants me to stay, I will. Even if it's just to bug the heck out of your mother."

"Jesus!" Adrian raked her hands through her hair and lifted her eyes skyward. "Is there a man around here who has any decency at all?"

James's smile tipped up at the corners as he took a look around. Hands on his hips, he looked right at home. "It's strange being back here. Where it all began. I passed the greenhouses on the way in. Made me more than a little nostalgic."

Adrian refused to think about the greenhouses and what had happened there.

He must have seen the tension vibrating through her. Taking a step toward her, he lowered his voice. "Look...if it makes you feel better, I'll swear another oath not to touch you."

She scoffed. "It's not that. Well, not *just* that," she added, eyeing the close breadth of his torso. Reaching up, she pushed him back so she had room to breathe at least. "My mother's already on my case about you. How am I supposed to convince her there's nothing between us if you're here?"

He frowned. "Well, for one, there *is* something between us." When she arched a warning brow, he ignored it and continued. "Two, if you decide it isn't any of Edith's business, it shouldn't be. Anyway, she should take you at your word."

"She won't," Adrian muttered.

James's brows hitched doubtfully before his expression cleared altogether. "Out of curiosity... how would you feel if I took Kyle camping next weekend?"

"Camping?" she asked, thrown off by the sudden shift in topic.

"Yeah. My Dad used to take me out to Fort McRee on the *Free Bird* every spring break. Kyle mentioned his is coming up. I'd like to take him, if you're willing."

"That's all the way to the Florida border,"

Adrian thought aloud. "You can't reach it by car, can you?"

"Not really," he admitted. "We'd sail there."

"Not on the *Free Bird*, I hope," she said doubtfully. "It's ancient."

"Mom sold the old daysailer after I skipped town years ago," he explained, pulling a regrettable face. "I've got a new boat. A catamaran."

She thought about it. "A catamaran. Sounds expensive."

"Well, I didn't exactly buy her," James admitted.

She cursed out loud. "You *stole* it?"

James laughed. It rumbled deep in his chest. "No, I won her. A year ago at the poker tables."

Adrian breathed a sigh of relief. "Oh, thank God."

"She's a real beaut," James told her. "Roomy, too, and safe enough for a daylight cruise to Fort McRee."

Adrian shook her head. "I don't know. I'm still mad at you."

James searched her eyes, the wide grin on his face slowly fading as he saw the truth of her wary words. His gaze dipped over her mouth and back to her eyes in a longing sweep. Lowering his voice, he asked, "What've I got to do to cure that?"

Weary, she began to lift her shoulders.

"Hey, Mom!"

They both pivoted as Kyle sprinted toward them. "Granddaddy said I could take Monty out for a ride. You haven't seen me ride bareback yet."

"I'll saddle up Stargazer and go with you," Adrian replied. "Just give me a minute, okay?"

As he ran back toward the barn, James narrowed his eyes. "Are you sure it's safe for him to be riding bareback?"

"Dad's been working with him." Adrian nodded. "If he says Kyle's ready, I hold my breath and do my best to trust him."

James lifted his hand to her hair and, although she eyed him sternly, he brushed his fingertips through her coif. "Don't worry about your mother."

Something echoed from years ago when he'd kissed her nail-scored palms after a particularly scalding run-in with Edith. The same words spoken the same, soft way. Her heart tugged her toward him and her hands tingled in remembrance.

Balling them into fists, she followed Kyle to the stables. A good, long ride on horseback would do her some good.

"Socket wrench?"

Without a word, Van handed James the tool. They'd been encamped in the barn with the vintage crop duster for much of the morning and afternoon. James didn't mind. It was grueling, dirty work, as the engine hadn't been cleaned in some time. Both his shirt and Van's were grease stained and their fingertips had gone black. It was the engine, though, that intrigued James. He wasn't familiar with it. It was easy convincing Van to let him dismantle it somewhat so that he could learn more about it.

Adrian's father's presence wasn't unwelcome. Van was a man of few words. For hours, they didn't speak beyond the work and the history of the plane. It wasn't until the light had shifted through the trees outside and an early-evening breeze wafted, light and cool, through the open barn doors that the past reared its ugly head between them.

Van raised a hand to his weathered, black ball cap, taking it off to wipe his sweaty brow with a dirty handkerchief. James's hands fumbled as he glanced up and his gaze seized on the jagged scar across the man's brow. It was faded and had gone white with time, but without the hat it was as prominent as Van's bushy gray brows.

As Van lowered the handkerchief, he caught James's stare. Unable to look away, James's eyes pinged uncertainly between those wise eyes and the terrible reminder of the attack that had brought James's time with the Carltons to an abrupt end.

After a moment, Van asked, "You got something you want to say, son?"

Son. The word was like a barb. James forced himself to swallow around the knot in his throat.

Van had called him *son* during his community service sentence. At first, he'd had to fight not to tell the man to quit calling him that. As the summer wore on, however, James had stopped minding. The relationship between him and Van might have been rough going at first, but a bond had grown. For James, it had been bittersweet since he'd rejected every other father figure who'd tried to impose himself on James's life. Van had been different. He never imposed. As the end of summer neared, James continued to work hard. He'd worked to earn Van's approval and to perhaps quiet the dark suspicion in Edith's eyes.

It had all been for nothing, thanks to Van's unknown assailant. And James's fast escape from Fairhope that had left Van's daughter alone when she needed James most.

Hands braced on the edge of the engine compartment, James looked away and cleared his throat. "I'm sorry," he said. The words seemed small in the face of everything that had happened.

Van covered his thinning hair with the ball cap once more and lifted a shoulder, turning his attention back to the engine. "If I remember rightly, my daughter vouched for your innocence."

The vote of confidence did nothing to assuage James's guilt. "I've been responsible for a lot of bad things. I hurt Adrian. By extension, I hurt you and Edith. I need to make amends. I want to."

Van frowned in concentration as he screwed a

bolt into place. "You get this plane runnin' again and maybe make Adrian smile once in a while, you'd be making fair progress as far as I'm concerned."

Van wasn't the type of man to hold grudges. Nevertheless, James was grateful for the chance at forgiveness. "Yes, sir."

It took another forty-five minutes, but after a sputter and a rusty moan, the prop turned for the first time in ten years and the engine roared to life. James, standing back to watch the propeller spin, beamed. Glancing at Van in the cockpit, he saw the old man's wide grin and the deep thread of satisfaction weaving its way across his face, washing away the age wrought there by time. James felt the weight of guilt ease more than a little. Even more so when they left the barn through the wide doors and Van clapped a hand over James's shoulder. "Good work, son. What d'ya say we grab a couple of cold beers?"

"That'd be great, sir," James said, "but I no longer drink."

Van eyed him, looking up from his five feet eight inches. Still, the approval James saw there made him feel at once three inches taller and like a small boy all over again. "Ah, well," Van said. "How 'bout a cold glass of lemonade instead?"

James splayed his dirty hands in front of him. "You sure Edith won't chase us out with a broom?"

Van chuckled. The sound was so rare, James

was almost certain he'd never heard it before. "All the better, son. All the better." He lifted his hand as they walked the fence line along the pasture. "Lookin' good, boy."

James's head turned and he stopped to watch Kyle trot over bareback on a tall, dark Tennessee Walker with a braided mane. Adrian was close behind him on her old bay mare, Stargazer. The pair made a picture, both looking as at home on horseback as he'd felt bent over an engine for the bulk of the day.

"Can I try jumping it, Granddaddy?" Kyle asked with a mischievous smile as he eyed the fence.

"No," both Van and James said at the same time. Van leaned on the top of the fence. "Grow a little in the saddle and I'll let you try some short jumps on Ajax."

"Okay," Kyle said with a small frown. "Hey, James, how'm I doing?"

James opened his mouth to tell him how steady he looked on the horse when a twig snapped loudly under Stargazer's front hoof. The Tennessee Walker started and sidestepped just enough to throw Kyle off balance. Adrian shrieked as Kyle began to pitch over the side of the horse. James vaulted the fence and managed to fold himself under Kyle's falling form just in the nick of time.

"Kyle!" Adrian cried, rounding the walking horse as Van clambered over the rail to tug on the reins so the horse's hind legs weren't in danger of trampling the pair on the ground. Adrian dropped to the ground and ran her hands over his head as Kyle sat up. "Are you okay?"

"I'm fine," the boy said, a bit wide-eyed. "James caught me."

"Thank God," Adrian breathed as she pulled him into her arms. Over his shoulder, she met James's gaze as he sat up. The look she gave him was equal parts parental terror and immense gratitude.

James gave her a nod and, as he came up to his knees, braced his hands on the pair to catch his breath. His heart was still hammering. He'd caught Kyle, but it would be a while before the image of him falling into open air faded. That knot was back in his throat. He ran a hand over Kyle's hair, in part to reassure himself that he was safe, whole.

"What happened?" Edith barked as she ran up.

"Nothing," Van told her. "Everything's fine here."

Edith's eyes snapped to her husband, latching on hard. "I told you not to let Kyle ride bareback, didn't I? I said it was only a matter of time before he fell off and busted his arm up, just like Adrian did when she was his age. It's stupid to let someone so young ride out of the saddle, especially on a horse as big as that."

"Edith," Van said sternly. "He's fine."

Edith's lips firmed, her face grew stony. "Get inside. It's time for dinner and we have a guest." When James rose, helping Kyle up, that hard gaze seized on him. "Not you. You'll understand if I don't want you coming inside, James."

Before James could reply, Van spoke up again. "I've already invited him."

Edith scowled. "I've already set the table. Five plates."

"We have other plates and other chairs," Van said. "You'll manage."

"Van—"

"Who else is coming to dinner?" Kyle's young voice pealed through the tense exchange like a hopeful bell.

Edith sent one last, seething glare at Van before answering. "Byron Strong."

Adrian looked up. "Byron? Why?"

James saw the alarm coating her face. Edith only raised a brow. "He finally got around to doing the books for the nursery. He's been working for the better part of the afternoon."

"On a Saturday?" Adrian asked, suspicious.

"I invited him to dinner," Edith told her. "I expect you to be pleasant."

Kyle looked pleased. "Byron's nice."

"Yes," Edith said, her eyes passing over James once more. "He's a very nice, respectable man. Wash up, all of you, and come in." Her eyes narrowed on James's hands. "You won't track anything in if you know what's good for you."

As Edith walked back to the farmhouse, James noted Adrian's look of exasperation. "You know Byron?" he asked casually.

She avoided his gaze. As Kyle walked ahead to help Van stable the horses, she explained, "Yeah, and if my mother had her way, we'd be married with five kids."

"Interesting," James replied and followed her to the house. It was going to be an interesting dinner, indeed.

CHAPTER FOURTEEN

"WOULD YOU LIKE another helping of mashed potatoes, Byron?"

Byron lifted a hand when Edith offered him the serving bowl with a smile. "That's all right, Mrs. Carlton. I feel as full as a tick as it is. That was a fine meal."

Edith all but simpered at him over the sentiment. Adrian scowled. *Speaking of ticks,* her mother was making a show of her attachment to Byron. "It's nothing you don't deserve, working the way you have. It's no easy labor making sense of Van's numbers."

"It's no trouble," Byron said, glancing at Adrian who'd "coincidentally" been seated next to him. "How's business for you?"

"It's steady," she told him, pushing her own mashed potatoes around her plate, avoiding her mother's expectant stare. "Spring's always a welcome comfort for anybody in the flower industry."

"Byron, do you play the guitar?" Kyle asked from Adrian's other side.

"Sure. I play a little. Not very well…."

Edith laughed, reaching to pat his hand. "Oh, I'm sure you're being modest, as usual."

Adrian looked across the table in time to see James eye Edith as though she'd sprouted horns. When James looked at Adrian, brows raised, she rolled her eyes and looked down at her plate again.

"Granddaddy and I are gonna play on the back porch," Kyle told Byron. "And James brought a harmonica. You can play, too, Byron."

"Sure," Byron said. "But only if your mother plays the tambourine."

Adrian sent Byron an arched look. When he smirked at her, she smiled back. In truth, she did like Byron. They had dated casually, but whether it was the pressure from her mother or the fact that they weren't interested in each other romantically, the relationship had gone no further than friend-ship, to Edith's deep and noisy disappointment.

James cleared his throat. "I think I'll be skip-ping tonight's performance, kid. My stomach's not settling well."

Kyle's protest was cut off by Edith. "Hmm. I guess a fine, home-cooked meal doesn't agree with everyone." Then she lifted her teacup to her mouth to hide a satisfied smile.

"Neither does crow," James muttered.

"Excuse me?" Edith snapped, blinking from him to Adrian as the latter coughed.

"Nothing," Adrian said, and frowned at James

when he lifted an innocent shoulder, shoveling the last of his pot roast into his mouth.

Byron looked at Adrian again. "So you and James used to know each other, huh?"

Before Adrian could offer a careful reply, Kyle said, "He's my dad!"

Byron's eyes widened as he looked from Kyle to James and back to Adrian. "Well, how 'bout that?"

"There are no other words for it," Van said with a soft chuckle.

"Oh, James is just one of Adrian's peccadillos," Edith told him. "What was that other boy's name before James? He had grand designs to be the world's next punk rock sensation, if I recall."

Adrian eyed her mother in warning. "Let it go, Mom."

"And then there was the one before that. The one your daddy caught you with in the back of his Chevy. Van had every right to shoot the boy, but he didn't."

"Sorry to disappoint you, my dear," Van said evenly, taking another swig of his beer.

"And then, of course, there was that disaster with Radley Kennard."

"Mom," Adrian said.

"What?" Edith asked.

"I'm sure this is what Byron wants to hear over dinner," Adrian said in an undertone. "Just how big a bullet he's dodged by not satisfying your wishes and marrying me on the spot."

"Ah…" Byron began, looking appropriately awkward.

Edith narrowed her eyes on Adrian. "Perhaps you're right."

"Edith," Van said. "Change the subject."

"Mind your own business," she replied. "I'm starting to realize Adrian might actually be right, for a change."

"Well, blow me down," Adrian muttered.

"Don't you sass me, young lady! I am your mother. How dare you speak to me in that tone? Our guest deserves better."

"Then why did you start it?" Adrian demanded.

"You started it with your pattern of bad decisions," Edith snapped back.

"Jesus, Edith. Would you do us all a favor and close your mouth for two seconds?"

Edith's mouth fell and every face turned in shock to James as he rose from his chair and towered over the table, throwing his napkin down on his plate. "It's no wonder I've got no appetite. You spew enough poison to make anybody within spitting distance hack and vomit."

She gasped, horrified. "I knew you'd be trouble tonight. I told Van he should know better than to include you. Are you satisfied?" she hissed at her husband.

James barked a laugh. "You've been giving

everyone in your family enough gastrointestinal problems to last a lifetime. Your problems started way before me."

Van placed his napkin on the table and motioned for Kyle as he stood, scooting his chair back. "Come on, boy. Time to tune up those guitars."

Kyle hesitated a moment before rising from his chair. No one said a word as he rounded the table and took his grandfather's waiting hand before being led out of earshot. James's throat moved on a swallow as he watched Kyle go. Then he looked at Adrian, remorse clouding his eyes. "I shouldn't have said anything in front of him. I'm sorry. But somebody at this table's got to stand up for you."

"James—" Adrian began but was smoothly interrupted as James turned back to Edith.

"If you want to blame anybody for the way Adrian's life has turned out, don't blame her," James told her. "Blame me. Not that there's reason to blame anyone because she's turned out fine. She's doing you proud and you can't even see it."

"I've about had enough of this," Edith said quietly, eyes hot on his. She hadn't risen from her chair but was locked in place like a spring on the verge of release.

"If Adrian's made mistakes, it's because she's lived her life," James told her. "Hell, we've all lived our lives. Now, I'm sorry for whatever's happened in your life to make you so terminally disappointed with everything and everyone around you. We're all sorry. But you need to let it go. More, you need to let Adrian live her life. Look at her, Edith. She's doing fine, just fine."

Here he stopped, out of steam and breath. His eyes strayed to Adrian. She stared at him, owl-eyed, unable to look away as silence reigned over the table. Finally, Byron lifted his glass and muttered a quiet "Hear, hear" before drinking.

Edith seethed, her mouth working silently. A couple minutes passed before she finally asked, "You remember your way out?"

"Vividly," James said. Dipping his head in a mocking bow to her, he turned to leave. "See you around, Byron."

"You owe me a poker night, Bracken," Byron called to James's retreating back.

ADRIAN HEARD THE front door slam moments later. It took only a few seconds for her to push her chair back and rise, muttering an "Excuse me" to Byron. She didn't look at Edith as she left the same way James had.

She caught him in the driveway, stalking toward the tree line where his sportster waited in the shade. "James!"

He glanced over his shoulder and stopped.

She huffed out a breath, walking to him at a fast clip. "Let's get one thing straight—"

He jerked a nod, eyes still heated from the con-frontation. "Okay. Let's."

"I don't nor have I ever needed you to fight my battles for me," she began.

"Is that right?" he challenged. "Then why is this still going on? Edith walks all over you. Why do you let her? Why do you let her make you into something small?"

"It's none of your business," she dismissed his words. "You weren't even supposed to be here tonight."

"That doesn't change the fact that she's still at it," James said, gesturing toward the farmhouse behind her. "And don't tell me it's because of your choices. She did this when you were seventeen. I saw it for myself, long before you made half of your *peccadillos*."

She flinched at the word.

"You're better than this, Adrian."

The words struck her off guard. Her mouth dropped. *"What?"*

"You let her flay you alive in front of your family, your friends. You should have learned to fight back a long time ago—"

"There's no point in fighting back!" she shouted.

"What I know is that if you thought more of yourself than she did, you wouldn't stand for it and you, Adrian Carlton, are stronger than that. I *know* you are."

She stared at him, at the truth on his face.

He nodded, knowing he had her there. "You've been through hell and you've fought—like a champ. You do what you love for a living. You're excellent at it and you've found success. And you are the best mother I've ever known. You deserve better than to be treated this way. And the fact that you're just now realizing it is a real damn shame."

He took a step back, turned and kept going. She didn't stop him.

It was some time before she heard footsteps crunching in the gravel behind her. Her body tensed. It wasn't until Byron eased up next to her and she realized that it was him that she relaxed again.

"Everything okay?" he asked.

She gave a tight nod. "Fine." She cleared her throat. "I'm sorry for the scene."

Byron gave a rueful smile. "What're you talking about? I got to see Edith barbecued for once. That's dinner and a show."

Adrian released a laugh on a watery wave. It halted as soon as it started, though, and Byron sighed, tugging her toward him. "Come 'ere."

She didn't want the comfort, mostly because she knew it would bring her closer to crumbling. But she stood for a moment in his arms, her face buried.

"Take a minute," he murmured, resting his chin on her head. "Just a minute."

Adrian breathed in slowly—then out—and she felt a bit steadier for it.

Then Byron added softly, "Loving someone isn't easy."

Her teeth gnashed together. "I don't love him."

"I was talking about your mother."

She frowned. "I know," she replied. The words pitched off-kilter.

Adrian could all but feel the doubt pouring off Byron as he replied. "All right." He pulled away. "Better now?"

"Yes," she admitted. Still, she took a couple of more breaths. "Thank you. I…I guess I needed the shoulder."

"Anytime." He reached out and touched her fondly on the chin. "Come on back to the house. You can watch my bad guitar playing and feel better about yourself."

She nodded. When he crooked his arm toward her, she lifted her hand to the bend of his elbow and let him lead her back into the lion's den.

"I'm THINKING ABOUT taking a personal day Friday. That all right with you, boss?"

James rolled his shoulders irritably. "Go ahead," he grunted, as he finished changing the minivan's back left tire.

"You wake up on the wrong side of the bed this morning or what?" Dusty asked.

Yeah, James had woken up on the wrong side

of the bed. His bed, as a matter of fact. Alone. "Don't worry about it," James said as he tightened the lug nuts, gritting his teeth when the last didn't cooperate.

"Does this have anything to do with Adrian Carlton?" Dusty asked evenly.

James chose not to answer that. Taking the tire iron with him, he went to the controls of the hydraulic lift to lower the minivan to the ground.

Dusty didn't take the hint. Instead, as the lift hummed, he followed James to the computer and said, "'Cause, you know, you're better off without that mess."

James whirled on him. "What do you know?"

"I've seen enough to know that Adrian Carlton and her folks are better off avoided."

"Why don't you enlighten me?" James asked, weighing him. "What's so bad about the Carltons?"

"I told you, dude, they ran you out of town. They put Radley in a bad place."

"Screw Kennard," James snapped. "The guy's a ticking time bomb."

"Ah, come on. Tell me you haven't bought into Adrian's victimized crap."

Anger knifed through James. His face heated and he stepped toward Dusty, fists clenched, before realizing what he'd intended to do—beat the living snot out of his friend.

Dusty paled, and for a split second looked worried. The savage look on James's face must've faded because Dusty lowered his hands and eyed him in a new light. "You're sleeping with her, aren't you?" he asked.

James scrubbed a hand over his face. "I don't want to talk about it."

"Why do you do it to yourself, man? Eight years ago, the Carltons worked you over like a pro. Now you're going after their daughter?"

"Maybe they were right about me," James said as he placed the tire iron on the shelf and began cleaning the greasy tools on the worktable. "I deserved whatever the Carltons dished out. Why do you think I left?"

"Nah, man," Dusty said. "They were uptight. Edith, she's as phony as they come. Going around town like a good Christian lady, trying to make everybody believe her family's perfect. And Van? The guy can barely put two and two together. He's as dumb as a brick."

James frowned deeply. "I'm going to ask you one more time to drop it."

Dusty scoffed. "If I didn't know any better, I'd say you were in love with her." When James didn't contradict him, he groaned. "Ah, hell. You're gonna wind up in the same state as Kennard."

"Kennard should be in jail."

"Ah," Dusty grimaced. "She's got you by the balls."

"He beat the living hell out of her!" James all

but shouted. "Can you tell me you never saw bruises on her while they were together? Bro code must go a long way for you to overlook spousal abuse."

"Maybe she pushed him to it. You gotta admit she's got a mouth on her."

James jerked his thumb toward the door. "That's it. Take off. You're done."

Dusty gaped. "You're firing me? After everything we've been through?"

"You're damn right I am."

"You're an idiot," Dusty retorted. "I'm just looking out for you. You wanna know how I know the Carltons are bad news?"

"I said take off, Dusty," James warned, at the end of his rope. "Now!"

"They accused you of attacking Van when we both know you didn't do it."

It took a moment to sink in. James narrowed his eyes. "How do you know it wasn't me? You weren't there that night." When Dusty only stared at him, clarity came with a numbing dose of shock. "Or were you?"

"Maybe I was," Dusty admitted, challenge lighting a match in his eyes. "What're you gonna do about it? Run and tell your new girlfriend?"

"You attacked Van Carlton eight years ago?" James asked, incredulity rising.

"I did it for you, back when I thought we were

friends," Dusty told him. "I thought if the old man was incapacitated, they'd forget about you and the community service and you'd have the Carltons off your back for good. But it backfired. And who was the first person those uppity do-gooders turned around and blamed?"

"You son of a bitch," James said, reaching out and gripping the front of Dusty's coveralls. "You almost killed him!"

"I was hammered," Dusty said offhandedly, without so much as a flicker of remorse. "My strength got away from me. You know how it is."

"Son of a bitch!" James said again and tossed Dusty back several steps.

"Big deal," Dusty said, straightening up quickly. He was solidly built, even if James had ten pounds of muscle on him. "It was eight years ago. The Carltons couldn't find the evidence they needed to lock you up so they dropped the charges and you split town." He spread his hands. "No harm done, if you ask me."

James thought about the jagged scar on Van's brow. Rage filtered through him, that familiar geyser that had once been a ready comfort. Cursing up a storm, he threaded his hands through his hair and began to pace.

Dusty licked his lips. "You're not gonna to tell anybody." When James's lips peeled back from his teeth in a snarl, Dusty's confidence leaked from his features. "You won't say anything if you know what's good for you."

James scowled. "Oh, you're threatening me now?"

"Depends," Dusty said. "You planning on keeping this conversation to yourself?"

James thought about it good and long, letting his fury fade, welcoming cool logic. He thought of Van. Edith. Adrian. Finally, he stopped pacing. "I won't tell anybody." Before Dusty could breathe a sigh of relief, James continued, "But you will."

"What?" Dusty asked, face falling.

James nodded. "I'll give you a few days to come clean with the Carltons. You can make your amends and they can decide what needs to be done."

Dusty looked at him as if he were crazy. "Come on. Be reasonable."

"I'm being a hell of a lot more reasonable than I want to be right now," James told him. "If by the end of the week you haven't confessed, I'll do it for you. Only I'll be talking to the police."

Dusty's expression hardened little by little and his eyes steeled. "If that's the case, then you and I are done."

James jerked a careless shoulder. "Guess you should've thought about that eight years ago."

Dusty eyed him for a moment before removing his ball cap with the Bracken logo and tossing it aside. With one last scathing look at James, Dusty turned and left the garage for good.

CHAPTER FIFTEEN

"TAKE YOUR NAUGHTY paws off my ride, Bracken."

James looked up to see Adrian's friend Olivia, with her hands on her hips. He raised his palm from the orange hood of the well-restored '80s model pickup that he'd been stroking in admiration. "This yours?" he asked, surprised, measuring her petite figure.

Her emerald eyes flashed indignantly. "Yeah. Now back away real slow-like and keep your hands where I can see them."

James couldn't fight a smile as he wearily stepped back. "Sorry."

Satisfied that he was no longer within reaching distance of her truck, Olivia relaxed. "Now, what can I do you for?"

"I'm looking for the little mama," he said.

Olivia snorted. "She lets you call her that and *live*?"

"I've been skinned a time or two."

Olivia let out a laugh. "She's coming around for lunch." They both glanced up as the sky rumbled a warning. "You should come on in. The bottom's about to drop. You hungry?"

"I could eat." James was about to accept the invitation when Adrian rounded the corner of the shop.

She frowned at him. "What are you doing here?" she asked, coming up short.

"Hello to you, too," James replied. For a moment, he simply looked. Wished. Wanted.

He hadn't seen or talked to her since The Farm—or since the run-in with Dusty in the garage when the truth about Van's attack came to light. Looking at her now, he wanted to blurt out the truth. Bring her the closure she and her family had needed years ago.

Two more days, he determined. He'd given Dusty his word, however harsh, and he'd keep it. He hoped to God his old friend did what was right and made his peace with the Carltons. Van deserved to hear the truth from the man who'd wronged him.

As James gazed at Adrian, the wanting turned into a long, hard burn. Christ, he needed to hold her, if only for a moment. Stephen had called that morning to update James. His mother's chemotherapy would be starting soon. They were pushing the treatment up in light of some new test results. James had been able to read between the lines. His mother's condition might be worse than expected.

Again, the thought of losing Mavis and the chance to make up for everything that had been lost scared James just as much as her cancer. He needed to man up and decide what role he wanted to play in her treatment and her eventual recovery. However, he couldn't hide the fact that, in the face of all his old demons, the urge to turn tail and run was itching beneath his skin at times.

Indulging in what he felt for Adrian helped ease those restless feelings. Even just looking at her helped. The distance between them…that was something he needed to fix. Right damn now.

Adrian frowned at the silent appraisal. "Look, hot rocks, I haven't got time for this."

"Aren't you on your lunch break?" he asked.

"Yes, but…" Adrian scowled. "I'm in no mood for your company."

James rocked back on his heels. "Ouch. Is this about your mother?"

"No," she said firmly. "It's about you bothering me."

James looked at Olivia. "It's about her mother."

Olivia glanced from him back to Adrian. "As much as I enjoy watching you two engage in foreplay, I don't feel like getting rained on." Pivoting on her heel, she called back, "Are you guys coming?"

James began to follow. Adrian blocked his path. "You're not coming in."

"She told me to," James pointed out.

"No, she didn't."

"Hey, lovebirds!" Olivia called from the tavern door. "Get inside! It's raining!"

A raindrop broke apart on James's nose. He looked around, saw the drizzle turning into a steady rain on the bay to his left. Without another word, he grabbed Adrian by the wrist and pulled her in through the open door beside him.

A mound of fur greeted James inside the tavern. It bared its teeth and emitted a low growl. James pressed his back to the door. "Jesus! What is that?"

"Rex," Gerald said, rushing over and laying a hand on the hairy beast's head. "Sorry, James. He's usually friendly."

"Good boy, Rexie," Adrian murmured, patting the dog on the back. She sent James a scalding look. "Such a good judge of character."

James felt the black mood he'd been wrestling with for days thunder down on him again. "All right," he said, pushing the sleeves of his flannel shirt up to his elbows as he veered around Rex. "Let's have it out, woman."

Adrian rounded on him, eyes firing. *"Woman?"* she echoed.

"Uh-oh," Olivia muttered. She grabbed Gerald's hand. "Incoming shrapnel. Let's get the hell out of here."

"No, stick around," James offered. "Grab some popcorn while you're at it. I'm not afraid to go at it with an audience."

"You made that very clear Saturday night," Adrian said.

"Did I embarrass you?" he ventured. When she only scowled, his lips tightened. "Is it Strong?"

"Strong?" She shook her head as if to clear it. "You mean Byron?"

"That's right," James asserted. "Byron Strong. You two dated, right?"

Her mouth dropped. "He's a friend. You know, someone who doesn't fly off the handle at the slightest provocation. Someone who can sit through dinner without making a scene."

James spread his arms. "Then why aren't you with him? Why aren't you two married and living at The Farm under Edith's thumb?"

"Oh, God," Olivia whispered. "It's like a train wreck. I can't look away."

"You've the right of it there, love," Gerald said, gripping his wife's elbow in case they needed to make a quick getaway.

Adrian walked to James and stabbed him with her finger. "What's between Byron and me is none of your business."

"If your mother had her way, Byron would be Kyle's stepfather." James was close to livid and having great difficulty concealing it. "I'd say that *is* my business."

"You're just jealous because you know he's a better man than you are," Adrian accused.

Damn it, she had him there. "Go on. Go marry him. I'm sure the four of you will be very happy together."

"The four of us?"

"Yeah," James retorted. "You, Byron, Kyle *and* your mother."

Adrian planted both hands on his chest and shoved him back a step. "Oh, why don't you just go back to whatever hellhole you crawled out of and disappear again?"

"You'd like that, wouldn't you?" he asked, voice rising above hers. "You'd like nothing more than to see me pick up and leave. Get out of the picture. Well, it's not gonna happen. No matter how hard you push."

She pushed anyway. "Why not?"

"Because I love you!" he shouted.

Adrian's face froze. Fear flashed across it. "Take it back."

"What?" James frowned. "I'm not going to take it back."

"Take it back!" Adrian demanded.

"No, I won't."

She advanced on him. "You take it back right now, James Bracken, or I'll—"

"I'm pregnant."

James and Adrian stopped. They turned as one to Olivia who had blurted out the unexpected words. Gerald's head swiveled sideways in her direction. For a moment, he stared at her, blank faced. He blinked owlishly from behind his horn-rimmed glasses. "What did you say?" he asked.

"I'm pregnant," Olivia said once more, facing her husband with her chin raised in challenge to mask the vulnerability permeating her expression.

When Gerald and the others only stared at her, Olivia shrieked, "Say something!"

Gerald blew out a breath. "Words. I'm…never without them."

"You could have fooled me!" Olivia said impatiently.

"Liv." Gerald gripped her arm in both hands now. "You're really…" He gestured to her middle in a silent motion.

"Yes, pregnant!" Olivia exclaimed. "You know? Knocked up. With child. In the family way…"

Gerald silenced Olivia by throwing his arms around her and holding her tight. He let out a choked laugh before lifting her off the ground and spinning with her. Rex barked happily from the floor.

Olivia placed her hands on Gerald's upper arms to stop him. "Whoa, whoa," she said. "Easy there, Shakespeare. I haven't been doing too great in the equilibrium department."

"I'm sorry," Gerald said, alarmed. "So sorry. You married a prat, Mrs. Leighton." Lifting her damsel-in-distress style into his arms, he turned awkwardly to James and Adrian who had been transfixed by the family interlude. He bobbed a short bow, unable to fight a broad grin. "You'll excuse us, won't you?"

Adrian waved her hand dismissively. "Go on, go on." She smiled as she watched the pair disappear through the swinging doors behind the bar into the hall beyond.

James watched Adrian as the couple went on their merry way. Her soft smile slowly faded. She didn't look at him but he could see that the fury was gone as was the fear. In their place was the fragile light of heartache.

Understanding it, James reached for her. She pulled back, dodging his touch once more. He let her because it was his fault. If he hadn't left, the news of Adrian's own pregnancy still might not have been welcomed by her family, but he would have had a chance to celebrate as Gerald had. To break out in a big, stupid grin and swing Adrian about until she glowed.

No, there'd been none of that.

On a ragged exhale, Adrian walked out of the tavern and into the rain.

James stared at the doors as they swung shut. Then he looked at the dog, Rex, who was eyeing him warily. Skirting the canine, he made for the doors and pushed his way out into the downpour. He trudged through the puddles to the front of Flora. He peered through the windows but the interior was dark. Going around to the other side of the building, he spotted her unlocking the doors to the greenhouse and made for her. As she removed the padlock, he gripped the door over her head and swung it open.

Adrian sighed. "I'd really like to be alone, James."

"No," he said.

That brought her gaze to his. "What do you mean *no*?" she asked, punching the last word out.

"I mean no, damn it," James said again. Gingerly, he tugged her toward him and into the greenhouse. Her resistance faded bit by bit as he wrapped her close.

He held her as the rain fell on the glass walls and roof, drumming around them in a steady cadence. She didn't fight him off this time. Giving in, she let him hold her amidst the hanging ferns and planters.

Finally, gripping his arms, she whispered, "Let me go now."

Without a word, he lowered his mouth to hers in a gentle, giving kiss that stilled her. It was the first time he had dared to kiss her since the morning he'd woken up with her in his bed. He'd missed this—missed her. He'd missed the burn and the peace she brought in equal measure. The answers. "I'm sorry I wasn't there for you," he murmured. "I'm sorry it couldn't have been that way for us."

Adrian shook her head. Her brow knitted. "Sorry doesn't change anything."

"I can change now."

She frowned. "I never wanted you to change. All I wanted was for you to stay."

And you didn't. The words echoed between them as if she'd spoken them. James grazed his thumb over the point of her cheek. "I'm sorry."

She closed her eyes and shook her head slightly. "James…it's done. That part of our lives is over. How many times do I have to say it?"

"Then what's keeping us from making a clean start of it?" he asked gently.

She licked her lips. "You didn't tell me the whole truth."

"I swear to you," he said, "I didn't know about the drugs in Huntsville."

Adrian's frown eased slowly. "I know that."

"You do?" he asked, surprised.

"Yes," she said.

"Then why the distance?" James asked. "Why all this tension?"

Adrian hung her head, dropping her hands from him. "Because you didn't tell me the whole story. I can live with the fact that you stole cars. I can believe you wouldn't have done it if you'd known they were full of drugs. But, James, you promised me the truth and you didn't deliver. Not all of it."

He nodded. He could agree with her on that. "I'm sorry."

She sighed. "Stop saying you're sorry. Just promise me, if you want to be a part of Kyle's life…and mine, you'll be completely truthful with us from now on."

"I will, I promise."

She hesitated before saying what she had to say next. "I saw your mom yesterday."

James faltered into silence once more.

Looking at him closely, she added quietly, "She was running errands in town, just like me. But she looked tired. And you were right. She is thinner."

James winced.

"James," Adrian said in a whisper. "Please tell me you've talked to her."

He swallowed all the conflicting feelings rising up his throat. "I'm trying."

The look she gave him was almost pitying. "I don't want to be the one to say it…but under the circumstances, time might not be a luxury you can count on."

"I know, Adrian, I know."

"Then why haven't you talked to her?" she asked, searching his face.

He scrubbed his hands through his hair. "Because I'm scared out of my mind. Because if this treatment doesn't go her way and I lose her, too…"

Adrian's lips parted when the words faded to an echo. "What? Are you…going to leave again?"

"No," he said quickly, meeting her gaze. "No."

"Are you sure about that?" she asked, the words cracking.

He saw the sheen work its way over her dark

eyes and pulled her into him again. He tucked her into his embrace and buried his face in her hair. "I won't lie to you, baby. I'm spooked. I'm feeling things—a lot of negative, cowardly things— that I haven't felt since my dad was taken from me. But if you understand nothing else about me, Adrian, know this. No matter what happens, I'm not going anywhere."

"But what if—"

"I'm not going anywhere," he said again. "I've got you. I've got Kyle. You need me. Both of you." Before she could think about arguing that point, he went on. "And I need you. No matter what happens, you're stuck with me this time around."

She didn't move for a long time. Finally she turned her face into his chest. He closed his eyes in relief when her arms wound around him, clinging after a moment's pause. "You're not really in love with me, right?" she asked in a halting, plaintive voice.

The laugh that broke out of James was every bit as healing as the peace she brought to him. Dropping a kiss to her brow, he pulled back enough to touch his lips to the line between her eyes. "I love you so much I can't think straight."

"Damn it," she groaned.

That brought a smile to his lips. "Not exactly the response I was hoping for. But I suppose it's better than the closed fist I had coming my way a few minutes ago."

Adrian fiddled with the top button of his shirt. "So, you still want to take Kyle camping? Am I invited, too?"

James all but beamed. He lifted two fingers to his brow in casual salute. "We set sail Friday, ma'am."

THE WEEKEND SPENT on James's catamaran passed by far too quickly for Adrian's taste. It had been so long since she'd been on anything resembling a vacation.

Friday afternoon they had set sail for the Florida Panhandle, reaching Fort McRee close to dark later that evening. They anchored the sailboat in the channel and made camp on the beach. As James and Kyle fished in the rushing gulf surf, Adrian lounged on the beach, basking in the warm, salt-tinged air.

A thunderstorm gathered as evening passed into the thick of night. They raced to the old fort to take shelter. James kissed Adrian as Kyle went around the cavernous walls of the fortress, making ghostly noises and flashing his lantern light to make shadows. As thunder rattled the old stone structure around them, Adrian lost track of time and space, giving in to James's long, hard form and opening her mouth to his.

It was Kyle who interrupted, as stunned to see them embracing as they were by his sudden reappearance. Minutes later, the storm crashed away into the night and they walked back to camp. James squeezed Adrian's hand and assured her, "I've got this." Reluctantly she watched James and Kyle settle by the fire with marshmallows before retreating into her tent.

In the morning, she found them nestled together on a pallet close to the dying fire, their heads cocked in the same direction in sleep and both their mouths open in twin poses. When they woke, Kyle was as chipper and full of energy as ever. James winked at Adrian when she asked if her son had taken the news well.

They'd spent the rest of the weekend fishing, swimming, surfing and sailing without pause. When it was time to return home, they did so regretfully. But Adrian couldn't think of a better way to end the weekend than by standing at the helm of the catamaran, James close at her back, watching the bow of the boat sail toward the sunset hanging low over the western shore of Mobile Bay.

By Monday, it was back to the Eastern Shore and reality. Which meant another big wedding for her and Roxie. Monday weddings were a rarity, but the couple had wanted their date to coincide with the anniversary of the bride's parents. Since Kyle was still on spring break, she drove him with her to work so that he could fish with Gavin and Cole at the inn.

"Hey, Mom?" he said as they pulled onto South

Mobile Street. "I think it's kind of cool that you and James are together."

Adrian turned her head to look at him. Kyle hadn't broached the subject since his talk with James at the campsite. And, truth be told, she'd been hesitant to bring it up. She licked her lips and turned back to the two-lane road. "You do, huh?"

"Yeah," Kyle added with a shrug. Adrian's brows drew together. She and Kyle had had a few conversations about James and the fact that he was Kyle's father, also about her own history with him and why things hadn't worked out. "What did he say to you on the beach?" she asked curiously.

"He said he was sorry," Kyle said thoughtfully. "He said that I was the man of the house and I had a right to know who you're spending time with." He wrinkled his nose. "And sucking face with."

Adrian choked back a laugh at the disgust coating his expression. "What James and I have is more than just sucking face. You know that, right?"

"Sure. And it's okay. I guess it would be kind of neat if things worked out," Kyle said.

Adrian pulled the car into Flora's parking lot and stopped, then reached for Kyle's hand. As he faced her, she saw the light of possibility in his eyes. "It's lovely that you think so," she told him. "Thank you for telling me. I want you to always tell me how you feel, especially if anything makes you uncomfortable."

Kyle made a face. "The sucking face does a little."

Fighting a smile, Adrian nodded. "Noted. But things between James and me have never been easy. And I don't want you to put all your hopes in this working out. Nothing's set in stone. Okay?"

Kyle's eyes narrowed as he thought about it. "He'll still live next door to us, though, right?"

"I wish I could say," she told him.

"But I'll still get to spend time with him, even if he doesn't?"

"Yes," Adrian promised, smoothing a hand over his arm. "If there's one thing I have learned over the past few weeks it's that James will never *not* be a part of your life again if you want him to be."

"I do want him to be." Kyle bit his lip. "I've been thinking about something else, too."

Because he seemed hesitant about it, Adrian patted his hand. "What's that?" she asked gently.

"Do you…do you think it would be all right if I stopped calling him James and started calling him Dad?"

Adrian's heart gave more than a gentle squeeze. "Yes. I'm sure James would love that."

"And you're okay with it?"

That her child could be so considerate, so sweet to ask, made Adrian closer to tears than she had been all weekend. She lowered her voice, afraid it might crack. "Yes."

Adrian spent the remainder of the morning

arranging flowers in the chapel for the ceremony and at Tavern of the Graces where Olivia would be hosting the reception. Still, as the ceremony wound down and the herd of guests trickled into the tavern that had been strewn with fairy lights, she couldn't get Kyle's face or request out of her mind.

She was almost ready to skip out of the reception altogether and join him on the inn dock when Olivia caught up with her. "You've been quiet today. Did you have a good weekend with the guys?"

Adrian glanced down into her champagne glass. "I've been meaning to apologize for what happened in the tavern last week."

"You're kidding, right?" Olivia let out a laugh. "Watching you two go at it like that was better than watching the Starz channel on mute."

Adrian's blinked in surprise. "You watch Starz on mute?"

Olivia lifted a shoulder. "Gerald left for his book tour a few days ago. I'm lonely. Sue me. And you dodged my question. How was the sailing trip?"

Adrian sighed. "Wonderful. It was wonderful."

Olivia smirked. "So, I take it the two of you made up."

"Yes," Adrian said. Sometimes, with Olivia, the truth was far less exhausting than evasion. "I suppose it is official now. We are seeing each other."

Olivia snapped her fingers over her head. "Hal-lelujah!" When Adrian laughed, she lowered her voice and said, "Okay, now tell me something else."

"What?" Adrian asked, smiling again. She was making a habit of the expression.

"Does he or does he not…steal kisses on the sly?"

Adrian's eyes rolled back and she turned her face up to the ceiling. "Oh, no."

"'Does he take time to make time?'" Olivia started snapping again and swinging her hips. "'Tellin' you that he's all yours? Learnin' from each other's knowin'.'"

"Stop," Adrian begged, covering her ears. "Make it stop, Ms. Springfield, please!"

Olivia belted out, "'Lookin' to see how much we're growin'!'" She stopped as several partygo-ers turned to see what the commotion was about. "I'm done."

"Thank God," Adrian breathed, reaching for another glass of champagne. "I'm having another one of these."

"Yes, drink one for me," Olivia told her. "You deserve it. One more question. Just out of curios-ity. The beard."

Adrian pointed at her in warning. "Let me stop you right there."

"No, let me finish," Olivia argued. A sly grin

grew across her face. "I just want to know how it feels when he—"

"Oh, look, there's Roxie," Adrian said, spotting her other friend across the tavern. "Excuse me." As Olivia cackled in her wake, Adrian crossed the reception space to where Roxie stood alone in the corner with an empty champagne flute. "Looks like another hit."

"Sure," Roxie said, jerking a shoulder.

Adrian frowned at her. She was wearing a somber shade of black, extraordinarily uncharacteristic for Roxie. Her eyeliner was a bit smudged and her hair wasn't nearly as neatly tucked into its business chignon as it usually was. "Are you okay?" Adrian asked cautiously.

"Yeah, fine." Roxie frowned, giving in. "I hate weddings."

Adrian stared, dumbstruck by the admission. "Um, no, you don't. You love weddings. They're your bread and butter."

"Not today," Roxie said, setting the glass aside. She hiccupped.

Adrian's eyes widened, her voice lowered. "Roxie...are you drunk?"

"That depends," Roxie said, crossing her arms over her chest. "If I were, would you judge me?"

The worry Adrian felt doubled when she read the grim light in Roxie's eyes. Something was very, very wrong. Her friend had a strict two-drink maximum at her weddings. She was the picture of decorum day in and day out. This was the first time Adrian could remember seeing her anything close to down or disheveled. "How many have you had?" Adrian asked.

"Counting that last one?" Roxie squinted to remember. "Like, six. Maybe seven."

Ah, crap. Adrian touched Roxie's arm. "In a minute, you're going to excuse yourself from the reception."

Roxie raised a doubting brow. "I am?"

"You're going to meet me and the girls in Liv's office, and we're going to have a chat."

A sad yet hopeful light wavered to life on Roxie's face. Tears crested in her eyes. "Sounds good," she agreed with a nod.

"Great." Adrian patted her gingerly on the shoulder, then went to round up Briar and Olivia. "Okay, wedding planner down."

"What's going on?" Briar asked, concerned.

Adrian cleared her throat. "Roxie's hammered."

"What?" Olivia said, looking around for Roxie. "That's not like her."

"There's something wrong," Adrian told them. "I told her to meet us in the office."

"Let's go," Briar decreed, leading the way as "Rock the Casbah" crashed out of the jukebox speakers and wedding guests crammed the dance floor. The noise dimmed as they headed out of the bar into the hallway. Roxie was waiting in the office, pacing the small space in her toothpick heels.

"What's going on?" Adrian asked, shutting the door behind them.

"I can't breathe," Roxie said, the heel of her hand pressed to her stomach.

"I've got it," Olivia said, going behind her desk. "I stocked these when the nausea started." Taking a brown paper bag from the top drawer, she shook it out and handed it over. "Breathe into that."

Roxie took it, put it over her mouth and took a few deep pulls. The bag inflated, deflated, inflated.

"Good," Briar cooed, rubbing her arm. "You're doing fine. Just keep breathing."

Roxie gasped as she pulled the bag from her mouth. "Oh, God. What's happening to me?" she asked, waving both her hands frantically.

Adrian steered her toward the couch. "You're having an anxiety attack. Just keep breathing. Liv, grab a soda from the fridge."

Olivia went to the minifridge and pulled out of can of ginger ale. Adrian pressed it to the back of Roxie's neck. "Does that help?"

After a moment, Roxie nodded. "Yes. Yes, that's good." She reached back and grabbed the can for herself, holding it in place.

Briar patted her free hand. "Are you okay? Can we get you anything else?"

"No, I'm fine," Roxie said with a faltering smile. "I just…something happened. I think…I think my life might be falling apart."

"Why?" Briar asked.

"Because Richard's sleeping with my sister, Cassandra," Roxie blurted out on a sobbing breath.

Olivia gasped. "No!"

Roxie nodded, closing her eyes. "I caught them this morning. I went back to the house after I left because I forgot my planner and there they were, tangled up together on the Aubusson."

"Oh, Rox," Adrian murmured. "I'm so sorry."

"That rat bastard," Olivia spat.

Roxie nodded. "You're right, Liv. He *is* a rat bastard. Men. They're all rat bastards." She glanced up at Briar and Olivia. "Sorry. But they are."

"No, you're right," Olivia said with a sage nod. At Briar's surprised look, she shrugged. "Pregnancy hormones. They make me want to jump Gerald's bones one minute and punch every other man I see the next."

"Maybe it's lucky Gerald's out of town, then," Adrian muttered.

"Why do you think he didn't stick around after I dropped the news?" Olivia asked pointedly.

Roxie gave a half laugh, half sob. She hiccupped again. "I should've throat-punched him. Richard. I should've throat-punched the both of them." She rose and started to pace again. "You know what I did instead? I apologized for barging in on them. Then I ran like a little girl. How *stupid* is that?"

"It's not stupid," Adrian said.

"The next time I see him…" Roxie balled her hand into a fist. "Ooo, I'm just gonna…*wham*, right in the—"

At that exact moment, the office door opened and Byron Strong, one of the reception guests, walked in. "Hey, Liv, we're running out of champagne—"

He was interrupted by Roxie's small fist in his solar plexus. He grunted, groaned and doubled over as the others stared in shock.

After a moment's pause, he gripped the door and wheezed, "Hell of a right hook you got there, Mrs. Levy."

"Oh, God," Roxie said, horrified. "Byron…I am so sorry!" The words trickled out on a sob. Roxie broke down, burying her face in the shoulder of Byron's tuxedo jacket.

"Um," Byron said, expression blank. When Roxie's back heaved, he folded his arms hesitantly around her, looking to the others for answers.

Briar rose to pat Roxie on the back. "You'll have to forgive her, Byron."

"Yeah," Olivia piped up. "She just found out her husband's been bouncing on her sister."

Byron's brows rose but before he could comment, Roxie hiccupped and muffled, "Men. They're such…p-p-pigs."

His hand rubbed hesitantly over her back and he said, "I, uh, I'm sorry?"

"Oh," Roxie said, stepping back enough to gaze at him. "Not you, Byron, I'm sure. Forgive me. I'm a mess. And I don't even…have a…a handkerchief."

Byron patted his pockets as she sniffled. Finding one, he lifted a white linen square to her empty hand.

"Oh, thank you," Roxie breathed. "Thank you so much." The words rose and died as she faded into sobs, pressing her face into the handkerchief and folding herself against Byron's tall frame once more.

Taking pity on the confused, helpless man, Adrian took Roxie by the arm and said to Briar, "Maybe we should take her to the inn. Let her lie down."

"Yes, of course," Briar said, taking Roxie's other arm as Byron stepped aside. "I'll make tea."

"Will she be all right?" Byron asked.

Adrian looked back at him and smiled at his genuine concern. "She will be. Liv, I'll be back to help with the reception."

"You guys take your time," Olivia called, tucking her arm through Byron's. "We'll handle everything from here."

CHAPTER SIXTEEN

JAMES CARRIED A bouquet of hand-tied, peach-tipped roses into the cancer center. Nerves crawled along his spine, chasing him as he went. He opened the door anyway and walked inside. Removing his sunglasses, he scanned the waiting area before crossing to the reception desk.

The woman behind it took one long look at his plaid button-down shirt and tattoos and raised a discerning brow. "Can I help you?" she asked.

"Yeah," James said, hooking the glasses into his shirt pocket. "I'm looking for Mavis Irvington."

Before the receptionist could answer, a voice from behind him said, "James?"

He turned and straightened. His mother was wearing a T-shirt he had seen on her before, but it looked bigger now. She also had on sweatpants and tennis shoes, but none of her subtle makeup, and the lack highlighted the gray shadows around her tired eyes and the pallor of her skin, especially with her hair pulled back from her face.

James's heart dropped as he looked at her. He swallowed and extended the flowers to her. "Here."

Mavis frowned at the bouquet. "What are those for? And what are you doing here?"

"Stephen called when he couldn't make it," James explained.

Mavis's mouth tucked into a firm, telling line. "Stephen."

James jerked a nod. He wished she would take the flowers. "Neither of us wanted you to be alone for your first treatment."

Mavis dropped her gaze from his face and rounded him to sign in at the counter behind him.

He waited for her, shifting from one foot to the other. When she took a seat nearby, he watched as she selected a magazine from the end table beside her and began flipping through it.

James inhaled deeply and crossed to her. As he sat next to Mavis she finally looked up. "What do you think you're doing?"

James pursed his lips, nonplussed, and looked around the room, ignoring several curious glances. "Well, I take it we're waiting." When Mavis only stared at him, brow puckered, he added, "I've been doing some reading on chemo."

Mavis's lips parted. "You read?"

"When the mood strikes," James asserted, nodding and ignoring the jab. He eyed the pillow and blanket folded together on the floor at her feet. "You're going the intravenous delivery route, right?"

"James."

"Probably waiting for a bed, then." He tried to see beyond the receptionist into the patient rooms beyond. "Want me to hurry this along?"

Mavis heaved a wary sigh. "James, listen to me—"

"I'm going to talk to someone," he decided and began to push up from the chair.

The hand that gripped his arm was cold and implacable. Mavis's eyes were like flint on his as she hissed, "Don't you dare."

He slowly lowered back to the seat, knowing better than to argue with that stern look. "At least let me find out how long the wait is."

"I'm fine waiting," she told him. "In fact, I'm perfectly fine doing this on my own."

As the words he'd feared reverberated through him, James's eyes combed her face. "But you don't have to. That's why I'm here."

"I don't need you to be here for me," she reiterated.

James did his best not to suck in a breath as the rejection sucker punched him. He shifted in the chair. "If you really don't want me here, I'll go. All you have to do is say so."

Mavis closed her eyes. After a second, the muscles of her face relaxed and she opened her eyes again. "This isn't your burden to bear."

"Look, I get that you're tough," he told her gently. "You're tougher than anybody I've ever known…and I've met a lot of rough characters in my time."

"I don't doubt it," she said, her voice laden with irony.

"I'm not here out of obligation. I'm here because I love you," he told her. When that made her fall silent, he reached for her hand. "I know you're going to give this thing one hell of a fight, and I want to be here when you do. I want you to know I'm in your corner, that I'm going to be here for you through all of this and that I'm not going anywhere."

Mavis's eyes lowered to their joined hands. They scanned the ink on the back of his hand and wrist. After a moment's thought, she squeezed his hand in answer. "It's a nice thought."

James stared at their fingers. Her hand looked so small against his. The bones felt hard and the joints looked stark. He cleared his throat as his brows came together. "Since Dad's funeral, I've done nothing but run away and hurt you. I behaved like a child, especially when you married Stephen. And I was mad because I thought that was my fault, too. If I'd been around more, maybe you wouldn't have been so lonely or felt the need to marry so soon." When she began to speak, he went on before she could. "I was afraid of losing you. That was part of the reason I stopped coming home. I was an idiot. Now we've lost so much time…"

He let the words trail off because he'd come close to admitting that he was scared of losing her now, too. For a long time, she studied his down-turned face. Her thumb began to caress the backside of his hand. Finally, she whispered, "I was wrong, too."

His face lifted to hers with a perplexed frown. Seeing emotion and remorse in her eyes, he fought the need to hold her.

"I should have found some way to reach out to you," Mavis explained. "Not only to tell you about your little boy. Every father has a right to know that he has a child. Just like every son has a right to know that the one thing his mother wants most in the world is for him to come home."

James caught himself squeezing her fingers a shade too hard and loosened his grip. Lifting his other hand to his mouth, he rubbed his fingers over his lips, then stopped and gripped the leather cord around his neck. Pulling the wooden cross out from under his shirt, he said, "I, ah…I want you to have this."

As he lifted the leather string over his head, Mavis's eyes softened on it. Holding it in her palm, she turned it over to see where the letters ZB were painted. She ran her thumb over them. "You still wear this?"

James lifted a shoulder. "I used to think it was Dad's old Corvette engine that brought me luck through the years. Now that I think about it, I believe it might have been this. And there's also this…" From his shirt pocket, he pulled out a wallet-sized photo of Kyle and handed it to her. "Adrian gave me some photos. I thought you'd like to have one. He is your grandson, after all."

A gentle smile warmed Mavis's mouth as she gazed at Kyle's school photo. "Well. There's no denying he's yours, is there?"

James let out a small laugh. "He likes engines, but he's smart as a whip. He gets that from Adrian, not me."

Her smile faded out slowly. "It seems you might be proving me wrong."

"About what?"

"I told you that the only thing you owed Adrian and Kyle was peace." She looked up at him. "Do you think you have what it takes to make them happy?"

James thought about it for a moment, then nodded slowly. "Yeah. I think I do."

"And is that what you want?" she asked curiously. "After everything you've seen and done, you're content with a life on the straight and narrow, juggling the responsibilities of family life in a small town?"

It was James's turn to smile. "I can't think of anything I want more. If they'll have me, of course."

Mavis touched his jaw, then she leaned over

and kissed his cheek. "My boy's all grown up," she said, her voice thick.

He chuckled. "About damn time, huh?" Sobering, he took the necklace and hung it around her neck for her.

Looking down at the cross, Mavis turned it to see the initials again. "When your father came home from rehab the last time," she said quietly, "he promised me that he would spend the rest of his life making up for all the pain his drinking caused. He told me that he would work to make you and me happy, to make us proud. And he did, James. He really did."

James nodded. "I wish I'd told him that."

"You do whatever you have to for Adrian and Kyle," she added. "They deserve happiness *and* peace. And so do you."

James was almost glad when a nurse entered the room and called for his mother. His eyes were stinging. He ducked his head as he stood with Mavis and picked up her bag, pillow and blanket before she had the chance to do so. Following quietly, he was relieved when she didn't protest his coming with her.

They talked quietly as the nurse made preparations for the intravenous administration of the drugs. James made sure to hold Mavis's hand as they put the catheter in...though she didn't so much as flicker an eyelash when they did.

She was tough, he thought. Stronger than he

was. Still, when the drugs began dripping into her bloodstream, she fell completely silent and he pressed his lips to the back of her hand in comfort.

YOU DO WHATEVER *you have to.* Mavis's words echoed in James's head throughout the rest of the day. It was late once he'd seen his mother home and made her dinner, making sure she was comfortable until Stephen returned. But instead of going home, James found himself at Hanna's Inn. He hesitated for a while before knocking on the kitchen door.

It was Cole who answered, not Briar. James exchanged a terse greeting with the ex-cop. After some hesitation, Cole opened the door for James to pass through.

The lights were low and all was quiet. Outside the windows, beyond a long tumble of green grass, James could see the water moving under the light of the moon. He'd always loved this spot on the bay. The inn hadn't changed much in a decade. As he took a seat at the round breakfast table in the center of the room, he realized it smelled the same, too—like cinnamon, cedar and delicious baked goods. Drawing the combined fragrances deep into his lungs, James said, "It's you I came to see."

Cole dropped into a chair on the opposite side of the table, unreadable.

Bite the bullet, James told himself when he

realized he was hesitating once more. "I, uh...I need some advice about something."

He told Cole everything—about the attack on Van, how he had been implicated, how Adrian had vouched for him, how eight years had gone by and the case had gone cold, and finally how he had learned about Dusty's involvement. When he was done telling the story, Cole's frown remained unchanged. "Why are telling me this?" he asked.

"You were a cop. Adrian knows you. She loves you. I'm sure that's mutual."

"It is," Cole said simply, sharp eyes never straying from James's face.

"The case has been cold a long time," James said again. "What do I have to do to get it opened back up?"

Cole thought about it, eyeing James. The look seemed to lose a bit of its acerbic nature as Cole thought the inquiry over. "You got any concrete evidence?"

"Aside from Dusty's confession? No. But the pieces fit. Van told police the guy wore a letterman jacket and was about my height. Dusty's the only guy I knew back then who's as tall as I am. He played football with me in high school so he had the jacket, like me. He wore it much more than I ever did."

"Do you know the name of the detective who was on the case?" Cole asked.

Another pair of hawkish, distrustful eyes entered James's head. "Randy Fleet."

"If Detective Fleet still works for the Fairhope PD, I'd go down to the station first thing in the morning and tell him everything you know," Cole said. "Whether it means simply taking another look at the case files or arresting your friend outright is up to them."

James nodded slowly, the idea of revisiting his old haunt, the Fairhope Police Department, and facing the leery Fleet made him feel like a twitchy teenager again.

"And," Cole went on after another moment's thought, "if Adrian means anything to you, I'd come clean with her. As soon as possible."

"Tonight." James decided. "I'll go over there tonight and tell her. It's late…we'll probably have to wait until tomorrow to go to The Farm. But I'd like to be there when Van finds out."

Cole's eyes narrowed as he watched James talk. "My wife keeps telling me to get over myself and accept your place in Adrian's life. I can't say that hasn't chafed a good bit."

James pursed his lips, letting the small, unexpected light of humor blink to life between him and Cole. "It's chafing me a good bit to sit here with you, if it's any consolation."

Cole frowned a moment before the muscles of his face eased and his chin lifted. "Then I guess we're even." He glanced over James's middle. "How's the baseball injury?"

James jerked a shoulder. "Mosquito bite."

"Guess you're as tough as you look."

James lifted a brow at the tabletop as he thought of his mother's treatment earlier that day. As he thought of digging up the past and telling the Carltons about Dusty. "No. I'm a softy."

Something close to a smile touched Cole's mouth as his eyes focused on the ceiling. "It's not so bad," he told him, "when the right one comes along."

James nodded. He stood and reached a hand to Cole as the man rose with him. "Friends?"

"Possibly," Cole said, looking as surprised as James felt. His fingers hardened on James's as they shook hands. "We'll see how you do."

THE DRIVE HOME gave James little time to go over what exactly he wanted to say to Adrian. One thing was clear. He *had* to tell her first. She'd vouched for him all those years ago. He wanted to be the one to tell her that her faith in him would finally pay off. Van's attacker would be brought to justice, even if the fact that it was Dusty who had done it hit more than a little close to home.

James parked in his driveway and walked the short distance to the cottage. She had given him a key days ago, so he went inside. It was late. Most of the lights were off. Kyle was clearly in bed and

had been for at least an hour if Adrian's strict bedtime rules were any indication. James followed
the sound of running water into the kitchen and
found Adrian washing dishes at the sink.

He watched her for a moment. In the light from
the stove, her hair looked burnished. She was taking her time, going about the chore leisurely, as if
enjoying a minute with her thoughts.

James leaned against the jamb and waited,
watching, as she finished washing the silver-
ware and set it aside to drain. She didn't hum as
she worked, as many others might. Her thoughts
were enough, it seemed. When she turned to put
another dish in the drainer to her right, he saw
her profile. There was a concentrated crease between her eyes.

He frowned. Something was weighing on her
mind. He walked to her and slowly wrapped his
arms around her waist. He felt her tense slightly
and rested his chin on top of her head so that she
would realize it was him.

Slowly, she relaxed in his arms, leaning silently
back into his embrace.

James held her a bit tighter. Yep. When it came
to Adrian, he was nothing but a big, hairy softy.
Still, he'd worked for weeks for her to trust him
completely. Her leaning into him might have
seemed simple to anyone else, but to him it meant
everything. Reaching around her, he twisted the
tap until the water shut off.

She turned her head toward him as he did so. "I wasn't expecting you."

"You're probably ready for bed."

"I was," she admitted. That bar between her eyes dug in a bit further. "It's been a hell of a day."

"Want to tell me about it?" he asked.

She placed her hands over his, rocking back into him. "Why don't you tell me about yours, instead?"

"I went to see her," James admitted.

"Who? Your mother?" she asked, eyes lighting at the possibility.

He nodded, pressed his cheek to hers. "I went with her to chemo. I thought for a minute she'd kick me out, but we talked. It was good. I stayed through it—the treatment. I held her hand."

Her lips warmed into a smile. "You did good," she whispered. "I'm proud of you. How is she now?"

"She's okay, I think," he told her. "I drove her home, fixed her a sandwich, since anything else I make is bound to turn out burned to a crisp. I left when Stephen got home. She was in bed." He'd made sure the blanket was tucked up to her chin… just as she'd done for him when he was a boy.

"And…how do you feel? Now that you've done it—taken the first step?"

James tightened his hold. "I feel like a fool for wasting so much time. But I'm in it. She's going to beat this, Adrian."

"I think so, too," she murmured. She paused briefly, then spoke. "I'm glad you're here. I wanted to see you."

"Oh, yeah?" he asked, finding a smile.

She nodded. Then she turned in his arms to wrap hers fully around him and rest her head on his chest.

For a while, they stood together, holding on, leaning into each other. Finally, he moved, touching his lips to the top of her head.

She lifted onto her toes and kissed him.

"Mmm," he said, surprised by the slow depth of the kiss. His hands tightened on her in reaction, as her palms swept from his shoulder blades down the small of his back. They went a step further, over his ass to rest just below.

He broke away. "Careful, baby," he said, hoarse. "Man like me might get the wrong idea."

She smiled, dropping back to her feet. Despite the movement of her mouth, her eyes remained serious. Taking his hand, she quietly tugged him out of the kitchen.

She led him down the hall, beyond Kyle's bedroom to a room at the back of the house he'd never seen—her room. She didn't give him time to hesitate, pulling him in after her and shutting the door quietly.

The fact that he was in her bedroom had more meaning than James could say. The last time he'd been in Adrian's bedroom—the one at The

Farm—he'd entered unannounced. Hell, he'd
climbed through the frigging window to avoid
running into either of her parents. She'd been
sleeping. He'd woken her by kissing the point of
her shoulder, once, twice…and though she had
been the one to turn to him, to pull him down to
her and happily roll him into her sheets, it wasn't
as it was now.

As she turned to him with her back to the door
and smiled quietly in the dark, his heart pounded.
His mind emptied of everything but her. He was in
her room. She'd brought him to her room and was
smiling the secret smile he'd once known so well.

That gesture alone made him ache. Closing
the distance between them, he kissed her heat-
edly, pouring the ache into her mouth as his body
pressed hers into the door. The slide from tenderness to something baser was quick and sultry.
His body bowed into the soft line of hers. The
arousal straining against the zipper of his jeans
felt as hard as a diamond. He wished he could
give her softer, sweeter. But tonight was something different, something more vital and he had
to show her…

They undressed each other. He took off her
pants and his own. She removed his shirt. He
wound her legs around his hips. He entered her
there against the door, holding her off the floor.
Even as his breath hitched and she moaned, he
kissed her, stroking. Sliding, stroking, repeating,

all the while feasting on her mouth, refusing to give up that link between them.

When her legs grew weak, slipping from his waist, he carried her to the bed. Desperate for more skin, for no barrier between them, he slipped off her shirt. As her arms linked around his neck, tugging him back to her, he dug his knees into the comforter and arched into her again. As he took and gave, their lovemaking became urgent, words grated low from his throat. "Love me. Love me."

Afterward, in the stillness, he held her so she was sprawled over his torso. Even though his arms felt weak, he kept them locked around her, unwilling to let go. No, there was no letting go. For him, there wouldn't be, ever again.

ADRIAN TRACED JAMES'S right forearm where the skin was mottled and pink, exploring the scars he carried. Her head was pillowed on his big shoulder. She could no longer hear his heart beating away at his chest like a wild thing. Still, she knew he wasn't sleeping. Though silence reigned in the aftermath of his loving, she knew without looking at him that he was just as awake as she was.

The harmony was a welcome oddity. She ran her palm over his before twining their fingers together, watching his join with hers, the distinction between his large, tanned fingers and her small ones. Tilting her head, she lifted their connected hands to the dim light filtering through the bedroom window. "Your thumb is crooked. It wasn't like that before."

"No," he said. The word came from deep in his chest. All the lazy satisfaction he felt echoed through it and she smiled.

Lowering their hands to her lips, she kissed the crooked joint, lingering for a moment before meeting his eyes, which were open and on hers. Holding his gaze, she did what he'd done a few weeks ago and gave the tip of his thumb a little nip.

The small lines at the corners of his mouth dug in. A light entered his eyes, the same she'd seen the night she first kissed him. It brightened, hardened just as it had then. Need flashed across his face. His fingers tightened on hers, readjusting so he could tug her mouth up to his. The kiss was long and deep.

He broke away. "I love you."

The words spilled out on a ragged breath. She sighed over them. "If you'd told me that eight years ago…"

"I was trying to find my moment. Pretty sure I would've found it sooner than later if I'd stayed."

"Then what?" she asked after a short pause. At his lowered brow, she added, "It still might not have worked out."

His chuckle sounded sour. "You still don't put much faith in me, do you?"

"I put a great deal more faith in you now," she admitted.

He cocked a brow, looking down as he traced the curve of her shoulder. When he remained silent, she rolled to her elbows, propping herself on them, eyeing him expectantly. "Go ahead," she said. "Tell me what would've happened if things had been different."

His face softened as he searched hers. "I wouldn't have let a day go by without you. Not because you needed me, but because I wanted— needed—you. Before I was arrested again, I was already in a place where I couldn't contemplate not being with you, and I didn't want to go back from that. I would've been damned if I hadn't found some way for us to be together. That would have been me standing with you in the church, baby or no baby. That would have been my ring on your finger."

Even as her heart leaped at the possibility, her rational, cynical mind denied it. "You can't know that, James. We were so young."

"And, most importantly," he continued, undeterred, "you would have been happy because there wouldn't have been a day go by that I wouldn't have worked myself to the bone to make you not regret a second of it."

At these words, something began to warm those defensive walls she still carried around. It strengthened, heating the stone of those walls until they began melting and the warmth penetrated the lonely, fragile place within. Her lungs strained as she searched his face once more, seeing nothing but truth.

She felt something else. The waves of warmth and light skimmed across something inside her she hadn't known was there…waiting all along. The willingness to forgive.

Rising up on her knees, she took his face in her hands. "In that case, I've got news for you, hot rocks." She spread sweet, reverent kisses from his cheeks to his brow, across the ridge of his nose to each closed lid, then over his sturdy chin and finally to his lips where they stayed for a long while. Her brow puckered with ardor and her eyes closed against the dampness behind them. She finally pulled away, only enough to say on a whispered rush, "You wouldn't have had to work that hard."

He made a sound in his throat, something caught between relief and longing. Grasping her behind the shoulders, he pulled her back down to him, into him, for another lengthy kiss, one filled with every what-might-have-been.

Eventually, he rolled her beneath him. She welcomed him to her as her hands tangled in his thick crop of hair. His fingers spread as they moved down her sides, over her hips and beneath to lift her up, against him. She opened herself to him freely and joined with him in one fluid wave.

In that moment, she, the eternal pessimist, believed that everything was right in the world—and would remain that way.

CHAPTER SEVENTEEN

WHEN ADRIAN OPENED her eyes the next morning, she was greeted by the fragile blue light that dwelled just before dawn. It was early enough that her alarm hadn't gone off. Still, something wasn't right. As she raised her head from the pillow, she saw that the other side of the bed was empty.

James was gone. She simply stared at the wrinkled, abandoned spot where he should've been. A chill went through her.

Then she heard the faint trickle of water hitting tile. Glancing over the edge of the bed, she saw the light under the closed bathroom door.

A breath washed through her and she lowered her cheek back to the pillow. He wasn't gone. He was in the shower.

A smile spread across her mouth. She felt foolish for the memory of waking up the morning after they were together in bed for the first time at The Farm and everything that had happened after.

He hadn't left her this morning. She'd forgiven him for leaving her before. Adrian was finally willing to bet that, in light of everything he'd told her about his mother and how he felt about her, she could lay her trust in his hands and keep it there.

She'd needed him last night. When she came home from the wedding reception, all she'd been able to think about was Richard's betrayal. Roxie had been thrown into upheaval. Adrian knew all too well the course she would take from heart-break in order to cope. Adrian had been there. First there was denial. Then anger, followed by months, maybe years, of cynicism when it came to all things love and commitment.

Adrian had felt guilty for smiling into her champagne for the first half of the night. In some strange twist of fate, she and Roxie had switched places—and the bitterness and pessimism wasn't something Adrian would wish on her worst enemy. Much less one of her closest friends.

Then James had showed up at her door. She'd turned to him because she'd been terrified of going back to living that way. This was all new territory for her—the hope, the trust and the wish that all would be well with her and James from here on out. But she didn't want to lose it. She didn't want to go back to being the bitter, cyni-cal Adrian.

The door to the bathroom opened quietly. With the light behind him, James stood there for a mo-ment, one of her towels wrapped around his waist. A grin spread across his lips before he reached over and turned off the light. He padded across the carpet to her side of the bed.

"Morning," he said in a lowered voice before dropping to the edge next to her.

"Good morning, yourself," she replied. When he turned his hand palm up, fingers spread, she placed hers over it. She let her palm graze back and forth over the top of his before lacing her fingers through his.

His lips lowered to her temple and he kissed her. "I like sleeping in your sheets," he murmured, a smile warming the words.

She beamed. "You might have to get used to it."

He chuckled softly, the noise reverberating over her skin. "I like the sound of that." He ran a hand over her hair. "How're you doing?"

She peered at him. "I think we both know you're not my first peccadillo, hot rocks."

His eyes were impossibly tender. "Just so long as you let me be the last."

Her heart struck up a quick beat. She watched him grin widely even as she felt her own lips curve. Twining an arm around his neck, she brought his mouth down to hers.

The phone on her bedside table rang. James groaned at the spoiled opportunity. Dipping his head to hers, he reached over and fumbled for the phone as he kissed her. When he placed the receiver in her hand, she turned her face away from his and answered. "Hello?"

"Did I wake you?"

At the sound of her father's voice, Adrian sat up, keeping a hand on the top of the sheet so that it stayed in place at her collarbone. She cleared her throat. "No, Dad. I'm awake. What's up?" Peering at the bedside clock, she wandered what Van could possibly be calling for before sunrise.

"I have some news," Van said. "It's, ah…a bit unexpected."

Adrian's brow furrowed. James had already put his fingers to good use rubbing the tension in her neck. "What is it?"

"I got a telephone call late last night from Detective Fleet," Van explained. "Remember him?"

Frowning, Adrian tried to place the name. "Fleet." As clarity struck her, she drew her knees up to her chest. Glancing back at James whose fingers had stiffened and stilled on her neck, she saw his eyes combing her face. "Wasn't that the detective who investigated the attack on you?"

"That's the one. It seems he's made an arrest."

"What?" she blurted. "How? I thought the case had gone cold."

"The attacker turned himself in. Guilty conscience or some such thing."

"Well?" she asked. "Who is it?"

"That Harbuck boy. The younger one, Dustin."

Adrian's eyes rounded. Looking over her shoulder she saw that James had sat back against her headboard, expression unreadable. "Dusty

Harbuck." She shouldn't be surprised. But how many times had she run into Dusty through the years? How many times had he and Radley had beers at the trailer? How many times had he looked her in the eye, knowing full well what he'd done? Anger burned the back of her throat. "You don't say," she added for lack of anything better.

"Seems so," Van replied. A pause wavered over the line. "Thought you ought to know before word spreads."

Adrian nodded. "Thank you for telling me. How are you handling this?"

Another pause. Then Van answered with, "I'm all right. Your mother's in a rare state, to be sure. But I've given a good deal of thought to the matter through the years. I'm glad Harbuck came clean. However, I made my peace with it a long time ago."

She licked her lips. They were as dry as her throat. "So you're okay."

Van laughed softly. "I'll keep, opossum. Don't you fret. Sorry I had to call so early."

"No," she said. "It's good that you did." Blinking against the sting behind her eyes, she added, "I love you, Daddy."

"Ditto," Van said in return. The line clicked as he hung up.

Adrian stared at the phone, brow knitting. True to form, her father was short on words. Funny how a simple "ditto" could mean more than the words themselves.

"Strange," she said finally, meeting James's grim stare. "Dusty Harbuck just turned himself in for attacking Dad."

"I heard," James said. His voice grated from deep in his chest.

As he held her gaze, she searched his. His eyes were watchful yet open. She saw a thread of remorse there in those Scandinavian blues. A confession all on its own. Her lips parted, went numb. "You knew," she said quietly.

His Adam's apple bobbed as her eyes narrowed. When he offered no reply, she scowled. "How long?" she asked, voice rising with the words.

His nostrils flared as he pulled air in. Pushing it out, he said, "Four days."

She stared at him for a moment, aghast. The anger at the back of her throat built until she tasted it. Finally disengaging her eyes from his, she arched a brow. "Well. Isn't that something?"

James straightened against the headboard. His hand closed over her shoulder. "There's an explanation."

She scoffed. "There usually is," she muttered, lowering her gaze to her hands in her lap. She felt cold. So cold.

His thumb began to massage the knots building in her neck. She shrugged until his hand fell away and then shifted, adding space between them. Enough to get her point across. "I suppose you were planning on telling me eventually," she said.

James looked pained. "If he didn't turn himself in. That was the deal. He had until the end of the weekend to come clean or I'd do it for him."

"Until the end of the weekend," she repeated, pursing her lips. "How kind."

His head tipped back slightly at the dark words as if she'd struck him. His jaw hardened but it wasn't in anger. More like resignation.

Adrian ran her tongue over her teeth. "Dusty's your buddy. My father's just the man who held you back for a summer. It doesn't exactly even out, does it?"

"Adrian," James said with a shake of his head. "It's not like that. You know it's not."

"Then tell me," she said with a jerk of her shoulders. "Go on. Tell me what I'm supposed to believe."

"I gave him four days to make it right," James told her. "That's all there was to it."

"Well, I'm so happy it can be so simple, so cut-and-dried for you," she said, and crawled out of bed.

"What are you doing?" he asked, not moving.

"I'm getting dressed," she said, picking up her scattered clothes. "I have work. Responsibilities. I don't have time for this."

He blew out a breath in disbelief. "That was fast."

"What?" she asked, wrestling her sweater over her head. "What was fast?"

"You," he said and lifted an empty hand. "Losing faith in me." He snapped his fingers. "That quick."

"Dusty Harbuck almost killed my father and you covered for him, however briefly!" she all but shouted. "What do you expect from me? A peace lily?"

James got up from the bed in a quick, deft move. He was towering over her before she knew it. "I came here last night to tell you. I got advice from Cole and then I came here, to you, because I wanted you to hear it first."

She braced her hands on her hips and said nothing.

"I gave Dusty four days to come clean because your father deserved to hear it from him, not me," James told her. "He deserved that kind of closure. But yesterday, the deadline elapsed so I planned to go to The Farm today and tell Van face-to-face with you beside me. But you don't believe that," he added before she could voice her doubt. "Because however much we've built together, however much you say you want me in your bed or your life, there's still a part of you that's holding back. And that part of you, however small, is riddled with doubt. Whatever's happened between us now, however many times you say that the past is dead, part of you hasn't let go of the betrayal you felt back in the day. And I'm starting to realize that no matter how long or hard I try, it never will. Am I right?"

"Really?" she tossed back. "You're accusing *me* when you know damn good and well that it's you on trial here?"

"I wouldn't be on trial if anything I've done over the last month meant anything to you. If you'd really started believing in me again," he pointed out. When her jaw dropped, he nodded. There was a grievous but certain gleam in his eyes. "But who can blame you, right? I'm just that guy who broke your heart. How does that ever equate to love and trust and all the things that come with it when it's real?"

As he scooped up his clothes, she frowned at the phoenix on his back. "So I'm the liar?"

"I should have seen it," he muttered, shoving a foot into his pant leg. "You were quick to leave the house after we slept together the first time. Even quicker to run when Cole accused me of transporting drugs. Now that I think about it... you've never had any faith in me. Not since I left. If this had gone down differently, if I hadn't gotten caught up in what was between us last night and had told you about Dusty, I wonder how many times I would have let *this* happen before realizing you were never mine. Not completely."

"What do you want me to do?" she asked as he shrugged his shirt over his head. "After this, you honestly expect me to see anything but your four whole days of silence?"

"No," he said as he walked back to her slowly. "And you know why? Because you might have feelings for me. You might even love me a little, but not near as much as you did eight years ago when you vouched for me. You were sound asleep when I left your room that night. You couldn't have known when I actually left. Given my history, you could've easily drawn the same conclusion your parents and everybody else had. But you didn't. Without hesitation you got in your car and drove to the police station so that I could walk free. Now ask yourself why you'd do such a thing then and why you can't do the same now."

He wanted her to make another leap of faith. A blind, reckless leap. She shook her head. "What if I don't know why?" she asked. It was a challenge. She tried desperately to hide the fearful plea behind the words. "What if I can't do it? What are you going to do about it?"

His shoulders lowered, deflating. "That's the kicker." He blew out a bitter laugh. "There's nothing I can do, is there? Except wait."

"You'd..." She blinked several times, doing her best to hold his steady gaze. "You'd do that?"

"Wait?" His eyes skimmed her features, the warmth of longing fighting against the bereft shadow in them. "Yeah. I'd wait for you."

"And what if I never..." Adrian sighed, trying

to loosen the knot in her chest. "What if I can never give you what you want?" *What if I can never give you all of me?*

James looked at some point beyond her. Defeat crossed his face and strengthened there as he rubbed his neck. "Then I guess you've got your reasons. All I can do is respect that—because I love you. I love all of you. Even that broken piece inside you that I can't seem to reach."

In the silence that followed, he stepped toward the door. "Y-you're leaving?" she stuttered.

"I'm going next door," he said, resigned, as he reached for the bedroom door. He looked back at her. "Unless you have something you want to tell me."

She didn't know how she was supposed to—not after he'd held four days of silence. Not after they spent the entire weekend together, close, and he hadn't said a word. She couldn't let that go. She didn't know how to. She shook her head, unable to summon the speech to tell him so.

It took a moment for James to grip the doorknob, turn it. Training his gaze on his feet, he scraped his knuckles over his lips with his first two fingers. "Then you know where to find me."

CHAPTER EIGHTEEN

THE SMELL OF bacon drifted up Adrian's nose as she pushed the strips around the pan. She frowned when James's face popped into her head complete with a lazy morning smile. *But I have bacon,* he'd said.

The frown deepened as Kyle said something from the table and she blinked, the bacon on the stove before her coming back into focus.

Damn it. Daydreaming again. It had been a week since James had left her bed, a week since they had spoken about their relationship. Kyle had been the only bridge between them, one where they only met halfway whenever Kyle transitioned from one parent to the other.

Things had been perfectly civil. Adrian had even somewhat learned to ignore the longing in James's eyes. Particularly at the end of any exchange when there was a long pause, during which he simply looked at her, clearly waiting for her to say what he wanted her to say.

It wasn't just about giving him the benefit of the doubt. It was the risk. Sure, she'd plunged head-first off that rocky cliff years ago without questioning him or anything else. It had been easy then...when she hadn't thought she had anything to lose.

"Mom? Are you okay?"

Adrian glanced at the table. Kyle sat with his mathematics textbook open, forgotten, in front of him. There was a pencil in his hand. He'd been chewing his lower lip, she noted. He did that when he was trying to work out a complicated problem. There was concern in his eyes and a line burrowing between them.

She worked to lift the corners of her mouth to show him things were fine. "Of course," she said. Turning her attention back to the bacon, she flipped the strips and asked, "Is there anything you want on your BLT besides bacon, lettuce and tomato?"

Kyle opened his mouth to answer but was interrupted by loud and sudden pounding on the front door.

They both froze. Kyle's head swiveled toward the entrance in the living room, then back to Adrian, his eyes wide with alarm.

"Come here," she said, dropping the fork with a clatter. He rose and rushed over to her. She wrapped her arm around his shoulders. Neither of them breathed as they waited for the pounding to come again.

Though her stomach twisted, her mind grasped for a desperate strand of hope. Maybe it wasn't who they thought it was. Maybe it was just Cole or James or…

The pounding came again. They both jumped. A voice echoed through the walls, insistent. "Aaaadriaaaan!"

"Mom," Kyle said, his hand tight on her wrist. She could hear the fear wavering through that one word.

It snapped her out of the cold, frenzied state Radley always reduced her to. Gripping both of Kyle's shoulders now, she looked at him. "Listen to me. I want you to go in your room and lock the door, just like you did the last time. Take my cell phone," she said, handing it to him from the pocket of the apron she had donned to cook bacon. "As soon as you're safe inside, call Cole and ask him to come over immediately."

"What about James?" Kyle asked. His lips trembled but he licked them as if trying to fight it.

The pounding came again. It sounded as if the door was rattling on its hinges. Adrian gave Kyle a push. "Go!" she said, guiding him from the kitchen. She watched him go down the hall, breathing a sigh of relief when she saw him enter his room without further question. Taking a deep breath, she waited for the door to close before going to the couch. Feeling in the scant space between it and the wall, she groped for the crowbar she'd hidden there after Radley's first visit.

"Adrian! Open up, you bitch, and face me!"

Gritting her teeth, she felt wildly for the cold steel. Her heart galloped in her eardrums as she pressed her cheek to the wall for better leverage.

"I've got a knife!"

"Oh, God," she said on a shuddering breath. Forgetting the crowbar, she dashed back into the kitchen. She reached for the back of the chair Kyle had been sitting in. Her damp palm fumbled over the wooden rail and the chair clattered loudly to the floor. Cursing, she picked it up and dragged it across the kitchen. Her eyes fell on the small kitchen window above the sink. She could see a light over the fence.

"James," she whispered. Yes, Kyle was right. She should call James…

First the gun, some distant voice in her head told her firmly. Radley had a knife. If he got through the door, she had little doubt he'd use it. Pushing the chair against the counter, she clambered on top of it and reached for the butt of the gun on top of the cupboard.

Just as her fingers locked onto it, the bay window over the table exploded. Adrian ducked and screamed, the BB gun falling to the counter and then onto the floor next to the brick that had shattered the glass. She looked up to see Radley climbing through.

His eyes lighted on her. They were grim and bloodshot. They were hungry for violence. His face was sheened in sweat. Perspiration soaked his shirt and he held a long buck knife.

"Come 'ere, you!" he said and lunged toward her.

The knife caught the light. She judged the distance between herself and the gun. The stove was closer. On impulse, she closed her hand over the handle of the bacon pan and swung it at him.

Bacon grease landed on him. Radley yelped as it dripped, thick, down one arm. Driven by success, Adrian took the opportunity to swing the pan up again and slam the bottom into his face.

Radley went down, hollering now in pain and rage. Empty-handed, Adrian climbed off the chair and leaped for the gun.

Fingers closed over her ankle, biting. She went sprawling. The edge of the kitchen island rose up to meet her. She twisted and the side of her rib cage connected with the granite counter before she tumbled onto the upturned chair beneath it. Her temple grazed off the point of one chair leg and her shoulder came down hard on another. She felt something crack in the area of her collarbone.

Pain, bright in intensity, filled her. A gray cast swamped her vision, blinding her momentarily as her teeth rang with pain. *Don't black out,* she willed herself. She was all that was standing between Radley and Kyle. *You will not black out.*

Choking back a whimper, gnashing her teeth as her ribs and collarbone added their own voices to the screaming inside her head, Adrian lurched across the kitchen floor on her knees and the heel of one hand until the kitchen island was between her and Radley.

He was cursing up a storm. "Damn it," he grunted. The words ran together. "Goddamn it, Adrian! If you'd've just listened to me…if you'd just listened to your husband…none of this woulda' happened."

Her lips peeled back from her teeth. "You're not my husband," she said between pained pants. She cradled her ribs, pressing her back to the island. Every move she made escalated the pain. She bit the inside of her lip to fight through it. "Husbands don't hit their wives, you trailer trash son of a bitch."

"Only whores have mouths like that," he said, closer now. She crouched at the corner and judged the distance between herself and the archway leading into the living room. "You're a whore, Adrian. That's why you left."

She shifted toward the door, ready to make a break for it. No matter how bad it hurt, she had to get to Kyle before Radley did. The toe of her shoe sent something skidding across the floor. The silver blade caught her eye.

Radley's knife. It had gone flying when she'd hit him with the pan. Her breath caught. Her hand went to it just as his fist came around the corner of the island and made a grab for her throat.

On a ragged cry, she gripped the knife handle hard and swung it toward him in an arc. It met his hand in the air.

The sound Radley made was something akin to a mauled animal. Blood poured from the wound. The knife hadn't penetrated all the way through his palm, but it was lodged there. As she scrambled away, making a break for the door, he used his other hand to pull the knife out of his hand. It clattered to the floor.

She ran for the archway. Her hand skinned the wall before his arm caught her around the waist and hauled her back. She flailed, but her ribs wrenched and she crumbled. She felt something tear as he turned her roughly to face him. His uninjured hand backhanded her in the face. She saw stars again as she fell to the floor and had to blink several times before his face came into focus above hers.

"Wives don't leave their husbands," he groaned. His breath fell over her face, sickly sweet. The stench was almost as bad as the reek of perspiration coming off him. "I don't care what the papers say. You're my wife, goddamn it, and you'll die that way."

Kicking, she almost managed to get a knee between his legs before his pressed heavily into her thigh. Arm flailing blindly to the side, she reached for something…anything. Finally, she felt something cool and warm. Metal and wood all wrapped up in one. The Winchester. She looked him in the eye, wanting the message to ring clear as she fought against the tidal wave of pain thundering down on her. She lifted the gun. "Get out of my house!"

She brought the butt of the gun down. He looked up at the last second. He jerked away and the blow skimmed the top of his head. Hissing, he gripped both her arms in a bruising hold and pinned them over her head. The pain in her torso reached the tipping point and she gasped, sobbed. The gun was useless in her hands.

Close above her now, he sneered in a twisted smile that chilled her to the bone. *He'll kill me,* she thought.

She saw his head come down to meet her in a head butt. Again, colors flashed behind her eyes. She swam through gray again, then white before a puke shade of green took over. "No," she muttered. "No, no, no…" Fighting to stay conscious, she thought about Kyle. Cole would be here any minute, right? Then Kyle would be safe and she could slip down into that milky-green fog and disappear for a while into a place without Radley.

Suddenly, Radley's weight lifted. She heard something other than his voice. A vicious growl that sounded like something wild. Rolling to her side, folding her arms over her ribs, she looked blearily through the haze clouding her vision.

The sight that came into soft focus made her heart stutter. James. His movements seemed slug-

gish. But then again, she was. Still, the fist that he
hammered into Radley over and over had no less
force in slow motion. She watched Radley's head
snap back again and again. Blood flew. Blood.
There was blood everywhere. She didn't know if
it was Radley's or hers or…

On a surge of towering strength, James let out
a roar, picked Radley up and heaved him into the
upturned table. Adrian jumped, the noise breaking
apart in her ears, deafening, whereas before it had
seemed dulled. As if she'd been underwater and
the sounds were carrying to her from the surface.

Cringing, she shrank against the wall behind
her. The look on James's face… She'd never seen
him look so enraged. So savage. He picked up
a chair and tossed it Radley's way. It splintered.
She cried out as he went for Radley again, a fist
coming down to meet Radley's marred face. She
got a hurried glimpse of James's knuckles. They
were bloody, split so that Radley's blood mingled
with James's…

She was sobbing when Cole finally barreled in.
He grabbed James by the shoulders and hauled
him back. James fought against his hold but Cole
locked his arm around James's throat. "Enough!"
Cole shouted in his ear.

"No!" James yelled, trying to throw Cole off
again.

"Look at him, for Christ's sake!" Cole demanded. "Much more and you'll kill him!"

"I know," James replied, breathing hard. He reached up to brush the back of his hand over his mouth. Blood smeared there. At that moment, his head turned and his eyes, wild and fierce, locked on hers.

Adrian cowered back against the wall. Little whimpers and cries were tearing out of her—she couldn't stop them. Her pulse was clouding her head. It felt like an insistent, tinny bell and it rang and rang until her head pounded with it. All the while, James looked at her and his eyes went from violent to blank, then shocked and fearful before softness took over. "Adrian…" he said in a choked voice. "Baby…" He took a step toward her.

She saw the blood on his hands and face and flinched. He came up short, alarm, hurt and dread slackening his features. She told herself not to be afraid. He'd taken care of Radley. He'd saved her. But whatever had taken over her, whatever was causing her to shake so badly she thought her ribs would splinter, had too hard a hold. She could do nothing but shrink into a protective ball and close her eyes against the mess that was her kitchen and the helpless expression that had consumed James's face.

That fog seemed like a safe place now. She heard Cole's voice, felt him near but she sank deeper into the fog. The further down she sank the more the pain and fear numbed, so she swam into it until the green and gray faded to black and she felt nothing. Nothing at all.

JAMES PACED THE waiting room in the ER. Several people tried to stop him. Briar implored him to sit and steady himself, but he couldn't stop. He had to move or else he'd fly apart at the seams or succumb to every desperate thought blazing through his brain. Adrian's screams. Adrian's limp form underneath Kennard's. Adrian's blatant, fearful cringe when James had tried to comfort her…

His heart knocked hard against his throat. He scrubbed a hand through his hair. He'd felt that look like a blow to the chest. It had gutted him. All that was keeping him from going to pieces right now was the fact that Kyle was sitting with Van and Edith in the corner. The kid was doing his best to hold himself together as the wait stretched into an hour and a half.

James owed him just as much. With his bloody hands and clothes, he was hardly a comfort. Several other people waiting had sent him wary glances. Olivia had all but ordered him to sit down and rest when she arrived. He ignored her, too. Cole at one point tried to wrestle him into a chair. Still, he continued pacing restlessly, like a caged tiger, until the sliding doors opened and his mother and Stephen walked in.

As he stopped and stared, Mavis spotted him,

scanned him, then made her way over. "Come," she said, taking him by the hand.

"But—" James began.

"No buts," she said sternly. "Just come."

She led James back into the white halls of the hospital until she found an empty exam room. "Sit," she said, jerking her head toward the bed. When he failed to comply, she arched a brow.

James heaved a sigh and went to the bed. He felt brittle. The numbness that pacing had brought was slipping away and he was starting to feel everything. His split knuckles. The pounding in his head. The desperation that threatened to go on a tear inside him if he didn't soon get the news that Adrian was okay. Scooting back onto the crackling paper surface, he shifted as Mavis brought forth a bandage and cleaning supplies. "Mom…" he began to protest.

"I don't want to hear it," she said.

James wondered how she managed to sound so sharp and gentle at the same time. He frowned when she handed him a wet cloth. "What's this for?"

"Clean your face," she told him.

Confused, he swiped the cleaning cloth over his features. When he pulled it away, he saw the blood. Suddenly, the looks from the people in the waiting room made sense. As he continued to wipe away the evidence of violence from his face, Mavis's smooth, narrow hands went to work cleaning his free hand and he made no bones about it as she peeled away the layers of dried blood. He felt a sting behind his eyes and cursed.

Her hands kept working and her gaze didn't stray to his, but she said in as gentle a tone as she could manage, "You're shaking."

Looking down, he saw the quiver in his hands and fisted them. She tutted and he winced when his knuckles split again.

As she finished cleaning and bandaging him up, the shaking worsened. He could feel it worming its way down into the marrow of his bones. He had no control over the tremors. And as she disposed of the adhesive strips and cleaning supplies, he felt the sting behind his eyes worsen, too. He muttered an oath, reaching a bandaged hand up to his face.

Mavis's arms lifted around him. He didn't question the embrace. He simply folded himself into her arms as the emotions he'd been fighting took hold and he crumbled like a dry leaf. She said nothing as his breath hitched and his shoulders heaved.

He'd been too late. When Kyle came flying into his house to tell him he'd snuck out of his bedroom window because Radley had broken in and was going after his mother, James hadn't thought. He'd told Kyle to lock the door behind him and had gone running, armed with nothing but his fists.

He'd heard the screams from outside, both from Adrian and Kennard. He'd seen the broken window and had gone charging through what was left of it. The sight of her on the floor beneath the big bastard, white as a ghost and unmoving, had stopped James in his tracks for a moment. He'd thought she was dead. After the crippling thought had crept through, a red haze had taken over.

He'd had every intention of killing Radley before Cole pulled him off. Before he saw that Adrian wasn't dead. The look on her face had killed him because he'd seen the glazed fear coating her expression and had known that something inside her had shattered, snapped.

A knock clattered against the door. James and Mavis broke apart to see Van standing in the door. His gaze locked with James's, stilled.

James reached up quickly to wipe his forearm over his face. It was wet. The sleeve of his shirt was no match for the mess that tears had made. Before he could speak, Van held up a hand. "I came to tell you the doctor's got some news for us," he said. "Thought you'd want to be there when he gave it."

James dropped off the table. Taking his mother's hand, he followed Van back to the waiting room. "Dr. Irvington," Van said quietly in greeting to Mavis.

"Van," she replied softly as they walked. "How serious is it?"

"I couldn't tell from the look of Radley," Van replied. "And I haven't seen Adrian." He glanced at James who *had* seen her.

James gulped. He couldn't find his voice so he dropped his eyes to the floor.

A hard hand came up to his shoulder, squeezed. It remained there the rest of the way back to the ER.

There, they found Edith and Kyle, Briar and Cole, Olivia, Stephen and—another surprise—Byron. They were standing around a small, gray-haired man in blue scrubs. Though the doctor looked unflappable, James could see that the others were all but harassing him for information about Adrian's condition. When he turned to find James, Van and Mavis approaching, he looked more than a little relieved.

Mavis dipped her head to him. "Dr. Jones."

"Dr. Irvington," he replied. His eyes shifted to Van. "You're the young lady's father?"

"Yes," Van said. "What's the news?"

The doctor eyed the large group. "It would probably be better if we spoke in private."

James began to protest but Cole muttered "Like hell" before he could. Mavis raised her voice so Dr. Jones could hear her clearly. "In this case, I think it would be best to break it to the whole family."

"Damn right," Olivia agreed.

Dr. Jones cleared his throat. "We did some

scans and it appears that Ms. Carlton is suffering from a concussion. I'm happy to say that she has regained consciousness and there appears to be no other trauma to her head."

James breathed a sigh of relief. Kyle edged closer to him. He wound his arm around the boy's shoulders, pulling him close.

"However," Dr. Jones continued, "X-rays show that she sustained other injuries. She has a broken rib on the left side. Thankfully, it doesn't appear to be in danger of puncturing her lung. She also has a broken clavicle."

"God Almighty," Edith murmured.

James winced. He'd tightened his hold on Kyle. Relaxing it, he inhaled slowly to calm the storm building steadily inside him.

It was Briar who spoke first. "What can we do?"

Jones raised an eyebrow as he looked around at the expectant faces surrounding him. "We'll keep her under observation for the night, just to make sure there's no further damage. She needs plenty of rest. Unfortunately, there isn't a lot that can cure the injuries except time and rest. Her arm will be put in a sling so that the collarbone can heal properly, but she'll feel the injuries for anywhere between eight to twelve weeks. Over-the-counter pain medication can be used to ease the discomfort."

Mavis nodded when James looked at her to

confirm this. "He's right," she said. "Thank you, Dr. Jones. If she is conscious and stable, I think it would be a good idea for her to at least see her son."

Dr. Jones looked at Kyle's pleading expression and nodded after a moment's hesitation. "I'll allow that. He can be accompanied by one adult. Does he have a guardian?"

Van glanced at James. Before he could speak, Edith did. "I'll go with him. I'm his grandmother."

James opened his mouth to argue but Mavis shook her head and he subsided. He watched Edith take Kyle by the hand and follow the doctor out of the waiting room.

"What about Kennard?" Byron asked. His gaze locked on James before dropping to his bandaged knuckles. "Please tell me you stoved the bastard's skull in."

"He's alive," Cole said grimly. "But he won't be up on his feet for a while. And when he is, there'll be a nice prison cell waiting for him. There's no way he can talk his way out of this one. He's done with civilian life."

As Byron made an agreeing noise, James remained silent. Briar walked over and hugged him. "How are you doing?"

James cleared his throat so that his voice rang clear. "It's her you need to be thinking about, not me."

"I am," Briar told him. "But you were there. And you love her."

James didn't argue with that.

Briar pulled away. "I was wondering if you'd like to come to the inn tonight with the others to wait for more news."

"No," he said. "I think I'll stay here."

"James, it's late," Briar told him. "Edith's bringing Kyle. There's a room for you at Hanna's. And in the morning we'll all be able to visit."

The terror James had seen on Adrian's face at the cottage filled his head once more. He wouldn't be visiting. He wouldn't see her unless she asked for him. "I'll stay here with Van," he said again, quietly.

Briar scanned his face. When he looked down at the tiles at his feet, she rubbed a hand over his arm, soothing. "Let us know if you change your mind," she said.

Mavis waited until Briar and Cole had walked off to speak with Olivia before turning to him. "I should go."

James looked at her. Her skin was pale. Damn it, he hadn't thought to ask how she was feeling. "Are you okay?" he asked, gripping her hand.

"I'm fine," she said with a smile that was somewhat convincing. "If there's anything we can do for the Carltons or you, you call us, James."

"Thanks, but you need to go home and rest," he told her.

Her brow arched. "Don't patronize me. And that wasn't a request. It was an order. Understand?"

He released a breath before nodding. "You didn't have to come."

Her expression softened greatly as she scanned his face. "Yes, I did." Lifting herself up on her toes, she pecked a kiss on his cheek. "Try and get some sleep."

"Yes, ma'am," he muttered, knowing full well he wouldn't. He nodded to Stephen as the man wound an arm around Mavis's waist and steered her toward the exit. James slid his hands into his pockets as he watched them depart. Then, finally, he lowered into the nearest chair to wait.

CHAPTER NINETEEN

ADRIAN WISHED FOR a lot of things over the next few days. She wished it didn't hurt every time she moved her torso. She wished it didn't pain her when she breathed. She wished she could cure the worry on her son's face.

But, perhaps most especially, she wished her mother would leave her alone.

"That pain medication is making you awfully cranky," Edith commented as she escorted both Kyle and Adrian home for the first time since the accident.

"They're over-the-counter drugs," Adrian muttered. "They're not known to be mood killers." *But I know something that is.* Biting her tongue as she had for the last day and a half, Adrian looked around her home.

The house had been cleaned. The bay window had been boarded up until the panes could be replaced. There were casseroles in the refrigerator from Briar and a high-priced bottle of Jameson's sitting on the kitchen counter with a ribbon around the neck from Olivia. It didn't take her long to locate the gift basket filled with lotions, bath salts and essential oils from Roxie.

"Wasn't it nice of Byron to drive us home?" Edith asked. "He didn't have to go out of his way like that. Did you thank him?"

"Yes, Mom," Adrian said. Because the pain was starting to edge back in, she lowered herself into an armchair in the living room and did her best not to move. Reaching up, she readjusted the sling, which was chafing against her neck.

Kyle appeared with a mug. "I thought you'd want some hot chocolate."

A smile touched Adrian's mouth. "You didn't have to do that."

He lifted a shoulder. "You always make me hot chocolate. You know? When I don't feel well?" He nudged the mug toward her.

"Yes," she said, taking it in her hand. When he hovered, she patted the arm of the chair.

Kyle sat and leaned over so that his cheek rested on top of her head, careful to keep his shoulder from nudging her arm and jarring her collarbone or ribs. For a moment, they sat together in the quiet of their home. Adrian closed her eyes. The scent of hot chocolate steaming up from the surface of the mug soothed her enough that she could almost convince herself everything was as it should be. Just a normal evening at home...

"Van, open up those blinds and let in some of

that light," Edith ordered. "Vampires could camp in here as it is."

Adrian shoveled a sigh out of her nose and lifted the mug to her lips. "Happy homecoming," she murmured before taking a sip.

"Why do you use bamboo blinds, Adrian?" Edith chastised as she watched her husband open the blinds in the living room. "Don't the regular, plastic ones let in more light?"

"It's an aesthetic choice," Adrian told her.

"A what?"

"An aesthetic…" When Edith only narrowed her eyes, Adrian shook her head, lifting the hot chocolate for another long sip. "Never mind."

"Have you thought about work?" Edith asked. "Who's going to take care of the shop? You're not closing up for a week, are you? Because that's at least how long it'll take for you to get back at it. You do realize that."

"Yes, I realize that," Adrian replied. "And no, I'm not closing. Penny's perfectly capable of handling customers. And I talked to Barb who worked for me for a few years before she had her second baby. She agreed to come in until I'm back on my feet. I'm not worried about the shop."

"What about Kyle? How is he going to get to school?"

Van spoke up finally. "I'm taking him."

"You?" Edith asked, eyeing him doubtfully.

"Yes," Van said. "I drive. I can get the boy to school just fine."

Edith frowned. "Maybe Byron could—"

"Byron works," Adrian pointed out before her mother could go there. "It's tax season. He's an accountant. He's going to be tied to his desk until mid-April." There was no way she was burdening Byron again. He'd done enough. And it would make Edith way too happy to know Adrian had called on him.

"Well, you're going to have to let go of your pride enough to let someone make you dinner for the next few nights," Edith continued.

"Look in the fridge, Mom," Adrian said. "Briar's clearly done it all for me. All I need to do is preheat the oven and start the timer."

Edith thought it over. Finally, she heaved a defeated breath. "I could stay, I suppose."

"No," Adrian said firmly. "We're fine. Some peace and quiet will do us good, trust me."

Edith's gaze sharpened. "Is that your way of telling me my presence isn't welcome?"

"That's my way of telling you that I'd like to be alone at home with my son for *one* night," Adrian said, her bad mood rising. "There's nothing to worry about. Not for the next twenty-four hours at least. We can take care of ourselves and we could both do with a little normalcy."

"It won't be normal," Edith warned. "You'll heal. You might be able to forget the whole ordeal down the road. But the neighbors, they won't stop talking. The town won't stop talking. People I go to church with every Sunday certainly won't stop asking about it."

"I'm sorry for your inconvenience," Adrian groaned, pressing two fingers to her temple. She had a headache brewing, in addition to the sharp pang in her ribs as she took a deep breath that should have helped calm her.

It wasn't working.

"What am I supposed to tell everyone?" Edith said, pressing a hand to her head as if the thought of facing her fellow churchgoers overwhelmed her. "That this is just the latest episode in the great Greek tragedy that is your life?"

"Mom!" Adrian shrieked, so loud that it echoed into the next room. "Stop talking! Just stop!"

Edith froze, startled. Kyle stiffened beside Adrian as the tension in the room came to a knife-point. She gripped the small hand that sought hers and fought to lower her voice. "For once," she said to Edith, "could you not be yourself?" When Edith's jaw dropped, Adrian set aside the mug and lifted her hand to stop her from replying. "I realize that I've disappointed you. I realize that my whole life has been a disappointment to you. But right now, I'm tired. I'm so freaking tired. Is it too much for me to ask my mother for one day without a guilt trip, without having to hear about my *peccadillos*? One day where my son doesn't have to hear two of the people that he loves most in the world bickering at each other like children?"

Edith stared at her, aghast. Her lips firmed together. "You're the one who raised your voice."

"Uh," Adrian groaned, exasperated. "Yes, yes. It's my fault. It's all my fault. Can we fast forward to the part where you leave me alone?"

"Edith," Van said. His voice was surprisingly gentle. When his wife's attention turned to him, he tilted his head toward the door. "Why don't you take Kyle for a little walk? The fresh air will do you both some good."

Edith hesitated. After a moment, Kyle rose and went to her, taking her by the arm. "Come on, Grandmama. You should meet my friend Blaze down the street. He's a piece of work and his folks say grace at dinner sometimes. You'll like him."

As Kyle led Edith out, Van opened the door, placing a hand on the small of his wife's back to usher her through. Edith sent him a long, cool look. The hand dropped and balled at Van's side before he closed the door behind them. Then he turned back to Adrian, his bushy silver-tinged brows raised.

She shook her head. "I'm not apologizing."

Van's mouth twisted into something of a smile. "Waiting for either of you to apologize is like waiting for a deluge in a drought." Lowering himself to the couch, he placed his hands on his knees and leaned toward her. "Ain't much point in that."

"How do you do it?" Adrian asked, at a complete loss. "You put up with it every day. How in God's name do you do it, Daddy?"

Van's face fell. "I'm no saint."

"Yes, you are," she said quietly. "You're the best man I know."

Van winced. "No, girl. I'm not."

Adrian frowned. "Living with that for thirty years pretty much qualifies you for martyrdom."

"There's a reason your mother is the way she is," Van told her. "And it's all to do with me."

"What are you talking about?" she asked.

Van lowered his gaze to the work boots he always seemed to wear. "We used to be happy. Your mother used to be different. There was a time nothing could bring her down. She was rosy cheeked and had a glow about her. She laughed easily, and she looked at me with all the love and admiration anybody could ever wish for."

He took a deep breath and continued. "Then I did something wrong. It was only a few months after you were born. I was out of town alone for an exhibition. While I was away, I slept with someone else, someone from my past."

Adrian's jaw dropped. "You..." She swallowed, not quite able to take it in. "You cheated on Mom?"

"Yes." He nodded, eyes still turned downward. He reached underneath the brim of his battered ball cap and scratched his forehead. "When I got home, I came clean with Edith. I told her everything. She was devastated, as you'd expect. I told her I'd do anything to earn her forgiveness. I'd wait as long as it took, if that's what she wanted. If she wanted to turn me out, I'd go. The ball was in her court. She chose to let me stay.

"But things weren't the same. I understood. I deserved to be treated the way she did, the way she still does. But as you started to grow, it became clear that you took after me more than her. You were reckless, impulsive. You made more questionable decisions than good ones, at least to her way of thinking. She saw a great deal of me in you, and it scared her." Van's gaze finally rose to Adrian's. "Are you starting to understand?"

Adrian shook her head. "She treats me the way she does because of what you did twentysomething years ago? That's not right, Daddy."

Van shrugged. "I'm not the judge of what's right and wrong, especially when I'm the one who's done wrong. You need to know, though, that your mother's bitterness has nothing to do with you. It's me she can't forgive. Your man, James, wasn't far from the truth the other night. My betrayal worked much like a poison in her veins and it's only spread through the years—so much so that it affects her behavior toward you."

"She could've left," Adrian thought aloud. "She could have found somebody else. She would have been happier. We all might have been happier."

"She stayed married to me because she wanted to punish me every day for the rest of my life. She knew I'd never leave her, just as she knew she'd never forgive me. The point of all this is that I'm not a saint and you've done nothing to deserve the way she treats you. It's me who disappointed her, not you."

Adrian's head was spinning. She massaged her temples, not knowing what to think of all this. Worse, she didn't know what to think of her father anymore—this man, her hero. "You probably should have told me this sooner," Adrian said.

"I'll give you that," Van acknowledged. "I was selfish. You looked at me the way she used to. I won't lie and say that didn't get me through some of the worst times." He straightened and got slowly to his feet. "But now you know. You've always had a right to know."

She licked her lips as her brows came together. She didn't know what to say anymore. Yes, her father had done wrong. But Adrian couldn't help but think that twentysomething years was a long time to hold a grudge against the person you love—or had loved, once.

She swallowed when the parallels hit her. Only, for the first time in her life, Adrian found herself in her mother's shoes…eight years ago when the person she loved had left her. That broken piece inside her hadn't been able to forget, even if she'd thought she'd been able to forgive. How could she tell her mother to forgive her father when she hadn't done the same for James?

"You're thinking about that boy, aren't you?"

Adrian looked up at Van, startled, and shook her head automatically.

Van let out a short chuckle. "He's all over your face." He reached down to give her cheek a fond pinch. "Maybe it's not my place—particularly in light of what happened between your mother and me—but you've gotta admit that what he did, what you're holding against him, is a whole lot more forgivable than what I did."

Adrian remained silent, studying some point on the wall behind her father.

He sighed. "Think of it this way. Will you forgive me, eventually?"

Her eyes veered up to his. She searched his face. Those gentle eyes, sober but no less adoring. She saw the lines there, the silver brows. It wasn't just from age, she knew now. It was from waiting, enduring, all these years. After a moment's hesitation, without a word, she reached for his hand.

His fingers tightened around hers. They held on for a minute, two. Then he leaned down and touched his lips to her head. "We'll get out of your hair."

Adrian listened as he walked to the door. Then she called, "Daddy?"

"Yes, opossum?"

Unable to turn around and face him because of

the strain on her collarbone and ribs, she closed her eyes and imagined his face. "Thank you," she said simply.

THE AIRFIELD WAS light on traffic. James had chosen it as the place to store his airplane because it was more private and further removed from the other airports that dotted the Alabama coastline.

He'd needed an afternoon to take the Cessna out. It had been a long time since he'd flown. When he'd brought Kyle to the airfield weeks ago, he'd let the kid drive the plane around the tarmac. He hadn't been able to go so far as to let him take off—that would come later when they were both ready.

It struck James as he soared above the coastline that he'd never flown over the beach before. He kept the Cessna out until the sun had almost sunk below the western horizon before pointing the nose back to the airfield and taking it in for a landing.

As he did his postflight check on all the gauges, James wished he'd taken off work an hour earlier so that he could've spend more time in the air. But the garage had been slammed. He'd had to hire an apprentice as well as a new tow truck driver. He would have to hire someone to answer phones. Bracken Mechanics was booming.

He was happy for it. The immediate success wasn't something he had expected. The garage had just been a pet venture, a dream he'd only had hope of getting off the ground.

Now that the business was up and running, James hardly had time for a sigh of relief. He was pleased with the work. It kept him busy.

Not busy enough, however. He hadn't slept a full night in two weeks. Not since Kyle came rushing up to the door of his house to tell him that Radley had broken into the cottage. The sick taste in the back of his throat hadn't faded, either. In quiet moments, thoughts of what could have been haunted him.

He couldn't sleep without her. He couldn't sleep knowing she was next door alone and hurting still. Although he'd waited, not once had she called on him for help. He'd seen Briar, Olivia, Roxie, Cole, Van, Edith and even Byron all stop by in a never-ending wave of visitors. He'd waited for the phone to ring. He'd all but stalked Cole and Briar for news of her. But he'd heard nothing.

He'd spent the weekends with Kyle after Adrian went back to work. They had been a short reprieve from the quiet, the waiting. He was grateful for the bond that was still allowed to exist between him and his son. But when it came time for Kyle to go home, he waited for her to come out of the cottage, to meet them halfway as she had done before the incident.

Nothing. The hole inside him burned. Today at the garage, he hadn't been able to contemplate going back to the house to wait in silence, so he'd driven to the airfield. He'd taken the Cessna out so that maybe for a little while he wouldn't have to think about that hole inside him.

It had worked, somewhat. Until he landed, of course, and was dreading the drive back to his empty house.

"So it's true," someone behind him said. "You do have a plane."

James turned, shocked to hear the voice. Adrian stood several yards away, eyeing him and the plane in surprise. It took a moment for him to find words. She looked normal. There were no longer marks on her face. She wasn't wearing the sling he knew the doctor had instructed her to use. She was wearing jeans and a light T-shirt. Perfectly normal.

Still, his throat burned much as that hole in him did, and it took a great deal of effort to stay rooted to the spot and not go to her—throw his arms around her, hold her and feel her so that he could assure himself that she was whole. That she had recovered. She was safe. "What are you doing here?" he asked. His voice sounded like a froggy croak.

She spread her hands to encompass the plane, ignoring his question. "Did you win this, too? In poker?"

James frowned, lifting his hand to the back of his neck to keep from reaching for her. He turned, glanced over the tail section of the plane and shrugged. "Not exactly. It was my first trip to Atlantic City and after a while it was just me and this bigwig sitting at a card table. Finally, he threw the Cessna into the mix and said, 'High card draw.' He pulled a king, I turned over an ace."

She raised a brow. "It's a Cessna."

"Well, yeah," he said. He studied her, perplexed. Why did she look so surprised? He thought he saw her eyes dive over his hips before they pinged away and she cleared her throat, shifting her feet.

"Huh," she replied. James watched her feet shuffle again. She looked off balance, as though she was suddenly rethinking being here with him.

Before she could think about retreating, he asked again, "Why are you here, Adrian?"

She lifted her shoulders after a moment's contemplation. "Hoyt, that new guy you've got working at the garage, he said you'd be here. So here I am."

He looked at her again, a good, long, lingering look. "Yep," he said. "Here you are."

"I figure we should talk," she went on quickly, dislodging herself from his stare. She walked to the plane's wing, pausing before lifting her hand to the white surface. "Again."

Knowing just how well their last talk had gone, he braced himself. When Adrian said they needed to talk, things happened. They either took a long step forward or a long step back. "About?" he asked.

She looked around the airfield. "Is there someplace we can go?"

He lifted his hand to the passenger door of the Cessna. When she only arched a brow, he tried smiling. "This is about as comfy as we're going to get here."

She considered, then walked to the door. He beat her there, opening it for her. He held out a hand to help her into the cockpit. She ignored it, pulling herself in by the handle above the door. He saw the quick flash of pain on her face and fought a curse. He walked around to the other door and boosted himself in. There was a gentle breeze over the airfield so he left both doors open.

"It's nice," she said, after a moment.

"Yeah," he said simply in reply.

"Do you take it up often?" she asked as another awkward lull drifted between them.

"Not as much as I'd like. You wanna?"

She turned to him, alarmed. "Now?"

"Why not?" he asked, trying to smile again. The muscles of his face wouldn't quite make it work.

"I don't think so," she said with a shake of her head. "Dad took me up once in the crop duster. Scared the bejesus out of me."

"I thought you were fearless," he said, then

cursed inwardly when the words echoed back to him.

She thought about that. "The old me was."

They dissolved deep down into another awkward silence. After what seemed like an eternity, she said in a lowered voice, "I never got around to thanking you."

"Don't. Don't go there, Adrian."

"Let me say this," she demanded. "I've been thinking a lot about it. Not just about what you did for me but also…what you did to him. In that moment, I…" She trailed off, took a careful breath. "I guess what I'm trying to say is that I'm grateful for what you did to Radley. He's never coming back. I'm okay and I'm free of him now. And it's all because of you." She looked at James. "I distanced myself from you. I saw the blood on you, his blood, and…something inside me turned away. I shouldn't have turned away from you."

The words grated at him, at all the guilty, remorseful pieces he'd been wrestling with since that night. "Don't apologize, Adrian. You don't owe me any apology. I wanted to kill him." He finally met her gaze, wanting to make her understand. "I would have killed the bastard. I fully intended to kill him, and if it hadn't been for Cole, I would have."

Her throat moved on a swallow. "But…it was to protect me. Kyle and me both."

He saw the earnest light in her eyes and

looked away again. It took a while for him to find the words to say. "When I saw you lying there…broken. You looked broken. For a minute, I thought…" He had to swallow several times, pausing to work his emotions back. "I thought you were dead. There was so much blood. Some of it was his." He reached up, scrubbed two fingers over his mouth. "You gave him a hell of a fight, sweetheart. But when I saw you, you weren't moving and you had blood on you. Your skin was like glass…"

He trailed off, unable to articulate the ruin he'd felt in that moment. "For weeks, I've relived that over and over and over again. I've been burned. I've been branded. I've been beaten. I've gone out of my mind. But, in that moment, Adrian…"

As he lost his voice, he sucked in a breath. There was something bubbling up his throat. It felt a lot like what he'd felt in the exam room when his mother had cleaned him up.

He couldn't break down in front of her. She didn't deserve to see that.

Her hand touched his. In the low light of the cockpit, he watched her fingers stroke the back of his knuckles, the same ones that had pounded at Kennard's face. Gingerly, she soothed skin where memories of the beating still ran deep. James stilled, watching her. It was the first time they had touched in…he couldn't think how long. He didn't want to think. He cursed. "That monster never would've been a part of your life if I'd stayed by your side eight years ago," he said. His voice shook but he talked through it. "I'm sorry for a lot of things, baby. But that…I'm having a hard time living with that one."

She touched his face. James lifted his gaze to hers, hoping very much his wasn't wet.

"I'm going to tell you something," she whispered. "Something I've come to understand over the last few weeks. I want you to listen, and listen carefully, because you need to hear it and believe it." Her eyes lowered to his mouth, scanned it for a moment as she gathered herself, then she looked him in the eye again and said firmly, fervently, "I forgive you."

When he started to look away, she stopped him, cupping his face in both hands. "I forgive you, James. For everything. I forgive you for leaving. I forgive you for not being there for me or Kyle. There's no need for me to forgive you for everything with Radley because that was my decision. He was my choice, not yours. I forgive you for coming back into my life when I didn't want you. I forgive you for Dusty. And, most importantly, I forgive you for making me fall in love with you again. Because, aside from the child we made together all those years ago, that's been the miracle of my life—finding the courage to fall in love with you *all over again*."

As it slowly began to sink in, James couldn't help but look at her. Just look.

"Now," she continued, "you need to forgive yourself. Because you deserve that. We both deserve the right to be able to move on with our lives."

He let loose a sigh. Letting his eyes close, he nodded slowly.

"Good," she said and kissed him.

He made a noise in his throat in surprise. When she pulled away seconds later, it took him a moment to catch up. "You're not...you're not saying goodbye," he realized.

She let out a laughing sob. "No, you idiot. I'm trying to tell you that I want you to come home. The three of us...I want us to be a family. I want you to be there when Kyle wakes up in the morning—not just tomorrow morning but every morning for the rest of his life. And I don't want to go to bed one more night without you beside me. I want us to have a thousand breakfasts and dinners together. I want to argue over what movie to watch on Friday nights, how much butter to put on the popcorn.

"James, I'm tired of living without you. You're my first love, my only love. I don't give my heart easily, but I gave it to you—on the night we first kissed and then again when you stood in my kitchen and told me you were there for me. You told me that you came back to Fairhope so that maybe you'd remember what it was like to have a home worth coming back to again. So I'm telling you—it's here. It's time. Come home."

"Yeah," he agreed without hesitation, smearing the tears on her cheeks and smiling wider than he thought he could. Lowering his mouth to hers, he gave her a quick, hard kiss. Then another. "God, yes, I'll come home to you, woman. And you can throw away the key once I'm there."

"No, that's just the point," she insisted. "You *have* the key. It's yours. Go wherever it is you need to go…just so long as you come back to us."

"Adrian, baby, why would I go anywhere when all I want, all I've ever needed, is right here?"

She tipped her head to his shoulder and he held her. They stayed that way as the light began to disappear from the sky. Content. Dear God Almighty, this was what contentment felt like. He closed his eyes, savored it, then spread his hand over the nape of her neck, touching words to the hair over her ear. "I will never leave you again," he whispered. "You hear me? I'm not going anywhere. I love you. I've always, always loved you."

She lifted her face back to his, lifting her fingers to trace the nautical star on his throat. "Marry me?"

He cursed. "Now wait a minute. I was about to ask *you* to marry *me*."

"I can't help it if you're slow," she said, a teasing light entering her eyes.

James laughed. "Would you let me ask?"

She squirmed a bit, impatient, but smiled nonetheless. "All right. But make it quick. This has been a long time coming."

"Damn right." His mouth hovered above hers as he grew serious. "When I came back, I came looking for home, but I wouldn't have bet big on finding it. Not only have you given me that, you saved me. You forgave me and you saved me. A lifetime won't be enough to thank you for that, but it's a start. So, Adrian Carlton, will you belong to me? Because I want nothing more than to belong to you every day for the rest of our lives."

"Yes," she told him. "Yes, James Bracken—I will marry you."

"Thank God." Swallowing her laugh, he kissed her, lingering this time.

They got swept away in it. His hands spread in her hair as she hummed, tilting her head so he could delve deeper.

He pulled away quickly, letting their mouths part. "Wait a minute—you don't like butter on your popcorn?" he asked, shocked.

She groaned, gripping the lapel of his shirt and bringing his mouth back down to hers. "Shut up and kiss me, hot rocks."

"Yes, ma'am," he murmured, grinning, and kissed her once more with everything in him.

* * * * *

LARGER-PRINT BOOKS!
GET 2 FREE LARGER-PRINT NOVELS PLUS
2 FREE GIFTS!

HARLEQUIN®

Romance

From the Heart, For the Heart

LARGER-PRINT BOOKS!

HARLEQUIN

Presents®

GET 2 FREE LARGER-PRINT NOVELS PLUS 2 FREE GIFTS!

PASSION GUARANTEED SEDUCTION

LARGER-PRINT BOOKS!
GET 2 FREE LARGER-PRINT NOVELS PLUS
2 FREE GIFTS!

H HARLEQUIN®

I N T R I G U E
BREATHTAKING ROMANTIC SUSPENSE

YES! Please send me 2 FREE LARGER-PRINT Harlequin® Intrigue novels and my 2 FREE gifts (gifts are worth about $10). After receiving them, if I don't wish to receive any more books, I can return the shipping statement marked "cancel." If I don't cancel, I will receive 6 brand-new novels every month and be billed just $5.49 per book in the U.S. or $6.24 per book in Canada. That's a saving of at least 11% off the cover price! It's quite a bargain! Shipping and handling is just 50¢ per book in the U.S. and 75¢ per book in Canada.* I understand that accepting the 2 free books and gifts places me under no obligation to buy anything. I can always return a shipment and cancel at any time, Even if I never buy another book, the two free books and gifts are mine to keep forever.

199/399 HDN GHWN

Name	(PLEASE PRINT)

Address	Apt. #

City	State/Prov.	Zip/Postal Code

Signature (if under 18, a parent or guardian must sign)

Mail to the **Reader Service**:
IN U.S.A.: P.O. Box 1867, Buffalo, NY 14240-1867
IN CANADA: P.O. Box 609, Fort Erie, Ontario L2A 5X3

**Are you a subscriber to Harlequin® Intrigue books
and want to receive the larger-print edition?
Call 1-800-873-8635 today or visit www.ReaderService.com.**

* Terms and prices subject to change without notice. Prices do not include applicable taxes. Sales tax applicable in N.Y. Canadian residents will be charged applicable taxes. Offer not valid in Quebec. This offer is limited to one order per household. Not valid for current subscribers to Harlequin Intrigue Larger-Print books. All orders subject to credit approval. Credit or debit balances in a customer's account(s) may be offset by any other outstanding balance owed by or to the customer. Please allow 4 to 6 weeks for delivery. Offer available while quantities last.

Your Privacy—The Reader Service is committed to protecting your privacy. Our Privacy Policy is available online at www.ReaderService.com or upon request from the Reader Service.

We make a portion of our mailing list available to reputable third parties that offer products we believe may interest you. If you prefer that we not exchange your name with third parties, or if you wish to clarify or modify your communication preferences, please visit us at www.ReaderService.com/consumerschoice or write to us at Reader Service Preference Service, P.O. Box 9062, Buffalo, NY 14240-9062. Include your complete name and address.

HILP15